The Canopy

Albert vande Steeg

Aakenbaaken & Kent

The Canopy

ISBN: 978-1-938436-88-8

Dedication

This is dedicated to my partner, good friend and one of the best policemen I was privileged to work with. His dedication to justice and to being there for any officer that needed backup or assistance was uncompromised. I was blessed to have him cover my back, and to know and work with a great cop and unique creation of God, Roger R. Remlinger. I miss you man, but you live in my memory.

Chapter 1

October 1978

The sound of the police helicopter flyover was fading away as the bagpipes began to play "Amazing Grace".

Amazing Grace how sweet the sound that saved a wretch like me. I once was lost but now am found, was blind but now I see

The words brought new tears to many eyes as they said farewell and "End of Watch" to a compatriot, partner, friend and all around great guy and good cop. Ricky Augustino was laid to rest, felled while searching for Henk Mueller who was running from the law after killing his drug dealer.

The cops that had some religion recognized this hymn. They reflected on those words and let their minds linger on the last verse, which brought comfort with the words, *"When we've been there ten thousand years, bright shining as the sun,"* referring to the time spent in heaven compared to the short time on earth. Even the hard-nosed macho guys realized that grace was what every cop needs to survive; they knew that this service could just as well have been for them instead of the man now named a hero for dying on duty. It could be their wife or mother who sat in the front row and received the flag from the chief.

As the notes drifted over them, each officer was aware of what the black band stretched across their shields or stars meant. The bagpipe squeezed out the last note as the bugle began to play *Taps*. Their hearts constricted as if the black band moved onto their hearts to squeeze them tight, bringing pain and anguish to even the most stalwart. Heads bowed as they turned and walked away across the cemetery grass, heading back to their rides. Some headed home, some back to their beat or assignments, while others gathered to swap stories, put down some suds or drink some hard stuff to hide the pain, sorrow and anger.

Life had been irrevocably changed.

As everyone drifted off, they recalled the words to *Taps*.

Day is done, gone the sun
From the lakes, from the hills, from the sky
All is well, safely rest
God is nigh.

Fading light dims the sight
And a star gems the sky, gleaming bright
From afar, drawing near
Falls the night.

Thanks and praise for our days
Neath the sun, neath the stars, neath the sky
As we go, this we know
God is nigh.

All was not well and only some realized that God was near. Those who knew it would draw comfort from God's presence in their lives, while the remainder would seek comfort from other sources, friends or from a bottle.

One group headed to the Canopy, the restaurant/bar owned by a former officer; there they swapped stories and grasped the camaraderie they needed in times like these. They needed to spend time with others who understood their emotions without having to say anything about feelings or be embarrassed for having emotions that may show, or maybe did not show on the outside. This was the main place to unwind after their work shift or "debrief" after working on an investigation past shift time. This was a "cop bar" and only cops, people who liked cops, and groupies hung out here.

Even those who worked the graveyard shift came in the morning; a couple of street cops performed janitorial duties at seven a.m. every day. The back door was open and drinks were poured for those in need. The food was great and the drinks were always full. The booze was measured by how it looked; forget the jigger and just make the glass look good.

No one mentioned Ricky's death or the memorial service. It was the number one item on each mind but the pain and anger were too much to deal with. So the topics of conversation were about happier times and events and arrests that brought back the routine. They avoided the anger about what contributed to the shooting death of Officer Ricardo Augustino.

"Hey, remember when we started working for OPD, and we

2

walked the foot-beat? Then we thought it was the worst assignment and couldn't wait to get into a patrol car. Now it looks like the best assignment we ever had."

Hillary Heyse began to tell the story of his first arrest; everyone heard it before, but today they had the patience to hear it again.

"I was walking the west beat," he said, "when it began to rain. Sergeant Grady told us that a good policeman never gets cold, wet or hungry, so I sought shelter. I know what you're thinking: why does a Brit worry about a few drops of water? Just because it rains most days in my hometown does not mean I like rain. Why do you think I came to sunny Southern Cal except to have better weather? It's not like I came to hang out with a lame bunch like you," he laughed.

"There was a used car lot right there so I checked the car doors hoping to find one unlocked. I found a 54 Dodge in the fourth row back and got in, took off my hat and scooted real low so traffic on Holt Boulevard could not see me. I kept an eye out for what was going on around me hoping to not be seen; I saw somebody checking the car doors. Thinking he was looking for a dry place, I watched, hoping he would find an open car and not discover me. He found a car in the second row and got in it. I relaxed until the car started up and drove out.

"Damn, a GTA [Grand Theft Auto], right in front of me. I jumped out, shone my flashlight into his face, and he stopped. I spread him out, cuffed him and then thought, *What am I going to do now? I am over a mile from the station.* We did not have radios back then to call for back up or transportation. I did the next best thing; I walked the perp into the traffic lane and stopped a passing motorist. I gave the driver a dime and asked him to go to the nearest pay phone to call the PD to send a squad car to help. Not knowing if the motorist would make the call, I repeated this with another motorist. I walked to the curb and waited for help. My first felony pinch and only on the job a week."

Everyone laughed. The air was tense, making the laughter a little too loud. Drinking without eating was fueling the comments and tension. Dee, the barmaid sensed this and came by to ask who wanted to eat. Orders were taken; the only items on the menu were the Texas Burger or Spaghetti Plate. The burger was huge. It came with fries, and was charred on the edges and juicy inside. It was a half-pound of health food with a little grease to coat the digestive

3

tract. The spaghetti was heaped on a platter with lots of sauce and meat that covered the noodles and flowed over the plate. Simple meals and a limited menu, but no one complained. The price was right, the quality and taste were over the top, and the company was comfortable.

"Hey, Jack! Tell these guys about your first day," ordered Heyse. He knew the story but loved to hear it told. Jack Hillberg grinned a little and then began the story. He was nervous that first day but now had the confidence to tell it and have it understood.

"I was working for Chino back then as a reserve officer. I was trying to get a feel for what a cop does to wet my feet to see if I would like doing it as a career, so I joined the reserves," he said.

"The very first night I report to duty; they issued me a badge and a six inch .38 revolver. 'Point this at the guy you're going to shoot or else leave it in the holster' was the only instruction I got. The officer I was going to ride with drove up at the rear door, and I got in a police car for the second time of my life. The first time was years ago and it was not good. I was young and stupid with too much alcohol, but that is another story.

"As we cruised the city, he asked me about my life and work; we got acquainted. He was evaluating me to see if he felt safe and better off with me in the unit with him or whether he should take me back to the station. Within thirty minutes we got a call that an escapee from Chino Men's Prison was at the GI Bar. He was described as a male Mexican (it was common and proper to use that term in the 60s, referring to anyone Hispanic), five feet six, one hundred thirty pounds, with black hair and brown eyes. Shit, that probably described half of the Hispanic males within one mile either way, depending on if they were wearing boots, shoes or moccasins.

"We were only five blocks away, so we rolled over. As we were on the way, my partner of thirty minutes said, 'You cover the back door and I'll get the front. I'll give you twenty seconds before I go in. If you hear shit going down, get your ass in there and help me out.'

"This freaked me out just a little. I had no training, had not shot a pistol in over a year and never shot the gun that was strapped to my side. There was no time to discuss the options as we rolled up next to the side of the bar. I ran to the rear and Jeremy went to the front. He stood just outside the doorway, waiting for me to get in place.

4

"As I went I was thinking, *What do I do? If someone comes out how do I know it is the escapee? If he is running that will be a dead giveaway. Okay if he is running do I tackle him, shoot him or just wish him well? Crap, what have I got myself into? Okay, no shooting unless he has a gun and I have no other choice. What I'll do is chase him down. I'm sure he cannot out run me, so I'll catch his ass and throw him down and cuff him up. Yeah that should be good.*

"I waited in the back. Nothing happened. No noise from inside – no shouting, no shots. It seemed like an eternity, but was probably less than a minute when I saw the rear door open. It opened slowly. I got ready to pounce on whoever came out.

"Then I heard Jeremy say, 'It's me, he is not here.' He had his helmet off and held it out the door before he opened it further and came out. When he saw that I was relaxed and did not have my gun out he put his helmet back on and we left.

"I was relieved! What if the dude had been there? What if I would have needed to shoot him? When we drove away I peppered Jeremy with lots of questions, questions that would give me guidance for future similar circumstances. Now days they would have sent out eight cops, surrounded the place, evacuated the neighborhood and probably called in the SWAT team. Then it was just us two. We had just considered it routine then."

Bernie Reed was the next one to tell a story. "I remember those days when we either had no radios or they had limited range. We did a lot of stuff then without the equipment or manpower of today. I pursued a speeder south on Archibald into the country and when I finally lost him I had no idea where I was or how to get back to the city. I had only been with the PD for a few weeks after working in Akron, Ohio. I found a farmhouse with lights on to ask for directions to get back. I told them that I was from Ohio and at first they thought I had chased the car from there, but when they saw my shoulder patch with Ontario Police on it they realized their mistake and understood what I meant. They had a good laugh but I felt like crap, just like the odor at that dairy."

Jack' said, "It's my turn. Let me tell you about my first night and my first arrest. Back then we did not go to the academy before we went to work. The city put you to work and if you passed probation, they would spend the money on academy training.

"Anyway, that evening I walked the east foot beat from eight to midnight with the man I was replacing. At midnight the

5

graveyard shift started and I was assigned to a patrolman who was to become my training officer. That night the sergeant decided he would do the initial training. He lectured me on gun safety and being there for each other while we cruised the city. At about one thirty we were cruising north on Benson from Holt when he spotted a car that was parked behind the trailer and camper supply store.

"He made a U-turn, doused his lights, and pulled into the parking lot. We spotted this guy standing next to the building's rear door. The sergeant lit up the inside of the vehicle with his spot light and I lit up the dude. He spread the guy out on the hood of the unit to frisk him for weapons or burglary tools then had him empty his pockets. Among his possessions was a pack of cigarettes. I picked up the cigarettes and felt a lump on one side.

"The dude saw me feel the pack and dropped his head onto the hood. 'Fuck,' he muttered. I shook the pack and out fell several double scored white tablets. They were called "Bennies", short for Benzedrine pills and it was a felony to possess them.

"My first night and we had a felony pinch. This made the sergeant feel good about my future. I felt good about myself, but knew it was just plain luck and curiosity. But I got my name in the newspaper like it was a big deal."

Many stories were told and many beers went down, until they all knew it was about time to leave before they were too drunk to walk.

Finally, someone said, "Sure hope Mueller gets the chair!"

Most everyone responded to this wish for Ricky's killer with "screw him," or "may he fry in hell," or other comments best not repeated. With that they downed the last of their drinks and solemnly rose as a unit and left.

The barmaid watched them leave and gave her usual parting words, "Be careful out there."

Tomorrow would be another day. A day to put up with the realities of life and the odd and crazy things out there to deal with, unlike the stories of old days. Tomorrow they would all remove the black band and it would be back to the realities of crime on the street and the bullshit from upstairs.

Chapter 2

June 1973

As the bureau briefing ended, the sergeant gave his usual admonition "to be careful out there" and then announced that if time permitted the "dicks" should do some preventive patrol after picking up coffee and donuts. He liked this idea because he thought the bad guys would see the detective cars cruising residential neighborhoods and this would make thieves avoid Ontario when looking for a house to break into. That is what he did the entire six years he worked in patrol division.

His plan for his police career was to get his education and move up the promotional ladder. College education was great but it did not guarantee good police work; the best street cops were those who worked in the real world for a few years and had experience working for and with people. This guy's idea of police work was that cops seen cruising the streets prevented crime. He had never made an observation pinch in his thirteen years on the force.

Every patrolman filled out a log sheet during each shift. The log recorded all of the activities of that shift. The first column on the log was where the activity originated: O for observation, C for call from dispatch, R for routine patrol, and S for report writing or other station activities. This sergeant's log consistently recorded C's, R's and Station; he seldom, if ever, observed a crime or initiated contact with the evildoers. The only O's recorded were traffic citations he issued, and there were few of those.

There was a noticeable distinction between those who were climbers in rank and those who came to do police work. The climbers went to school and hated making arrests, because making arrests often meant staying late to finish the report. Then, when the case went to trial the court time interfered with class time and doing homework.

Ray and Jack were both working cops; they attended all required classes, went to as many training seminars as they could, but had no illusions or desires of attaining rank. They loved finding and outsmarting the crooks. Their theory was that keeping Ontario safe required a policeman on every block twenty-four hours a day; the only reasonable alternative was to find the crooks

7

and apprehend them before, during or after committing a crime. Patrol did the first two and the bureau [detective bureau] primarily did the later.

Jack Hillberg was an immigrant from Belgium. His name was Americanized from *Jacobus Hoogeberg* when they arrived at Ellis Island. Jack spoke Flemish, French, Dutch and English fluently and without an accent, having come with his family when he was not yet ten years old. He had the old European values of justice, fair play, integrity and earning your keep. He learned them from his parents when his family lived through and survived the Nazi occupation of World War II. There was not a day that passed in which he did not cherish liberty. America was the greatest place on earth. A place where justice was valued and hard work produced results. Jack believed and practiced that belief. Every day you worked it was your responsibility to do your best. It was not about being seen or not seen working; it was about personal integrity to earn your keep.

Ray Follett was a military brat who lived in many parts of the States, Japan, and Germany as he grew up. His father retired from the army as a full bird colonel. He chaffed under some of the rules of life and of the police department. He obeyed all of the rules that made sense and that he thought had value, but the others he only paid homage to. Circumventing them was always a desirable challenge. He was scrupulously honest and had a keen sense for justice. However, he did have a weakness for the ladies. His supervisor was known to say, "Ray is probably the brightest and best cop we have, but is a pain in the ass to supervise."

Both scored in the top ten of four hundred applicants when they were hired on, and scored in the top three in the promotional test for detective. Neither one had any desire to promote higher since that would take them off the streets and thus limiting their interaction with the public. They loved caring for and tending to the needs of victims and got great satisfaction in cleaning up the streets.

They attended Pomona Police Academy where Jack bested Ray by a mere one-tenth of a percent. The ease of how they learned and accomplished the tasks caused them to refer to this portion of training as "Peter Pan Prep." It was a good academy. They mastered firearms training and excelled in the classroom as well. Classes included: Arrest, Search &Seizure, Patrol Procedure, Interview Techniques, Handling of Evidence, Investigation, Self-defense, and Use of Force.

The only thing this academy did not have that future academies had was physical fitness training and stress training. Stress training was some wacko's idea of preparing the troops to deal with the stress of working the streets and to deal with pressure. Those academies harassed the trainees, got in their face, and yelled at them over perceived faults or lint on the uniform. They were demeaned and punished for these incidents until the trainee wanted to punch out the sergeant, but he had to restrain himself or lose his job.

Stress training created animosity and a deep dislike for the drill instructor, and instilled the idea that everyone a cop had to deal with while enforcing laws was a scumbag. Sure, they could handle the stress, but they also wanted to be more violent toward arrestees. Shooting or beating up suspects was not seen as bad; it was a means to vent against someone that was seen as being of less value. The rage an officer felt against his DI (drill instructor) during training could not be seen or vented; however this rage against a suspect could be vented with creative tactics and creative report writing. The only benefit of stress training was to the training officer who seized the opportunity to lash out and vent his emotions on the hapless trainee. In reality the DI acted as the bully he was supposedly training the officer not to be.

The academy should teach future officers to value people and respect cultural and ethnic variances. Stress training made the officers look for conformity, viewing anything different from what they were taught was the norm with distain and suspicion.

Ray had a natural or God-given talent to relate to people that could not be taught at an academy. When Ray interviewed an arrestee, it often resulted in confessions and admissions of multiple crimes. The officers and the district attorney's office were awed by his knack for understanding the criminal mind and using that to bring about admissions. The defense attorneys spent a lot of time cross-examining Ray and tried to uncover some type of coercion or violation of the Miranda rule, but to no avail. Ray was just that good.

Ray and Jack started out working adjoining beats in 1967 while in patrol and grew to respect each other, develop a working relationship that created a bond of friendship and commitment to each other's welfare. They worked so well together that they seldom had to talk about whom was to do what. They were kindred minds and each knew what to expect of the other. And they never let their partner down.

As they began this workday, Ray and Jack each grabbed a donut and coffee, talked for a few minutes with Bert, the shop owner, and then headed south. As they crossed Mission Boulevard, patrol received a call of a burglary in progress. Ray looked at Jack, gunned the ride, and said, "Let's do it."

They jumped the call, which pissed off the beat cop, because he was left with the crime report while the detectives got credit for the arrest and only had to make the booking report.

They arrived first. Ray went to the rear yard and Jack covered the front while he waited for the black and white. Ray noticed a washing machine on the patio, under an open window; the curtains were blowing outside through the window and there were fresh scuffs on the dirty concrete, indicating that the washer was moved to provide access to the window. As he assessed the likely point of entry and thought about what to do next he saw the doorknob of the rear door turning.

"Shit!" It was too late to wait for backup or to decide what to do. It was action time.

The door opened and the suspect stepped out onto the stoop with his arms full of goods: a rifle, a pillowcase bulging with items, and a small television. The perp saw Ray and immediately stumbled back into the house.

A call went out for help, stating that the burglars were armed.

Ray called for the crook to come out with his hands up. The front door opened and not one, but two men came out with their hands up. Jack was relieved that they gave up without a gunfight. The black and white slid to a stop, just in time to take the PC459 burglary report. You've got to love preventive patrol!

Chapter 3

July 1973

Ray and Jack were actually assigned to vice and narcotics. They finished their part of the burglary paper work and then headed out to the truck stop at Milliken and Interstate 10 to see what might be happening there. The info on the street was that this had become the place for purchasing drugs, especially uppers and marijuana, and to be pleasured by the talents of the many hookers.

They added a CB radio to their ride; it was on channel 19. The air was full of chatter about where friends were, what schedule they were keeping, and where the next load was going. Once they arrived on the lot, the word was broadcast that the "fuzz" was there. Ray used the CB moniker "Grasshopper" because, as he said on the air, "I love jumping the ladies." Jack moniker was Frenchie. He chose that because most truck drivers and hookers did not expect a cop to be bi-lingual unless he knew Spanish.

As they drove along the line of semi-trucks they saw a passenger door open, and a young woman stepped onto the top step. She was nude on top and was talking to the driver of the truck that was parked in the next space. She did not see the approaching police car. Ray stopped the car and Jack jumped out and approached the young woman. Instead of going back into the truck she jumped off the step right into his arms. She pushed her breasts into his face, laughing and asking if he liked them.

The drivers of both trucks rolled up their windows and acted like they had nothing to do with this and had no idea what was going on. Ray stepped up onto the step of the truck she came out of and told the driver to roll down the window and step out of the truck.

When the driver stepped down Ray asked if he could look in the truck for the woman's things. Permission was given. He entered the truck, found the girl's blouse, bra and a small handbag. Her identification was in the handbag.

The bare-bosomed woman saw Ray look at the ID and she took off running. Jack loved a good foot pursuit. He ran four miles almost every day just to be ready for times like this. He ran after her.

It is a little dicey to stop a half nude woman. Normally the pursuing officer would give someone he was chasing a little push so the perp stumbled and fell. Then he would put a knee into the back and place the handcuffs on. It would not look good if this was done to a young woman who obviously had no weapon on her; a push onto the asphalt would give her nasty scrapes and bruising. Later Ray said it might have been fun to remove grit from her boobs. But grabbing her might look bad too.

He got it done by tapping her shoulder while he ran next to her. She looked at him and knew the race was over. She was convinced to give up.

Leading her back to the patrol car was a bit of an experience, since truck drivers were standing around jeering and making rude, sexy comments and expletives. This was the type of attention that brought citizen complaints and spread false rumors about what police did. If they held her too firmly it was abuse, if too loosely she might attempt to escape again. The observers might think the cop was playing up to her and looking for sexual favors.

Jack took a firm grip on her wrist and walked fast. She had to keep up with his long strides; it was just the right move to eliminate false ideas or accusations.

Ray retrieved her clothes from the truck and told her to dress herself. Her bag contained make up, Kleenex, some money, and half a dozen condoms. She needed those condoms if the money she had was any indication of how many tricks she did a day; so far she had six twenty dollar bills. Truckers were not great tippers, so had she already turned six tricks before noon.

They ran a check on the name on the library card she had for ID. She actually told the truth as the check returned with the information that she was fifteen years old and was a runaway from Kalamazoo, Michigan. Debbie was a really sad story.

Ray phoned the parent's home and spoke with the mother to inform her that her daughter was found and in custody. Her mother asked how they found her daughter and what she was doing which got her picked up. Not wanting to create a hassle or further problems, he told the mother she was found at the truck stop.

"Probably giving blow jobs to truckers, wasn't she? Just like she was doing to my husband when I caught her, and then she ran away."

Jack and Ray had a conference with Debbie. "What's with your step-father?"

"That creepy asshole has been forcing me to have sex for two years and my mother thinks it is my fault. She thinks I wanted to have sex with her creepy old husband? She is nuts. He has raped me for eight months already."

"When you get back will you tell the police what he has been doing?" asked Ray.

"If I do that both of them will beat me and I will have no place to stay. I may as well stay gone," said Debbie.

Jack said, "Well, we are including the rape in our report and will notify Kalamazoo PD of the abuse. Hopefully you and they can find a way to protect you."

Debbie began to sob, her shoulders shaking. She was a broken, lonely girl in a messed up world. She hugged both officers and thanked them for being kind and actually caring about her.

"Nobody really cares about me. My mom is such a worthless piece of shit, she only wants me back so she can collect child support and welfare. That creep she is married to hardly works and drinks every day."

Jack had a sister-in-law in the Kalamazoo area. He called her to see if she could find a church or youth group to look after Debbie, and then gave Debbie some contact numbers she could reach out to for help. With tears running down her face, she got on the transportation to Juvenile Hall and awaited her return home.

Ray and Jack saw that this truck stop was a zoo, so they made a plan to send undercover operators to clean up some of the mess, bust up the prostitution and buy some dope. Everyone knew it could only be controlled and not eliminated, but they had to give it their best shot.

Chapter 4

Bureau briefing came to an end with the usual reports of burglaries, thefts and busts patrol made since yesterday. They were reviewed to see whether any of the busts might be a good candidate to interview for further info and maybe develop into an informant.

Ray and Jack were pulled aside by Sergeant Sturm.

"Got a little job for you," he said.

They hated these assignments; there was almost always some jerk who needed something special. Little did they know just what they were getting into. Sergeant Sturm told them a parole officer needed back up.

The parole officer was a female (first sign of trouble) who needed assistance checking on a parolee. Usually these parolees were guys that were out of prison for a short time and had gone back to using drugs. Therefore they skipped their parole meetings for fear of being asked for a urine test, which they knew would be dirty. Skipping their meetings got the parole agent's attention. The agent might wait a few days or a week while he or she kept trying to make contact, but eventually would realize that it was time to make a personal visit. When the parole officer anticipated taking the parolee into custody they asked for police help, especially when the parolee had a history of violence.

This particular parolee, Robert Brown, was living with a brother who was also on parole but had been doing well. The only violence on the brother's record was a problem when he was doing his time in Duaell Institute in Tracy.

"Let's go get this done so we can get back to our caseload," grumbled Ray.

They met the parole agent (PA) at a gas station a block away from the last known address of the parolee. This guy had a record of armed robbery, drug use and sales. The plan was for the police to cover the front and back while the parole agent knocked on the door. If anything odd was heard or seen Ray would kick in the door and secure the room while the PA went to the rear door to let Jack' in, if Jack was not already coming in.

The parole agent knocked on the door. It opened about six inches and then slammed shut. *Ah, not so fast!* Ray did not have time to get his foot into the space but he was ready to kick the

15

door, so his foot hit the door just before it latched. He took the parolee down and was cuffing him when Jack came in the back door.

A juvie was sitting on a beanbag watching the events in front of him. He was in a fog, too loaded to move or say anything. The parole agent stayed with him as the pair of cops made a quick check of the house for anyone else.

In the first bedroom closet there was a pile of clothes and a blanket. Ray nudged the pile with his foot and realized there was a body in there. Pulling his .45 caliber auto, he gave the order to come out real slow. The pile moved, slowly as ordered. Two hands appeared, and shoved the blanket and clothes aside. It was the parolee's brother. He put his hands on top of his head. He had seen too many movies and had been busted before so he knew the ritual. He was handcuffed and brought to the living room. Both suspects were searched.

Suspect one had a pocket full of coins, totaling nearly twenty dollars. No guns or drugs on either one. On the sofa was a pile of cigarette cartons. It was odd that they were a variety of brands: Marlboro, Salem, Winston, Camel and more.

"Hey what do you smoke?" Jack asked.

"Lucky," said suspect one.

"Who smokes these?" Jack' asked as he pointed to the variety on the sofa. "There are no Lucky Strike cigarettes there, mostly Marlboro, Camel, Salem, Winston and Kool."

The heads all dropped, and all eyes were on the floor. No response. Silence from everyone. Something was up. There was more to this than met the eye.

With their antennas up the cops began checking what was really going on. Further observation showed that these cartons had red paint on portions of them. It looked like over-spray from a paint sprayer or spray can was on many of the cartons. Assuming that the cigarettes were stolen from somewhere, the policemen arrested all three suspects. The parolee and his brother were transported to West End Sheriff Substation. The juvie was taken to the station holding cells, interviewed and then held for transportation to Juvenile Hall.

Ray sent a teletype out to other agencies regarding the cigarettes, describing them and the paint over-spray. Soon a reply came from the Sheriff's Valley Station to ask about the cigarettes. A service station was robbed in Etiwanda and cigarettes were taken, along with cash and coins from the till. The attendant was shot and found dead by a customer at about 4:30 that morning.

Jack worked on the reports while Ray went to the West End DA's office to obtain a search warrant. The office was in an office trailer next to the court buildings at Sixth Street and Mountain. Two hours later they went back to the house and met with two deputy sheriff detectives. These detectives were watching and protecting the house to keep the place undisturbed and to prevent pollution of any evidence that might be found when the warrant was served.

The exterior of the house was the same as when they left earlier. The doors and windows were all closed and locked. Jack had kept the keys they used earlier to lock it up and they used them to enter to search for further evidence of the robbery and the homicide. It was a typical doper pad, with furniture of assorted type, style and color scattered here and there. It was good furniture except it was all filthy and disheveled. Cushions were strewn on the floor, along with the clothes and towels that were scattered around. Towels? Why towels? Don't they use the bathrooms to dry off and hang them up?

They pushed the piles and odds and ends of clothes that were scattered around and shoved blankets that lay on the floor with their feet. The floor that had not been vacuumed or swept for months, or at least not since they moved in, and likely would never be swept or vacuumed as long as they lived there.

The kitchen was equally bad. How did anyone eat food prepared here? The pots and pans were on the counter with leftover beans, and other stuff that had become indescribable, both inside and on the lids. The stove was filthy. Refried beans that were gathering mold and the remains of macaroni and cheese were in pans on the stovetop.

The sink was a similar story. It was piled with unwashed dishes and plastic forks and butter knifes with peanut butter crusted on them. Apparently they washed what they needed next and ignored the remainder for another time. The odor was as bad in the kitchen as it was in the bathroom. Spoiled food and moldy towels and clothes were about the same. But this was home for someone. Ray looked up, but there was no "Home Sweet Home" sign.

They really hated this part of the job. Going through the filth was part of what it would take to do the complete search.

17

Occasionally they stopped and washed their hands, letting them drip dry. This was where they learned to always wash their hands prior to urinating; they never knew what they had touched and did not want to cause infection on their private parts. All narcotic detectives washed prior to using the rest room and seldom after. For them, signs in public restrooms had the order in reverse importance. Ray was fond of saying, "The best thing I learned in the academy was to not pee on my fingers."

The search warrant included finding proof of who lived at the residence, such as medical, utility and tax statements. Then the search extended to finding clothes that might have gunpowder residue or blood on them; hopefully they could connect the residue to the shooter. Of course, any place where a gun could be stashed was searched for the weapon used in the homicide.

Including small items on the list in the search warrant gave the opportunity to check small areas, such as drawers and pockets of clothes. If they found things not related to the original crime, the items were then admissible for evidence for additional charges.

Jack opened a kitchen drawer and jumped back as he shook off several cockroaches that ran up his arm. "Shit," he muttered as he used a spoon to paw through the items. In one drawer he found a phone book with a list of numbers written in pencil and the Edison electric bill with one of the arrestee's name, Robert Brown. On the table there was a letter from the parole office addressed to Frank Brown. Both brothers definitely lived there. This search proved very successful. It produced ample evidence of the robbery and homicide.

Ray searched the bedroom where he found the dude hiding under the pile of clothes and blankets. He picked up each item and threw them behind him. He yelled at Jack to come over. There under the blanket, lying on the closet floor where the brother had been hiding was a Ruger .38 revolver. He realized that the suspect could have shot him without ever exposing the gun. He shivered as he thought about the words in "Taps", indeed God was near!

A polo shirt was on top of the pile of clothes under the window. It looked like there were some flecks on the right sleeve near the wrist. Forensics later showed that these flecks were gunpowder blowback. A stash of drugs, some meth and a baggie of grass were found in the bathroom drawer.

It had been an almost casual event; after all it was only a parole check, but they exercised due caution and had controlled

18

the situation. Jack was well aware that it took only one small slip-up or loss of focus and death could come, like it did to Ricky. Everyone realized that Ricky had been living under pressure and was not on top of his actions. The due caution that Jack and Ray used this day had undoubtedly saved their lives. Who would have thought these guys had just committed a homicide? Jack shivered when he thought about what could have happened.

Ballistics showed that the Ruger .38 was the gun that fired the bullets that killed the service station attendant. It was another lucky day for law enforcement. No one was hurt and two crooks were in custody.

Another long day, which started out with a simple assignment to help a parole officer, had culminated in two homicide arrests, filing and serving a search warrant, investigative and booking reports and verbal reports to Sergeant Strum. Now it was time for debriefing.

Jack and Ray headed to the Canopy. A couple of beers and that half-pound Texas Burger sure looked real good.

The stories of the day's events brought out other stories of escapes from near death or stories of good arrests coming from unexpected sources or events. One of the patrol officers related an event that happened just a few weeks earlier.

He and a trainee, who was a cadet officer, were working Beat Four, the north east section of the city. The cadet officer was not yet old enough to be a peace officer and therefore was not armed. Beat Four's officer came in one hour early to start the swing shift at 2pm. Beat Four and Beat Two started an hour earlier than the others to provide patrol cars on the street during the regular shift change at 1500 hours, 3pm.

Ray began his story with, "It was Sunday afternoon and so far it was quiet like most Sundays. At 2:55 we received a call of a family 415 on North Amador. This is a nice blue collar area. All the houses are single story, three bedrooms, working family homes with well-kept yards.

"We walked up to the front door and before we could knock the door opened. The woman standing in the doorway was disheveled; her clothes were messy and torn, and she held a portion of her dress to keep her breast covered. Her hair was really weird, like it had been pulled or maybe she had just experienced an electrical shock. The most striking thing, which caught our attention, was that one side of her face was blue and turning black in areas. It was strange because it seemed like her face was divided exactly in half; one side of her face was normal while the other side was a mess of mottled color."

"What happened?" we asked.

"She replied that her husband had beat her and tried to suffocate her with a pillow. 'He tried to kill me!' she whimpered. She was shaking and her eyes were full of fear. She stepped aside, holding the door so we could come in.

"I asked her, 'Where is he now?'

"'Oh, he is in the living room,' she said and stepped aside, motioning for us to come in.

"As I stepped into the living room I saw the husband sitting on the sofa with this twelve-gauge shotgun. I was in the doorway with no place to go fast enough to escape. He had his shotgun raised up; it was aimed at my stomach. 'Shit!' I couldn't back up or jump sideways without him being able to shoot me. I was in the open with nowhere to go. I motioned with my hand for my partner to keep back. He took a quick read of the situation and headed to the patrol car to call for a backup. We did not have a portable radio with us; all the operating ones were in use. There were three waiting to be sent out for repair, so we just did without. Just another typical budget problem.

"It was 3pm and there were no other patrol units on the street. The officers were all checking out their units and loading their gear in their rides. Besides we were at least two miles away from the station. The trainee was unarmed and did not have the key to unlock the shotgun in the unit. We were on our own.

"When you are looking at the business end of a shotgun, that barrel looks really big; the first thought I had was, 'That is going to be a huge hole in my guts when he pulls that trigger.' Nothing was said for what seemed like an eternity; both of us were watching each other figuring out what to do or what would happen next. The dude looked a little wacky, just not quite there; you know, like a few bricks short of a load, or the light was on but the bulb was dim."

"Well, obviously you did not get shot, so what happened?" asked Jack.

"I was looking at the gun and just started talking to him about what a nice gun it was and that I had one almost like it at home that I used for pheasant hunting. 'Do you hunt too?' I asked him.

"He responded with a story about hunting pheasants in China

20

when he was in the Merchant Marines and how he loved that gun because it was so accurate and easy to shoot. Talking about hunting expanded to ducks and geese and grouse, as well as his favorite - pheasants. I could see the tension slowly going away from his face, so it seemed like a good time to see if he would give me the gun so I could admire it more closely.

I said, 'Can I see that beautiful gun?'

He said, 'Sure, mister,' and handed it to me.

Whew! The strain drained from my body as I took the gun and passed it to my partner who had returned and was standing just at the edge of the door. Then I grabbed the chump and cuffed him up.

We heard the sound of sirens coming from several blocks away and soon two units slid to a stop in front of the house. Too late! God already did the entire backup I needed.

Two hours later, after telling the story of the day's events to the boys and the barkeep, Jack and Ray headed for home. Twelve hours of work and one hour to kick back and unwind. That was what they needed. Now it was time to go home to a safe place where people loved you and worried about you. They did not like it when their wives worried, but it did mean they cared. When they got home they would tell their wives about their boring day and all the hassles of helping the Parole Board do their job.

Jack wife, Gail, knew he was not telling her the complete story. If it was all so boring, why did he need to go to the Canopy and come home this late? She realized that Jack had a tense day and was protecting her from worry, but she worried anyway.

Ray's wife, Lystra, didn't believe him either. She suspected he might have spent some time with another woman, but was not sure, because she knew that when Ray was with Jack, that Jack was not party to any of those things. So, she too realized that his story was to protect her from fears.

Only the next day would they calmly say that they had gotten lucky to find and arrest two suspects for homicide; they made it sound casual, with no danger involved. They never said anything that might make the wife or children worry or need to pray more. Do not fear. God was near.

Chapter 5

September 1973

Working vice or narcotics requires information-inside information which is extremely difficult to get. Good useable information is found only on the streets or with great luck or by developing circumstances. Informants are the backbone of such information or grapevine for investigators. A small pinch of a good guy caught up in something he wished he never got into might result in a cache of information. Other informants might be small-time crooks who exchange information for lighter sentencing or it might be concerned family members who were trying to remove bad influences from someone they loved. The motivation to be an informant varies with the crime.

Jack had the luck or great skill of finding such people, who were not only willing to tell everything they knew, but in spilling their guts they were often relieved to unload the burden of keeping a secret. This time the information came from the drunk Jack helped out several months ago while working patrol, before he was promoted to the Dick bureau.

You never knew when a good deed might come back to help you. When Jack patrolled his beat he would make occasional bar checks. Walking into a bar had a great effect on the clientele and the barkeep. Jack stayed just a few minutes to chat with the bartender and look around at who was there and who was trying hide their faces. He scanned the place to take in anything or anyone that might look out of place or suspicious and merited checking out.

The good bars liked this service, while those who lived on the edge and dealt in illicit behavior were not too pleased to see cops come in, but even then the bartender learned to be cordial. They knew that if they pissed off the officer he would come back with help and do a complete search. He would search the bar for liquor violations, such as liquor bottles that were empty but still whole. Alcohol and Beverage Control required the immediate breaking of liquor bottle necks to prevent barkeepers from putting cheap liquor into pricy labels. Officers might shake down the clients for ID checks and do other things that were not good for business.

One night Jack walked into Johnnies Bar on West Mission to

do a bar check where he found Clifford passed out, sitting on a stool with his head on the bar. The bartender was worried, because it was not legal to serve alcohol to a person who was already drunk. He explained that this guy came in regularly and drank too much; tonight he came in, walked to the stool and ordered two beers. He said, "Before he finished them he flopped down on the bar and passed out. I was letting him sleep a bit before waking him and sending him home."

Jack realized the drunk was probably a poor working stiff with no home life and he needed alcohol to survive the pain of life. The bartender thought that he lived in the motel across the street. Realizing that arresting this drunk would prove nothing and would cause more hardship in the poor guy's life, Jack picked him up, threw him across his shoulder, and carried him to the unit. He found the address in Clifford's wallet. *How far down are you when even the DMV has the room number of the seedy run-down motel you live in?* He must have lived there for some time. Jack drove there and deposited him on the sofa, locking the door behind him when he left.

Satisfied that he did the right thing, he sat in his patrol car thinking about this man's poor miserable life. He had worked with people like that prior to joining the PD. For a month he provided transportation to a co-worker on the construction crew. The guy had been a good worker but it took a half pint of vodka to get him going in the morning, two tall 16-ounce beers for lunch, and by four he faded into not being able to work. Jack was glad he had not gone to college and then straight into law enforcement, because he would not have understood or cared about people like this who are trapped in misery. Poor soul. He was a man who probably worked hard, never committed a crime except being drunk and had no hope for a better life, but he did not hurt anyone other than himself.

Two days later Clifford called the station to ask to meet Jack. After he thanked Jack, he promised that he would call whenever he had some info. He said, "You will know it is me when the message is 'your touch' wants to see you." Jack smiled as he thought about Clifford; a simple mind was going to help the police and make it deeply mysterious. He figured that Clifford watched too many old movies, and probably loved James Cagney flicks.

Not much good had come from this source, but now he said he had information about gambling, bookmaking, football cards and high stake poker games. The info was sketchy but sounded like it was worth checking into. Jack told him what he needed and asked if he could get more names and maybe addresses and license numbers.

"Sure, I can do that, just take a few days."

"Okay, but be careful and do not get too nosy; that would mess this up and get you hurt."

He thought that would be the last he heard from Cliff. But four days later his sergeant handed him a note as he said, "What goofy guy is this?"

The note said, "Your touch wants to see you."

"Yeah, Sarge, it is an informant who loves the intrigue and mystery of working with cops. He is little screwy but his info is good."

They me at the sandwich shop at Mission and Mountain where he bought Cliff some good food and a drink. Cliff slid a sheet of paper across the table with all the info Jack needed to start surveillance at the fruit stand just a few blocks south from where they were eating. Who would have thought that a guy selling fruit and vegetables was big in making book and running numbers and sports gambling?

He began surveillance on the reported bookmaker. Interesting things began to happen. It was discovered that one of the runners was also a city employee, working in the building department as a field inspector.

A friend at General Telephone provided phone numbers and calling records that aided in knowing where to look and who to watch. The list of those involved became interesting: lawyers, car dealers, business owners, concrete Ready-Mix drivers, city hall staff, building inspectors, and a raft of people who came and went without buying an apple. All of them were creating a quarter-million-dollar pool each week.

Jack realized that this was a big deal and even worse, influential people were involved. He became really concerned when the assistant city attorney was seen having lunch with Augie, the produce stand owner.

Jack and Ray discussed what this meant and what they should do. No one knew they had been working on this and now they were really glad they had not said anything. They decided to keep mum about it and work it when time permitted while they did their normal assignments. They knew it was going to get dirty, so they would take it slow and easy.

Days went by and they decided to do a little surveillance after the duties of the day. Using a department undercover car, they tailed Augie as he made several stops at bars, a laundry business on Euclid, an automotive shop, and the Frozen Food Locker on West California Street.

A few days later they were parked watching the fruit stand where Augie was talking to a supplier. He bought some fruit, left and went straight home. The next day he was followed again, to a meeting at Squires Restaurant. Again, he went straight home and stayed there. Something was wrong. It seemed like he knew he was being watched; the "Dick" (detective) cars must have been spotted.

Ray had numerous contacts with car dealers up and down West Holt: Citrus Ford, Mark Christopher Chevrolet, Rungle's used cars, and others. These guys had all been victims of shysters at some time and victims of burglars and vandalism. He helped Citrus Ford and Rungle's with employees who stole and used drugs. He made a few contacts with them and hit them up for a loan, to borrow one of the used cars they had for sale.

"Sure, no problem. Just bring it back without bullet holes," said Lou.

Rotating cars every few days worked out well. Augie was doing his rounds and then he met with the city attorney and some dude who rode in a limo. He made his regular stops at the Ready-Mix plant, appliance store and a couple of body shops. Three days later, Augie and the others again began to act like they knew something was up and they stopped making the usual contacts.

"What the hell is going on?"

"How do they know when we are there?"

The next day they found out that something was really screwed up in Ontario.

After briefing, Sergeant Smith pulled Ray and Jack aside and asked, "What the hell are you guys doing? The captain wants to see you now, before you go anywhere! Anything I need to know about? Are you getting me in trouble too?"

"Beats me! I have no idea what he wants and we haven't done anything wrong, at least that I know of."

Jack and Ray walked out and went upstairs to the captain's office. On the way they looked at each other with apprehension. They both knew that this was not looking good but had no idea

26

just what was going on. No arrests or contacts had any reason to complain, no cases the DA was upset about, nothing. They also knew that when the brass got on you that shit was about to come down.

Keeping a cool attitude, they strolled into the captain's office.

"You want to see us boss? Got something you want us to take care of?" asked Ray. He hoped to set a positive tone and wished this meeting was about a new assignment and not a butt chewing.

"Shut the door and sit down," commanded Captain Lee.

They sat, one near the desk and the other against the wall. They tried to appear confident and nonchalant.

"Hear you guys have been checking up on a few people. What's going on?"

They both responded at once, "What are you talking about? What people are we supposedly checking on?"

"If you are doing some side work or investigating things not on the books, I want you to leave it alone," said the captain.

Ray showed his frustration when he said, "What the hell are you talking about? Just what the f.... are we supposed to be doing that is wrong?"

He immediately realized that he just screwed up. The captain was used to hearing and using vulgar language, but did not like it used when anyone was talking to him. Oops.

Captain Lee glowered at Ray, and then said, "The word is that you guys have been doing some surveillance on people who have some connections, and they do not like it." Then he threw in the clincher, "The chief says we have more important things to do, so whatever it is, leave it alone. Just stick to your case load. Am I understood?"

Nothing was said about what had been done or who with, but the message was clear. We know what you are doing, so stop it and stop it now! Someone had connections to the chief's office or in City Hall.

"Yes, sir," both dicks said, and they walked out.

Ray and Jack headed out to the donut shop to get a cup of dark roasted coffee and an apple fritter to share. Worried about being overheard or even taped, they had not mentioned anything in the station or in the detective unit. Now with coffee in hand they went outside to talk. It didn't take a brain surgeon to figure out that there was a leak some place, and they knew it was not either of them. How did the crooks know? Who do they know? What now?

All they had were questions with no sure answers, except that they agreed to keep working on it and to be more discreet in what they did. This looked even bigger than they thought and the people involved had really good connections.

"Maybe we need some help. Let's go see the DA."

So they made an appointment to have a private conversation with the Chief Deputy, in charge of the West End District attorney's office.

Lawrence "Pug" O'Brien relaxed in his chair. He sprawled out his legs, leaned back, lit his pipe, and looked at Jack and Ray. He knew them both pretty well since he had prosecuted several big cases they investigated. He knew they were good cops and took their work seriously.

He said, "Okay guys, what's up. Why are we having this meeting?"

Jack leaned forward, looked O'Brien in the eye and told him that this meeting must be kept in strict confidence. Pug pledged that this conversation would not ever leave the room.

"Good!" said Ray. "Our careers and our lives may very well be at risk. We do not know who we are dealing with except they have connections in high places. Our jobs are at stake if our chief finds out we had this conversation with you."

O'Brien reassured them and promised them again that nothing would leave the room. He said he would help guide the investigation to assure the case would be solid and search warrants well grounded. "Trust me; I am the top enforcement officer under the DA. I am on your side."

Two days later, Ray and Jack were at a car dealer to pick up another surveillance car when their radio called out, "Ontario 167, 10-19 Chief's office."

"Oh shit," they both said, looking at each other. Dread fell over them as they realized that something was seriously wrong and they were probably in deep doo-doo. No one got a call like that over the radio unless the chief was upset.

They went back to the station and announced themselves to the chief's secretary, who immediately ushered them into the inner sanctum. The chief looked up at them; his face was red, even redder than normal. He did not tell them to sit, so they stood at semi-attention waiting for what was coming. Were they being terminated? They wanted the chief to say something and at the same time dreaded what they were going to hear.

Finally the chief cleared his throat and began to speak. He reminded them that they had a conversation with Captain Lee, that they had been advised to work only the assigned details, and to leave whatever they were investigating alone. He reminded them that they had more important things to do than surveillance on good citizens. He ended his tirade with the admonition to knock it off and to not talk to anyone about the investigation. It was over, done! He concluded with the fact that this conversation was between us only. "Understand?"

When they left, the chief reached into the bottom drawer of his desk and took out a bottle of Maalox. He drank straight from the bottle, replaced the cap and put the bottle back, muttering to himself, "Hope those gung ho bastards listen."

"What just happened?" Asked Ray.

"What the hell did we get ourselves into?" mumbled Jack.

They called in Code-7 and went to In-N-Out to eat and to have a place to talk about what just happened. Paranoia crept in, so they ate outside as they wanted to be sure no one was going to hear or tape their conversation.

"Pug snitched us off! What an ass! And to think we trusted him!" Ray said with disgust, spitting on the asphalt. "What a lowlife, creepy puke sack."

"What the hell are you going to do when the district attorney's office cannot be trusted?"

"Who is all involved in this? It looks like mafia stuff! Do they have fingers into City Hall, the police department and the DA's office? Shit!"

They analyzed what they knew: a city administrator was involved, big business people, power players, the city attorney and now the Chief Deputy DA and the Chief of Police were somehow connected, aware of, or somehow aware of this. The conclusion? Could Organized Crime (OC) be in Ontario?

They talked about the class they attended where the FBI agent taught undercover tactics and problems that appear when criminals have powerful people looking out for them and helping them. He related his work in Los Angeles, working undercover in the mafia with Mickey Cohen's organization. How many agents had been ratted out to Mickey before they figured out how deep they needed to go and how secretive the investigation needed to be so as not to be discovered?

It can't be! OPD had detectives working Organized Crime in the Intelligence Unit. They never indicated mafia stuff was happening in Ontario. Were those guys also complicit with the crooks? Certainly this was not happening in Ontario! Mafia? Here in River City? No way! It can't be!

But their guts told them it was real.

They decided to lay low for a while and see what happened. Wait to see if anyone else talked to them or they heard something through the grapevine. You never know what your informants might come up with and tell you about. Maybe Clifford would hear something and call them. They knew they could not contact him for fear of getting him into trouble too.

The next day after his tour of duty, Jack noticed a dingy green Chevy a few cars behind him. *An ugly piece of shit*, he thought. As he turned south on Euclid he noticed that the Chevy made the same turn. He looked in his rearview mirror and noticed that the car was still there, only a little further back when he crossed Mission Boulevard.

Since he had attended the Department of Justice Surveillance training in Sacramento, he began to take notice of his surroundings. When he made a right turn on Francis, he noticed that the other car did too. Now he was quite certain he was being followed. So he headed to San Antonio, went north and stopped in at the Canopy. An hour later the vehicle was gone and he went home.

The next day he told Ray about it and they both watched for tails the next day. Sure enough, they each had a tail following them. They both shook them off by going to the Canopy again. This was messing up their schedules and home lives. They felt a surge of fear, knowing they had stepped on some big toes to get this much attention.

Who was following them and why?

Was Organized Crime looking for a way or a place to take them out?

A chill ran down Ray's back as he thought about that. Would his wife become a widow and his children orphans? His heart throbbed as he thought about how much he loved to play with his son and daughter. It felt great when they came running into his arms when he came home.

He planned to discuss the whole thing with Jack tomorrow. He figured they might have stepped on OC's toes, but not enough

30

to have a hit put on them. Besides, they would not need to be followed to make that happen. They could hit them lots of ways and not need to follow them home to do it.

Was the city or chief behind this to gather information to discredit them? Were they looking for information that would lead to reprimands, disciplinary actions or possibly termination? That was intriguing, because there was obviously nothing about their duty time that might bring discipline. Hmmm!

When Ray got home he called Jack to ask him to meet for breakfast the next morning. They did not mention where for fear that the phone was tapped.

The next morning that dingy Chevy was back, but they were smarter now. The Chevy dropped off and a Ford Pinto took up where the Chevy turned off. This was going to be fun! Ray sped up, made two quick right turns and then a left, pulling over in front of a parked truck. The Pinto had not kept up, so he went on his way. Ray circled Joanie's Cafe a few times to be sure Jack did not have a tail, and then they went in to eat and make plans.

They decided that the surveillance was looking for something to use against them, either in blackmail, picked up for drunk driving or getting reprimanded or fired for embarrassing the city. Neither of them had girlfriends or drank too much, so that was not a problem. They decided that if this was as big as the chief was making it, they should not drop it, but pursue it by getting some one trustworthy involved. The feds might like to look at some corruption, or at the least, a large gambling operation.

They set up a meeting with Agent Holder of the FBI Los Angeles Office. The meeting was held in Covina on a Saturday morning. It was safer to take time on a day off when it was expected they would be with family. They headed west on the San Bernardino Freeway, keeping an eye out for a tail. They took the Via Verde off- ramp, went into Forest Lawn, and then made a U-turn. No one followed them, so they proceeded onto the freeway. At Grand they got off, and immediately got back onto the freeway, now satisfied that they were not being tailed. They met Agent Holder at Denny's.

Chapter 6

Officer Pete Heller was on routine patrol when he received a burglary in progress call. He was only six blocks from the address. The dispatcher stated that the car was parked down the street from the house and a suspect had been seen breaking the glass on the front door.

The adrenal rush hit Pete fast; this was what every cop wanted to do-catch a burglar in the act. Quickly, he spun a U-turn on Fourth Street. The sound of skidding tires filled the air. Pete thought it was his tires pealing out until he felt the impact.

Then everything went black as the unit rolled onto its side from the impact of the crash. His shotgun and his helmet fell out as the unit skidded to a stop against a Southern California Edison power pole. The unit was lying on the right side and Pete was hanging in the seat belt harness. He never knew that he was removed from his unit by the firemen he had coffee with that morning at Station Five.

When he woke up he was in the emergency room in San Antonio Community Hospital. He felt the pain across his chest and his head throbbed worse than the tequila hangover he had last weekend. His groans brought the attention of a nurse, who assured him that everything was all right and they were taking good care of him.

Then he realized that his sergeant was also there, taking information for his report. Pete asked what happened. He had been broadsided by a pickup truck when he made the U-turn, but he was the only one hurt. He remembered getting the call and thinking that he had plenty of room to make a U-turn.

Puzzled, he asked his sergeant, "Where did that pickup come from? He must have been really hauling ass."

They wheeled him out to surgery. His spleen had been broken, his left kidney was bruised, and his liver was lacerated, along with other internal bleeding. After three hours of surgery and two more hours in recovery he was back in the land of the living. He felt no pain. He was just happy to be alive and that nobody else was hurt.

He spent a week in intensive care and then had a few weeks of bed rest at home. He felt pretty good considering how beat up his body was. It would be months before he would be allowed back to work.

As he improved, the IA (Internal Affairs) called to ask him. "When can we come to visit you and discuss the incident?" *Incident*, he thought? It was an on-duty crash, not an incident. What were they making out of this? Yes, he had screwed up, but it was a TC not an incident. Incidents meant discipline. *Damn.*

Internal Affairs had read the report and found inconsistencies between what he told them and what they perceived as the evidence in the case.

Had he been drinking?

Was he on drugs?

He was called in for an interview, which he willingly submitted to, not that he had a choice. When IA called you would either talk or be terminated. The State of California had a Police Officer's Bill of Rights which allowed for the officer to have representation with him during any questioning, but there was no choice; he had to be interviewed.

Pete had not done anything wrong, other than making a U-turn at the wrong time. But hey, it was done in the line of duty as he tried to nab a burglar in the act. He would not be in serious trouble for that, would he? But doubts crept in because IA was investigating, not the Traffic Bureau.

Pete called his OPOA (Ontario Police Officers Association) representative, Jack Hillberg, after he received the latest call from IA. Previously he had not felt the need to be represented during the interview, but now he was getting worried because he had an appointment with the San Bernardino County Sheriff's crime lab. He was scheduled to take a lie detector examination.

What lie did they think he had told? It was a simple clear-cut case of making a stupid U-turn. He had told the truth throughout the entire report on the event and the follow-up questions. Now he was afraid-afraid of his own department. Were they setting him up to be fired, or for other disciplinary actions? *Come on*, he thought, *we are in this together. What is this crap? Is it coming from the Chief's office?*

Was there someone at City Hall who was gunning for him? Sure, he had gotten into a bar fight six months before. He had been really stupid, but it was no big deal because no complaints were filed and he had not received a letter of reprimand. In the future he would avoid drinking too much or hanging out at bars. He had several "Atta boy" letters in his file. He was a good cop. What was up?

Pete remembered that he lost his off-duty weapon during the bar fight. Well actually, if truth was told, it was taken away from him during the melee. But it was returned and everyone was okay. No arrest, the gun was recovered, apologies were made, and he had a new respect for how cops help each other when trouble came.

Pete called the officer who recovered the gun to represent him during the lie detector test. He knew that Jack had visited the bartender and two patrons who were involved in the fight. Jack put a lot of pressure on them. Somehow he convinced them that it was in their best interest to return the gun. If Internal Affairs knew what Jack had done, Jack would likely be in trouble. Pete knew who he could trust to look out for his welfare. It was not the chief, City Hall or IA. Jack had gone out on a limb for him so Jack was where Pete placed his trust.

Chapter 7

Ten o'clock in the evening, 2200 hours in police time, the doorbell rang. A uniformed patrol officer was at the door, accompanied by an attractive young lady. Officer Breen told Ray that there had been a minor traffic collision (TC). This young lady had struck a parked car. She had been drinking but passed the field sobriety test. To show how sober she was she stood on one foot and smiled.

Breen asked if Ray would give her a ride home, since she had no one to call. Breen knew about Ramjet's weakness for pretty ladies, so he thought it would be a favor for both of them. After all, she only lived a mile away. Ray did not miss his opportunity to make suggestive comments and to tease her. They soon arrived at her apartment in Montclair.

Using an old come-on, he said, "If I followed you home would you keep me?"

Smiling, she goes, "Yes of course!" She kissed him as he walked her to the door and followed her inside. As the door closed the clothes began to drop to the floor leaving a trail to the bedroom. All but forgotten were the wise words of the training sergeant at the police academy. He had emphatically instructed the class, pointing to his badge, "This badge can get you a lot of pussy." Everyone laughed and joked until the sergeant finished what he had to say, "But one pussy can take this badge." All of those lectures about how booze, broads and bills could destroy a career were ignored and forgotten as lust took over and they spent the night together.

When they woke up the next morning she said, "That was good. Wish I didn't have to go to work so early."

Not being one to turn down an obvious invitation, Ray followed her into the shower. She held him a moment and then said, "I wish we could, but I need breakfast and then I have to leave. Call me tonight."

Breakfast and a friendly kiss goodbye and it was all over.

As Ray drove away he thought about all the sex available out there for a cop. He knew he had done a stupid thing, but chances were that she was happy that she did not go to jail and had a good time besides, so nothing would come of it.

This liaison was not like the call last week.

A lady called to report that a prowler was looking in her bedroom window. When Ray got there she was waiting at the front door.

"I think he ran away when he heard me call the station. But come in I have some pie and coffee waiting."

He sure was tempted. She was wearing a see through negligee that showed off everything she had. She looked pretty good too, as he remembered her nice shape. He knew he was not going to get messed up with sex on duty like Pacheco had. But then, that was Pacheco's own fault. He got hung up on sex with a hooker.

Hookers could be easy marks for horny and indiscriminate officers. This one had been rousted working the truck stop. She was a heroin addict, which made her very vulnerable. Pacheco talked her into giving him oral sex to make him go away and to stop hassling her. He promised her that he would call her whenever the vice squad was working the Stop *if* she would take care of him when he needed sex.

He told her, "I'll look out for you. We are going to get along real nice, huh?" He patted her on the butt as they exchanged phone and pager numbers.

This arrangement worked fine until the night the Vice Squad finished a surveillance assignment early and decided to spend a few hours at the truck stop. She climbed into the big-rig and offered to take care of both narcs. When she was busted, she put up a protest. She told them she had this arrangement to avoid being busted.

Instead of booking her the narcs made a new arrangement with her. They took a urine sample to check for heroin use, which they all knew would come back positive. The marks on her arm indicated that she shot up twice a day and sometimes three times. She told them, "When I have a little extra cash I use it." The arrangement was that this prostitution arrest and the under the influence case would be dismissed if she cooperated in investigating Officer Pacheco.

"No problem. I'll do it for free. That guy really crejackeps me out, but I'll take the deal, thanks."

The next night she met the narcs to be wired with a microphone and given instructions on what to say. She called Pacheco and asked him to meet her in the parking lot of the city library. Late at night it was great out of the way place where they could talk.

When he arrived he pulled up next to her yellow Mustang so both drivers' windows were next to each other. He parked far enough away to get out of the cruiser and walked over to talk to her, unlike cops do when they want to talk to another driver.

Meanwhile the vice squad was pleased because with him leaning into the Mustang's window the mike picked up the conversation much better. Besides monitoring the conversation, they also had a camera and began taking photos of the scene.

He no more than said hello when his radio blared out, "Ontario 105." Damn! That was him getting a call. He was upset and so were the dicks that were recording this. They expected the whole thing to fall apart and they would have to reschedule. However, the horny man saved the day. He reached in through the cruiser window and answered the call, put the mike back, and went back to the hooker.

"Got to go," he said. "Call me later."

Then he did what the vice squad was waiting for. After all, this guy's actions compromised their work and could put their lives in danger. Getting shot over pinching a hooker was about the dumbest reason to die on duty.

"Quick," he said, "put your finger in it and let me smell it."

"What?"

"Put your finger in your pussy. I want to smell it before I go."

The next sound they heard was Pacheco saying, "Aaah that's good."

Then he jumped back in his unit and drove off.

The report and recording would be on the chief's desk the next morning.

Pacheco received a call from the chief's secretary when he came into the station that day at 2pm, to see the chief. He denied any improper actions or being involved with prostitutes. Chief Brookings shoved the tape recorder to the front of the desk. Without saying a word, he punched the play button. The recorder began playing the conversation.

Pacheco became angry and started to open his mouth. "What the hell…" was as far as he got before the chief silenced him with a motion of his hand. Pacheco was embarrassed when he heard the part about what he wanted to do with her finger. He just hung his head.

39

"You put officer's lives in jeopardy, would you like to resign?" asked the chief as he stood up.

"When?" asked Pacheco.

"Today! Go clean out your locker!"

Sergeant Coleman met Pacheco at the door and ushered him to the locker room and out the door. The sergeant returned with Pacheco's ID card, badge, and the safety equipment purchased by the city.

Grinning, Ray reminded himself that not all the sex a policeman saw involved a cop. He recalled one night when he was working patrol and he was dispatched to the semi-rural area of south Ontario because a child had reported, "There is a car parked down the street and the lady is screaming. Somebody is hurting her." There was a car parked where the kid had said. Ray lit the car up with the spotlight, unsnapped his holster, and walked up to the passenger side. The couple lying on the seat was having such a good time they had not noticed the light. The groaning and screaming stopped when they heard Ray walk up on the gravel. Embarrassed, they apologized, and Ray left them after he said, "Keep the noise down, okay?"

Chapter 8

Detective bureau briefing was over. Everyone shuffled off to their desks or headed out for the first interview of the day, except Jack and Ray. They were summoned to the chief's office. No longer baffled by the bull that was going on; they headed up the hallway wondering what was coming next. They both knew to not say anything or volunteer any info, for somehow it would come back to bite them in the place you sit.

The chief's secretary looked up when they entered. She said nothing, just pointed them to the connecting door to the chief's office. Trying to read the look on her face they wondered what the message was for them. Was she feeling sorry for them and silently approving of what they did? Or was she sorry for what she thought or knew was going to happen?

Standing straight, they faced the chief. He was sitting behind his desk and the bureau captain was sitting on the far side of the room. Saying nothing, they just waited for the hammer to fall.

Looking up and trying to keep an impassive expression the chief said, "Which one of you or did you both go to LA to see the FBI?"

So, he found out already. It had been three weeks, so at least they knew the FBI had not burned them. The chief was exploring, hoping to figure out what happened or what they might have done. He was carefully checking his options. Tough spot: powerful people telling him what to do and being limited in how to do it without being in trouble with the law.

Speaking at the same time they said, "Not me, Chief."

At least it was not a total lie. No one went to Los Angeles. We only went halfway, meeting in Covina.

The chief growled and fumed when they asked, "Why would we go to the FBI, Chief?"

He knew he was stumped, because if he said anything about the gambling/bookmaking investigation it would implicate him and he needed to stay out of it. They realized that he was being pressured by someone. They almost felt sorry for him but it was not their fault he didn't have the balls or moral compass to stand up to the pressure for fear that his job would be gone. It also showed how little confidence he had that the council supported him.

41

There was a standoff of sorts. The chief was sure that they contacted the FBI about the bookmaking and gambling but he couldn't prove it and needed to be careful not to implicate himself. Both detectives knew they did it and realized they could not mention the bookmaking investigation for then the chief would know they had talked to the FBI. Confession would result in discipline for failing to obey orders. They all knew that they all knew, but nothing was going to be said.

The chief's anger showed as he stood up and told them that the captain had a new assignment for them. It was something that was neglected for a long time.

"Since you guys are some of our best detectives we want you to take care of getting control of the unlicensed yard sales, and to make some progress with the Malicious Mischief cases that have been neglected. The victims are tired of having no one to look at the reports and pursue justice for them."

A smile spread across his face as he saw that they were getting the message. They recalled him saying, "We have more important things to do" when they were told to stop the investigation. So malicious mischief and garage sales were the important things he alluded to?

"Yes, sir," they said. After snapping a salute they walked out.

Later when they were away from the station house they nervously laughed out loud.

"What a joke, he hasn't got a bone in his spine! What a chump."

"He sure does not want this investigated, does he?"

"Wonder what the FBI did that alerted them? Did they get burned in surveillance or did they file a search warrant, what?"

They knew that this assignment would give them time to do a little checking up. They also knew that they did not want to get caught. Besides, the FBI was apparently on the job and would not need their help.

Three weeks went by while they worked Saturdays and took Sunday and Monday off. It was a great assignment. There were no call outs. They came to work at 8am and went home at 5pm, and that was it. No one asked for reports or follow-up info on garage or yard sales, no citations were written, and no Malicious Mischief cases were solved. They knew this was not a real assignment and no results were expected.

Captain Lee called them in and assigned them back to the old caseload. They had some catching up to do since no work was done on their cases and new ones had been added. This was what was called, "Having your career developed."

Meanwhile, the FBI did wiretaps, served search warrants and interviewed lots of people. No one was privy to the results. Jack and Ray got an oral report from the field agent. No one was happy to do these investigations and seldom was everyone happy with the result.

The FBI had recordings of calls made from the bookie's phone to someone at the police department asking for information on vehicle registrations. The recordings were found during the execution of a search warrant. Most of the vehicle information that was requested was on cars the DMV had on record as being on car lots for sale, and others were cars that belonged to citizens who spooked the bookie by being in the area where he was.

The voice was identified as one of the detectives at OPD. He was known to drink a lot. He liked playing the horses, and made frequent trips to Las Vegas and Indian casinos. On the recordings he was heard saying, "I ran the plates. DMV says the Chevy is registered as in transition at Citrus Ford. Yeah, you know who is driving it." Another conversation was about another car and the bookie described the driver. The detective said, "That sounds like Ray, one of our narcs, and the car is registered to Rundle's."

The FBI busted the bookie and one of his runners. Case closed. No politicians, city employees, or detectives were interviewed or arrested. The end result was that after the arrests, playing the horses was difficult, but numbers and football cards somehow survived. Nothing else came of it.

A phone call was made from a public pay phone to the FBI office.

"What are you going to do with the phone recording of the detective giving info to the crooks? What about the involvement of the chief and deputy DA?"

Agent Proctor replied, "You are not going to like this, but this is all we are doing. We got orders from above. They are not satisfied, but if we do more it will interfere with another case. Sorry."

Damn it, how do we get some justice? We risked our jobs, reputation, career advancement, had our lives scrutinized, for what?

43

Of course Jack and Ray knew that it was the norm. Both knew that their careers were limited. Promotions would not come soon, if ever and they had better watch their backs. They were fully aware that this was not the end of the matter. Now they lived in a fish bowl; they did not know just who or how many were watching them.

Chapter 9

The next morning Jack and Ray went to Bert's for coffee. Still smarting about what had been going on, they said nothing. They just looked at what cases they would follow up on that day. Just as they finished, the sheriff department's Intelligence Officer came in. He seldom came there and when he did it was with Souza, OPD's intelligence detective.

He talked about the good time he would have this weekend, fishing out of Balboa on Saturday and partying Saturday night and Sunday.

"Hey, why not meet us for fishing? There is lots of space on the boat," said Don with a quizzical smile.

It sounded good, so Ray and Jack decided to go fishing, get away from the pressure, and relax. They arrived in Balboa at 9 am.

"No need to start early," they were told, "this is a fun trip. Catching fish is just a bonus; we will have a good time."

Sure enough, the plan was for a good time: they had three cases of beer, a case of wine and another case with liquor. It was enough for a dozen or more people, not the six of them.

They fished until 2pm. Most of the beer was gone and the deli sandwiches were good, and necessary to keep the booze from totally messing up their heads. They fished off San Onofre and the huge kelp bed. They caught a few calico bass, a barracuda and one yellowtail. As they stepped off the boat, Don invited them to his condominium to clean up and eat.

They sat around admiring the view while they drank a beer. It was nice to relax after washing off the smell of the anchovies they used for bait and the odor of the diesel fuel. They ordered a pizza and drank a few more beers.

Don and his two friends from OPD, Souza and Penneli, talked about how much they enjoyed coming to the condo whenever they wanted to or had time for it. Looking at Jack and Ray, Penneli said, "You can enjoy this, too."

Jack smelled a rat. They had been set up to be recruited, or at the very least tempted, with outside benefits for doing or not doing police work.

Ray did not immediately grasp this, so he said, "Really, wow, that would be great."

45

Souza replied, "Yes, this can all be for you, too. Plus, sometimes we get some girls to entertain us too if you know what I mean. Actually three are going to be here in an hour. All you have to do is let us know if you want to come along."

Jack said, "You know that I am too much of a straight shooter to mess around with women. This is nice but my wife is more important than this, sorry."

Nothing more was said about it. They finished the food and Jack and Ray headed for home, leaving the others there for the night and whatever else they had planned.

On the way back Jack looked over at Ray with a concerned and scared look on his face. "Have we just been recruited? Are these the guys that gave the information to Augie when we were watching him? I thought it a little strange when Dan just happened to come by for donuts."

"First they used the chief to put fear in us and now they send these guys to lure us as friends. How deep does this go?"

"If we get involved with these guys, and use the condo and fishing boat, we will be beholden. You can bet they will have women there the next time and some nice photos will be taken, shots our wives or chief will not like."

Two weeks went by, and Agent Holder called. He wanted to meet somewhere out of town. They agreed to meet at Bob's in Pomona on Holt next to the Baptist Church. They ordered coffee and pie, and exchanged some pleasantries and regrets over how the investigation was stopped.

"That is why Proctor and I are here," said Holder. "This is between just you and me, but you have the right to know why and what is happening."

Having said that, he pulled an envelope out of his coat pocket, removed some photos and he laid them out for viewing. The photos were of a boat, actually a very nice boat, it was a fifty-foot yacht. The Coronado Bridge was off in the distance, so they knew the photos were taken in San Diego. The second photo was of three men standing along the railing. All of them were holding wine glasses and seemed to be conversing.

Jack said, "Hey that is Souza!"

"That's right," said Holder. "Do you know the guys with him? They are the mobsters who took over Mickey Cohen's operation."

Holder put the photos away and said, "Just thought you

46

should know what we are up against. Our investigation would be jeopardized if we pursued what happened to you. Now they think it went away because of the influence they have in Ontario. So let us handle it, okay?"

They told Holder about the fishing trip and the invitation to join the group in the future. Holder leaned forward. His eyes bore into both of them.

"You did not have sex or make agreements to come back did you? Cause you are totally screwed if you did."

Chapter 10

"Hey, Jack I need some help or advice. They want me to take a polygraph test."

Jack was the newly elected President of the OPOA. Part of his role was to represent the troops in disciplinary cases and head the negotiations for wages and working conditions. OPOA was not a union, but an entity that served as an independent labor group. Police Officers Associations or Police Benefit Associations were by law independent of each other, with no umbrella organization they reported to. Most of them did belong to PORAC (Police Officers Research Association of California). PORAC provided insurance, programs for health, auto and legal defense, plus lobbies with the State Legislature for or against bills in the Senate or Assembly, but had no control over member associations.

Jack called the head of IA to see what this polygraph was about. It seemed unusual to have truth tested for a TC in which all the photos and statistics were carefully calculated. They knew how fast the unit was going and how fast the pickup that hit it was going. The tires were checked and skid marks were measured and calculated. Everyone knew that in his haste Pete made an unsafe U-turn and got clobbered. They even took blood tests from Pete to see if drugs or alcohol were involved. So what was up?

"Just routine, to be able to give the public the assurance that we are watching our own; we want to be transparent," said the sergeant.

IA was good at spouting off crap to cover what they did. Maybe they thought street cops were stupid or might even trust them to be open and truthful. Something did not seem right or smell right. Polygraphs were rarely done, and this was the first one for a TC. Normally they only used polygraphs for investigations involving fraud, embezzlement, theft and such problems. Caution and distrust of his own department made Pete decide to have an association rep accompany him at the lie detector test.

The day of the test arrived. The sheriff deputy installed all the wires and set up the machine, while the head of IA and Jack watched. The sample questions were asked, the background questions read and approved, and the test began. About a third of the way into the questions regarding the traffic conditions prior to the collision another question was thrown in.

"Do you drink a lot?"

"No, at least not very often."

"How much do you drink in a week?"

"Wait a sec," said Jack. "Where did that question come from and what does it have to do with the TC? These questions are not on the list of questions you provided either."

The deputy stopped. Then he asked, "Who are you?"

Jack told him, "I am his association representative."

The deputy's face paled, he looked over to the IA and turned the polygraph off, saying, "This test is over."

The IA sergeant turned pale when Jack asked, "What are you up to? What is going on? Is this a witch hunt?"

No reply.

The deputy was still undoing the wires, which gave Jack time to step in front of the IA sergeant. "Tell me what the hell is going on. This whole thing was rigged, wasn't it? No wonder we do not trust you!"

The IA sergeant's face turned red with anger as he spun around and walked out. "I'll call you later," he said to the deputy.

Jack turned to the deputy, "You tell me what's going on. What are they after?"

"I am only doing what I'm told. I cannot and will not tell you anything."

Jack was upset. Pete grabbed him and pushed him out the door. "Leave it alone or we will both be in trouble."

Glad they had taken their own vehicle they left and went back to Ontario.

The next day Jack went to see the chief to find out what just happened. Jack got right to the point. He was known for cutting to the chase. "This whole thing looks like a set up to screw somebody out of a job," he said. "Why Pete? Why the polygraph? Why deception and trickery? What are you fishing for?"

The chief turned bright red again, as usual when he was pissed off or put into spot he didn't want to be in. "We have been having too many vehicles damaged. Guys are being careless and we need to make a statement the officers will understand."

"So, we are going to use deceit to crucify an innocent officer to teach bad drivers a lesson? What about when Herschel was chasing rabbits in the vineyard and damaged his car? Nothing was done. Come on, he even covered it up by taking the unit to the body shop during his shift time, and had it fixed and painted before the end of his watch. A few months later he was promoted to sergeant. Maybe that would have been a good time to instruct the troops! No, he is one of the favorites, so nothing was done. He not only damaged the car, but he took the car to that body shop, took another officer off his beat to fix the unit and paint it, costing the city over nine hours of paid service. He never would have gotten caught except the paint was not dry at shift change and the next officer to use the car got paint on his uniform. Where is the justice we all promised to bring to society and fair play for the troops?"

Chapter 11

The evidence room is the most protected and regulated place in any police facility, with the exception of the armory, because the proper handling of evidence was crucial. When evidence was saved for further investigation or to be used in court testimony, it went through a careful process. The process accounted for where it was discovered, who found it, who collected it, and who stored it. Evidence was tagged with the case number and the date and time it was placed into an evidence locker.

The officer who placed the item into the locker removed the key from the lock and deposited the key into the slot that dropped the key into the evidence room. Whatever dropped there was only accessible by the technicians and police personnel who worked in the evidence room.

To remove items from the evidence room required a written request, stating who was to receive the item, what the purpose of taking it was and when it was to be returned or what the final disposition was to be.

During a trial the chain of possession was tracked in the testimony to ascertain that the item was the exact item placed into the evidence locker and that the item identified was exactly in the same condition, unless it was processed by a criminologist or other laboratory personnel. If they handled it, the evidence tag would reflect who handled it and why, and a report would explain all the circumstances.

Tracking the chain of possession and the condition of each item was crucial during a trial. If anything was missing, altered, or the chain of possession was broken it created cause for the defense to make a motion to have the item of evidence rejected as evidence or to limit the scope and use of the evidence. No officer, detective, or prosecutor wanted to damage testimony or the validity of the case by mishandling the evidence.

After a case was adjudicated in court the evidence was disposed of by orders of the judge. It might be returned to the PD evidence room waiting for the appeal process, returned to the owner, destroyed, or any other disposition the court deemed appropriate. In the case of firearms, the gun might be turned over to the police armory. Other valuable items were sold at the police annual auction, and the proceeds went to the city General Fund.

The auction would include found but unclaimed property. Guns were sold at the auction back in the good old days prior to the new gun laws, since then guns are destroyed.

Therefore, it was extremely urgent to find out what happened to the money that was discovered during a raid on a cockfight. It had been a mess from the beginning. Ray and Jack had been called out at 8pm because a cockfight was in progress.

Hastily, they raced to the station, assembled the team, and made the plan of attack. The cockfight was in a semi-rural area southwest of downtown, where homes were on half-acre to three-acre lots on Fern Street. The beat officer gave a description of the area and what he knew of the site.

The lot had two houses, one facing Fern and the other behind it facing south. The property also had two old wood-sided sheds and an aging weathered gray wood barn. The cock-fighting pit was in this barn.

Plain-clothes officers led the way. Four uniformed officers would roll up immediately after the plain-clothes officers exited their vehicles. All went well until the lead team cleared the back house. That was where the lookout was. The lookout whistled and then ran toward the barn screaming, "*Policia, Policia!*"

It was like the walls of the barn exploded as men and chickens went in every direction. Live chickens were dropped as the owners ran. These birds were now more frightened than before, when they were waiting to fight. They ran squawking and pooping, with feathers and chicken poop flying everywhere.

Many cars escaped through a previously unknown opening into the neighbor's property, thereby avoiding the blocked driveways. Other guys just ran on foot and disappeared into the darkness.

Four arrests were made and two live roosters were taken into evidence, along with ten dead roosters. Blood and feathers were everywhere and the smell of chicken shit and blood filled the barn, overpowering the smell of beer and urine. Chicken droppings smelled bad enough in normal conditions, but when cocks were fighting the fear and rage they had caused the excretions to have an even more powerful pungent odor.

Several hundreds of dollars were also picked up in the barn, and forty thousand dollars was located in the attic of the front house. Jack searched the attic by placing a ladder at the crawl space and found the money in a paper bag behind the second ceiling joist.

One of the arrestees lived in the front house. The others were illegal aliens who gave bogus addresses. Those three were turned over to Border Patrol and sent to Mexico.

The court case was over. The resident pled guilty and sentenced to six months in county jail. The defense lawyer made a request to have the cash returned because the arrestee wanted to use it to pay his attorney fees.

Thirty thousand dollars was missing! Everyone who worked the case and everyone who worked in the evidence room were interviewed. The money was tracked into the evidence room and no one had taken it out. It had never been brought to court for evidence because there was no trial. The money was suspected to be drug sale receipts because drug packaging and scales had been found in the house, but no drugs or narcotics. Therefore there was not enough evidence to file charges for drug sales or manufacturing.

It was never proven, but Sergeant Washburn, the Evidence Room supervisor, or the chief of police, who also had a key, were suspected of absconding with the cash. Chief Ward gave up his key to remove the possibility of blaming him if this ever reoccurred. He also resigned within a year to become chief of police for a San Francisco Bay area department.

Tighter controls were installed and nothing was ever mentioned outside the PD to prevent defense attorneys from casting a cloud of mistrust on how evidence was handled and lost, so they would not raise the issue when evidence was brought to court for defendants they represented.

Chapter 12

1982

Gloom and anger was rampant throughout the PD. The California State Department of Corrections called. Ricky's murderer who had been convicted and sentenced to death had just escaped. He had been removed from death row when the California Supreme Court ruled that the current death penalty was cruel punishment. Henk Mueller escaped while he was being transferred from San Quentin to Folsom.

Expressions of anger at the courts and the entire justice system were heard in the hallways, bureaus, offices and on the police radios as the notice went out to be alert, just in case he was headed back home. Two detectives were detailed to watch Mueller's sister's house. Everyone hoped he would dare to show up there because that would ensure that the justice system's errors would be corrected. Mueller was as good as dead if he showed up.

This time there was no "Do Not Shoot" order coming down. Every man in blue was still rankled about that order when the first hunt for Mueller was on. Then he was wanted for armed robbery and homicide. He shot the dude that was trying to rip him off for drugs and money. That order came from the top, via transmission by the dispatcher: "Do Not Shoot." The chief wanted him alive and anyone who shot him without permission would be in trouble.

"How the hell can he give such an order? We are the ones on the street. We are the ones whose lives are on the line when we find him. We have the training and know policy. We should make the decision to shoot when it is necessary."

Somehow everyone knew that this time Mueller would not surrender. He would go down fighting. He knew his chance of leniency from cops would be next to nil.

The day ended with no sightings or word of where Mueller might have gone. Late that night a new break came on TV. A house was broken into in Roseville, California. Prison blues were left at the house and clothes, food, a handgun, and a hunting rifle were taken. The homeowner's pickup was stolen, but found abandoned in a parking lot in Chico. Mueller was loose, armed, and headed north, making it unlikely that he would return to friends. He was more likely to go to friends he made in the joint.

57

Then nothing was heard, not a word. Nothing for days, that stretched into weeks. No sightings, no contacts, and no information from family or friends. Nothing! Who picked him up in that parking lot? Who was he with and where did they go?

The memories about Ricky and how he died again haunted every officer. Many prayers were said. Most included a request to have God put Mueller into the sights of their guns. The day of reckoning was coming. There would be no black bands issued this time.

Chapter 13

Viva la Raza! Chicano Power became the sign of the times. There was turmoil on the streets and turmoil in politics. The cops were caught in the middle of the tussle for power. Hiring and promoting Hispanic surnames became the political thing to do. Fortunately, Ontario had been ahead of the curve in hiring, but minority promotions were few due to the meager positions available. There was also a movement calling for civilian supervision in the records and administrative areas.

Working the barrio became hazardous. The corner of Sunkist and Sultana became a war zone. Young men would hang out on the vacant lot at the corner and throw bottles and rocks at passing cruisers. T stops (traffic stops) required several units as back up and often crowds would gather jeering and yelling abuse at the cops.

It was a Sunday night when the call came about a fight at the corner. Terry and Wes were nearby and rolled up just as two homeboys dragged another by the arms into the house next to the vacant corner lot. The guy's feet were dragging on the ground and snagged on the door sill. The door slammed shut and the crowd came back together, although all of them were now watching the cops as they arrived. The backup units started rolling in and tried to disperse the crowd. Meanwhile Terry and Wes went to check on the injured person they saw being dragged into the house. The crowd shifted to the front yard to prevent Terry and Wes from going in the house. Forcing their way through the crowd, they knocked on the door and without waiting for response went in leaving Jack to cover the door.

The noise level grew louder and louder. The crowd grew more agitated and vocal as they pressed into the yard and yelled for the cops to leave. Jack tried to explain what was happening, and that the officers in the house were required to check on the safety of the injured person. The noise increased until nothing could overcome the clamor. They demanded that the cops leave the house and free the people in the house. The agitators were at the back of the crowd urging them forward, pushing the crowd toward the door.

"Damn the pigs, we can kick the *putos* out," yelled the leaders as they urged the crowd to rush the house.

It was the phenomena that leaders push from behind, urging others to do what they themselves were hesitant to do. In these types of riots and mob actions the agitators pushed the crowd, rather than lead it. There was never someone up front yelling, "Follow me!"

Jack was the only person between the crowd and the two officers in the house. *Shit, now what am I going to*, he thought. *I can't shoot them and I can't fight thirty or forty people either. Well, here goes.* Out came the night stick and three people fell down from being jabbed in the stomach, neck, or solar plexus with the end of the stick. The crowd was being pushed and kept coming.

He was about to pull his .357 Magnum to protect himself and take out at least some of them. He figured that if he was going to die he was not going alone. The judgment seat of heaven was going to send some to hell while he was going the other way, up.

Just then a voice was heard from just outside the back of the crowd, "Is that you Officer Jack?"

"Yes," yelled Jack with some relief, because the voice sounded familiar and friendlier than the agitators who pushed the crowd.

"Knock it off! That's Officer Jack and he is cool."

The crowd looked for a way out. They did not want to get killed or go to jail, so they backed off.

Jack snapped the strap back on his holster. Still shaken, he stepped aside when Terry and Wes came out with a person in custody.

Jack Hillberg realized that God was taking care of business when he recognized that Frankie Armijo was the one who just rescued his ass. He had arrested Frankie twice, once for burglary and once for possession of drugs. Treating those he arrested with respect and dignity just paid off in a huge way. Jack was relieved that this crisis was past and grateful that Frankie spoke up when he did. He realized the truth and benefit of what his training officer had taught him: "When you are right you can afford to be gracious and when you are wrong you cannot afford not to be." Today that professionalism and being gracious to an arrestee had paid off. It cost nothing to treat people respectfully no matter how bad they were.

In an attempt to bring peace to the corner, the city created a community center in the small empty building south of the vacant lot. At one time it had been a small church but now it was just gathering dust. Thus the Chicano House was created. A city employee and several volunteers staffed it.

It worked while it lasted. The gangsters stayed away and the Chicano House. The staff reported all police activities in the area. One of the volunteers liked to play the role of a tough guy and leader of a movement. Whenever a police officer was writing a citation or doing other law enforcement work he would investigate. Then he became bolder and started giving advice to the suspects. He acted like a street lawyer, asking questions of the officers and accusing them of harassment and violations of policy. He was advised to back off and stand back many times, until one day he stepped between the officer and the person being cited for failure to stop at the sign. He was arrested for interfering with a police officer doing his duty.

The arresting officers were called into the chief's office to explain their actions and admonished that it was a foolish thing they had done. Didn't he know they were trying to make peace and improve relationships in the barrio?

"You can't go and arrest the city employee who is the liaison," growled Chief Ward. A call was made from IA to the West End Jail to have Jorge Armanderaz released on OR (own recognizance).

The officers were indignant. This would not be done for the average citizen. Why was a rabble-rouser who was causing lots of problems to street cops getting preference? Jorge was suspected of being the leak from City Hall. Someone there who had access to personnel files had given names, addresses and home phone numbers of officers to the Chicano House, where that information was passed on to anyone who wanted to know where a cop lived.

Jack, who lived out of the city, came home one morning after working late to find that someone had been to his house and spray painted "fuck you" and "Puto" on the driveway. He cleaned it up before he went in the house; he did not want his kids or wife to see it or know that someone had been at their home during the night while they slept. Fear and anger coursed through his mind and heart, as he thought about what could have happened.

These were not just misunderstood or mistreated citizens as Ward claimed; they were cowards that snuck around at night. If they had other ideas of doing violence his wife would not hesitate

61

to blow them away with the sawed off shotgun they kept next to the bed. Jack was glad to have prepared his wife with the gun and with hands on instructions for its use. The shotgun was legal, but not by much. She wanted it as she knew it was easier to hit someone in the dark with a shotgun then her .25 Semi-Automatic.

The next week his home phone rang and his saintly seventy-five-year-old mother-in-law answered. She was visiting for the winter to get away from the Minnesota snow. The caller swore at her and told her that he was going to come rape her and burn the house down. When the officer came home she was too embarrassed to repeat the words he said. She was still trembling with fear, afraid and worried that she, her daughter and grandchildren were in serious danger.

"Do you have to be a policeman?" she asked.

Jack began to worry too. What could he do? Every man wants to protect his wife and children, but what could he do when he had to be at work or be gone? Who would protect those he loved when he was not there? Worry and rage at being helpless to protect his family swept over him. Where could he go for help? Who would be there for him?

The only thing the city did was to relocate the personnel files to a safer place, but the damage had been done. No investigation, no reports, no discipline. Just lower morale.

Ray had a friend in the court and another at the sheriff department. He made them promise to call him when the warrant of arrest was issued for Jorge, because everyone figured that Jorge would be given special treatment again. Think so?

Three weeks went by and Ray got his phone call. He took Cary with him to City Hall, walked into the Community Services Office, and arrested Jorge. With hands cuffed behind him he was lead out of City Hall and placed in the unit.

By the time Ray got to the unit his radio was calling him, "Ontario 105, Ontario 105." With a huge grin across his face, he reached over and turned the radio knob to off. He knew he had just pissed off the chief, the mayor, and probably the entire city council, but he also knew that every officer and police station employee was rooting for him. All of them wished they had the balls to do this.

Still grinning, he walked into the West End Sheriff's jail. The jailer looked at him and said, "You are in deep shit, buddy. The phone has been ringing off the hook to see if you were here. You better call your captain now." He handed the phone through the bars.

He placed the call and he was put through to his captain. The captain did not say hello or anything nice, just, "Do not book Jorge, take him directly to Department #3. Do it now and when you are finished come to my office."

Wow! He didn't cuss, threaten, or go nuts, but he was ticked.

Ray did as directed, taking Jorge, still in cuffs, to Court Room #3 as directed. There he removed the cuffs and Jorge stood for arraignment as Judge Ruttle took the not guilty plea and released him OR. Bob left knowing that Jorge would be free to go but still need a ride back to City Hall. That return ride was not going to be in his police car. Cops only gave rides one way.

"What the hell do you think you are doing?"

"Why do you try so hard to get into trouble and piss everybody off?"

The questions kept coming. The captain did not wait for answers. He already knew the answers. He knew that the men in blue were not happy with how the city and the chief of police were coddling the enemies of the field cops.

"I want a report on this entire matter before you go home today! I want to know how you knew the warrant was issued and why you did not respond to your radio calls."

Not wanting to burn the source of information, he wrote that he had called the court to check on the warrant's status and just got lucky. As to the radio, well apparently he had accidentally turned the volume down too far because he did not want to disturb the employees when he was parked outside City Hall, and he forgot to turn it back up.

You could feel the tension and apprehension throughout the department, especially during briefing time. Everyone waited for the axe to fall. Everybody rooted for Ray because he did nothing illegal and he did what most of them wish they had the guts to do. But they also knew the chief hated to lose face. The Chief would not ignore this personal affront. No one else saw it as personal toward the chief. They mostly saw it as a response to the practice of favoritism for troublemakers. After all, this was the guy who put their wives and families in jeopardy.

Two days was all it took for the response. A letter of reprimand was placed into Ray's personnel file: "You are hereby

63

reprimanded for leaving your assigned patrol district without proper authorization or purpose."

Ray had gone two blocks outside his beat to make the arrest.

They had to find something, didn't they!

A collective sigh of relief swept through the briefing. Smiles returned. Nothing was said and Ray got a slap on the back from each officer when they walked out.

Chapter 14

Technician Ian McDougal found a custom gripped S&W .45 stainless steel handgun in an intake locker of the evidence storage. An officer recovered the semi-automatic pistol and a stereo when he arrested two burglary suspects placed it in evidence.

Ian logged in the gun and ran the serial number. Something was wrong! He checked the serial number and ran it again- same result. That gun was registered as evidence at the Ontario Police Department. It had been taken from a suspect who was arrested for a robbery five years ago. How did it get back on the street?

How did it end up in the possession of a local hype? Panic hit him like a ton of bricks. His reputation was on the line. Nothing went out of evidence without his knowledge and without his approval. He would have recorded the chain of evidence and who had the authorization to remove it, all nice and neat in the log book.

Ian pulled up the case report that was listed on the evidence tag. As he read it his eyes got bigger. He could not believe what he saw. The gun was recovered from the PC459 (burglary) at the home of an Ontario Police Sergeant, and not just any sergeant either. It was the only other person who had a key to the evidence storage room: his superior, the sergeant in charge of Records and Evidence, Zak Washburn.

Ian went through the log book but could not find any notation that the gun was assigned to be destroyed, removed or any other disposition for it. The case had been closed, fortunately, or a serious problem would occur in the court room. This case had been adjudicated, appealed, and the defendant was serving his time somewhere in the California Prison system.

Karen, his assistant, noticed Ian's concern and worried expression. She talked to him and looked at what he had been working on. She soon figured out what the problem was. Sergeant Washburn took the gun home. Ian knew that Karen was not known to keep secrets, so this news would soon spread through the station.

Ian went to the Chief's office to report what he knew and to seek guidance on what to do next.

Listening to McDougal's tale brought more angst to the chief. Just what he needed! Some idiot was going to embarrass the department and the chief. He had enough to do dealing with the racial and political tensions of the city. He reached into his drawer for two Tums to help settle the rising acid. Damn! He couldn't buy big enough jars to keep his heartburn in check. He threw the empty bottle into the trashcan.

"Write a report to me and I will have Internal Affairs look into this. Thanks for bringing it to my attention first McDougal," said the chief as he rose from his chair. He shook McDougal's hand and asked him to return with his assistant.

When Ian and Karen returned they were instructed to keep this between the two of them and the chief, and to speak to no one about this except IA. They agreed and left. They were spotted coming out of the Chief's office by one of the clerks, who insisted on knowing what was up. By the end of the week everyone at the PD heard that a gun recovered from Washburn's house burglary was a gun that was missing from the evidence locker.

When would the axe fall? It was against department policy to remove items from evidence without logging them, and to keep anything was theft, in this case a felony since it involved a firearm. There was no way to prove the intent was not theft, because the grips had been modified and a new spring and firing pin had been installed. The new grips were the same favorite grips Zak had on his other guns.

Months went by and nothing more was said. Tension mounted. No one knew what IA did or recommended. Discipline was always secret, but somehow it became public anyway. Maybe the janitor read the files! For certain, the chief's secretary was not the leak; she was very professional, which earned her the respect of everyone.

White wash! So much time elapsed that everyone expected a whitewash. Did Zak have information that would harm the chief? What's the deal?

Jack as the Police Officer's Association rep asked the chief what the disposition was. They had an interest and a limited right to know because they represented the rank and file officers in disciplinary actions, and expected equal and fair treatment for any violation of law or department policy.

"It is none of your business," It was an unfortunate indiscretion on the sergeant's part and we have handled it. The case is closed."

Being a thief was now seen as an indiscretion? *Hmmm.*

66

It was good to have friends in high places, or at least places that had access to information. Rumor was that the District Attorney's office had been asked by Internal Affairs to investigate and write a legal opinion. Several personal contacts were made, because phone calls were too easily overheard. The first contact was with a secretary in the DA's office. Ray flirted with her numerous times while he filed reports or sought search warrants. She liked and trusted him, so he thought he would see what she could do.

Several days went by, and then a phone call came to Ray's desk. A female voice said, "I found what you want, see me." Then she hung up.

At 11am Ray said he had a dentist appointment and then was going to lunch. "I'll be back at 1:30, just in case anyone cares."

The guys in the bureau laughed .They did not care where he was going or when he would be back. In fact, they suspected he was making this announcement to cover his time for a noontime tryst with one of his girlfriends. McIntyre reminded himself to ask Ray what the oral exam the dentist did was like when he returned, but he forgot.

At 5:30, Ray and Jack walked out of the station. The day's work was done until tomorrow when they would pick up where they left off. Ray told Jack to follow him. They drove west on Holt and went to the parking lot of King Cole Market at Holt and San Antonio. Ray got into Jack's car and handed him a file folder. "You are not going to believe this."

The folder contained a letter from Pug O'Brien, DA, to the city manager, and copied to the chief of police and the city attorney. It also contained the reports written by Sergeant Washburn regarding the .45 caliber pistol that had been stolen from his home during a burglary.

The report made by the sergeant was actually two reports written on two different dates. In the first one he had difficulty remembering what type of gun it was and just what the circumstances were, but the second report was precise, with dates and details. His memory improved. Why?

The first report said the gun was possibly a .45caliber that he checked out for test firing. It was in the "To be destroyed" cardboard box. The report continued,

I simply wrote on the box that I had the weapon, the weapon's description, with serial number and the date.

67

However, upon racking my memory, it now seems this __may__ have been the same weapon that was subsequently stolen from my home.

I am not completely clear on the sequence of events. However, it seems that after test firing this weapon and ascertaining that it was not operating properly, I attached a note to it, outlining same and placing it in the upstairs armory locker. The reason seems to be, that I didn't want the weapon destroyed, as it appeared to be repairable.

I checked into the case report from when the weapon came in and ascertained it had been consigned to the Department armory. A day or so after this I sought and received the Chief's permission to take the weapon home and repair it.

I am at this point clear in my own mind that I checked the weapon out by leaving a note in the upstairs armory locker.

Respectfully submitted
Sgt. Washburn

The box containing the weapons to be destroyed was normally taken to Kaiser Steel for smelting. That ended the possibility of determining whether a note had been written on the box, besides who writes official records on the flap of a cardboard box?

The second report had more exact details; the memory was now clear. "Weapon stolen from my home" was the title of the report dated November14, 1974

Sometime in early August 1973, I had occasion to check out and fire a Department .45c pistol. While firing it, I could tell it was not functioning properly. The slide would hang up and shells were not being ejected properly (it was actually unsafe). I returned it to the Department armory. (Weapon was consigned from Evidence to the armory in 1972).

A day or so later I mentioned this weapon to the Chief. I asked permission to take it home and work on it. I have always had an interest in weapons and the ability to work on them.

The weapons assigned to the Department armory have always been available for Department and personal use, when properly checked out. I checked this weapon on August 23, 1973, by leaving a note in the locker with my name and weapon description on it. However, this note is no longer available.

After working on it extensively and replacing several of the moving parts, I had it functioning perfectly shortly before September 24, 1973. On that day my home was burglarized and the weapon, along with other personal property, was stolen.

Due to the parts and labor I put into the Department's weapon, I estimated its value as $350 when it was stolen. I inquired of our Department gun expert, who has a certain expertise in firearms appraisal, what he thought the value of the weapon was prior to repair. He stated that it was worth no more than $160.

I have reimbursed the City $160, the value of the weapon, and collected the new value from my insurance company.

Respectfully submitted,
Sgt. Washburn

OPOA had written a letter to the chief of police and copied to the city manager about this weapon and how it had been misappropriated from the evidence room. Now they had official letters to see how it had been handled. The end result was that the city was paid for its property and everyone was satisfied that no crime or criminal intent had occurred. No mention of how the gun left the evidence room and got to the armory. There was no penalty for false reports, improper evidence control, misappropriation of property, or stealing. Equal justice for all? Maybe it was Sgt. Washburn who makes the liquor store runs for the chief. Delivering to the chief's house a case of booze: one week from Slim's and another week from Downtown's?

Chapter 15

The TA truck stop at Milliken and Interstate 10 continued to be a problem. Drugs and sex were sold and semi-trailers were stolen at an increasing pace. It was time for vice and narcotics to spend some time there to quiet things down. Two days a week would be spent at the truck stop.

Jack and Ray got the assignment and were promised all the help and backup they would need. They exchanged looks and agreed that this could be fun; but there was nothing worse than getting into a shoot-out over some sleazy hooker. They made plans to come in late afternoon and work until midnight. Jack had a friend who owned a Mayflower Moving Company. They went to his office and spent some time joking and telling stories of interest to Roy, the owner.

Jack finally got around to the reason they were there. They needed a truck. They asked Roy if he had a truck and trailer that might be available for them to use for the evening. When they promised they would bring it back undamaged Roy consented. Roy knew Jack had driven trucks in the past, but he also knew he did not have a Class B license. What good were buddies if you couldn't trust each other? The arrangement was made.

It had been three years since Jack drove anything bigger than his pickup truck, but by the time they got to the freeway they were comfortable, and drove east on Interstate 10. They pulled into the truck stop and found a place to park. There were hundreds of trucks parked in long rows. They found an open spot that they could drive through and not need to back into. Backing a semi was difficult for an amateur. Once they parked, they put an empty beer can on the dash and popped a cold beer and a coke, they sat back to wait.

A Lincoln with two women drove up, the blond rolled down her window and waved. Ray waved back and she pulled up a little and asked, "Are you looking for a date?"

Shit was happening and happening soon!

The second girl was a brunette with a little extra weight on her. What the heck, they were not looking for girls to spend their lives with. This was only a job that would hopefully end with an arrest.

Both girls climbed into the truck.

The brunette grabbed Jack's arm and said, "You're first. Let's get into the sleeper."

The blonde set a container of handy-wipes on the dash and took a big drink from the beer can. She reached over and groped Ray's crotch while she said, "Sure hope they hurry up so I can get some of this."

Ray was not too happy. This was his first time with a hooker and suddenly he felt intimidated and self-conscious.

Meanwhile, Jack was settling down on his back on the bed.

The girl asked, "You want a blow job?"

"Sounds good to me, How much is it?"

"Twenty bucks," she said as she pulled his zipper down.

Ray heard the zipper going down and was ready to end this and make an arrest before anything foolish or dangerous happened.

"10-15?" he asked, using the police code for suspects in custody. Both girls looked up and said, "Is it that late already?"

Ray and Jack busted out laughing as Ray said, "No, it is only eight, but you are busted."

He flashed a badge and took out the handcuffs. The hookers were quickly cuffed before they could leap out of the truck or make a scene. They placed a call for a patrol unit to transport them to West End. When it arrived they walked the hookers to the back of the truck and put them into the unit.

Ray and Jack walked to the restaurant to wash their hands and see what action they might get into there. Before they got there they were stopped by two of the homeliest black women they had ever met. "Hey you guys want to date?"

"Sure, but we need to use the pisser first," they responded.

"How about buying some lunch for us first? We will show you a really good time after. Okay with you?"

What would they do? It was the city's money and they were hungry too, so they agreed. There they were, drinking coffee and chatting with these ugly hookers, who also needed to bathe or use a powerful deodorant. Jack and Ray were not having fun, and were wondering what they got themselves into. Then the door opened and three couples that attended the same church Jack went to came in. They were good, respectable people who lived on a dairy farm just a mile or so down the road. Jack wanted to crawl under the table.

Ray had no idea what was going on, so he just started eating

72

his greasy burger. Jack was silently talking to God, asking Him to keep these people from church away from them, for a variety of reasons. He did not want to be exposed as a police officer. He did not want them to even see him, because he was sure that one of the women would gossip about it, as usual, and call or tell everyone she met that she saw him hanging out at the truck stop with some provocatively dressed woman.

God does hear prayers! The church people did not come over or even acknowledge that they recognized them, and no one called his wife or mentioned anything at church the next Sunday.

After they ate, they walked to the truck and made conversation about what they were going to do and what the price was. Both girls said they only gave head, and charged twenty dollars. Another patrol car came and transported them to jail.

As soon as they were gone, Ray looked at Jack and asked, "Do you think they were guys? They were too ugly to be women."

Jack called the jail to alert the desk to what might be coming in. It turned out that nope, they were both women.

They both felt dirty and wanted to clean up and finish the reports without too much overtime, so they brought the truck back and called it a day. Then they went to the Canopy to debrief with the swing shift that was just coming off duty.

The next week they returned to the truck stop. This time they had two trucks, each with a team of narcs, and two detective units to transport the arrestees to the hold cells at OPD. Someone in patrol had complained about having to do the booking reports and transportation for the dick bureau. Now they had to do it after they shut down at the truck stop for the night. They would probably log some overtime; overtime that they did not need. They had enough compensatory time on the books already. It would shut down the bureau for a month if they used it all.

This time the action at the truck stop was fast and furious. They just turned off the engine when the truck next to them started rocking, and the laughing and howling was going wild.

The window opened and the hooker called over, "Do you want to be next?"

A man's head appeared next to hers. He promised that this was a wild one and they would have a great time.

Jack opened his door and the hooker switched trucks. Her boobs were hanging out for all to see and her skirt was caught up at the waist. She noticed it and giggled uncontrollably, grinned

73

from ear to ear, and said, "Oh well, it just makes things easier."

This one turned out to be a speed freak and she was flying high. Her face looked like forty miles of bad road; all wrinkled and missing teeth. She looked forty years older than she really was.

After the two teams had each made four busts, the CB's came alive. Drivers were arguing about whether the cops were there. Most of the drivers, at least the ones on the radio, were angry. The vocal ones called for action. They wanted to chase the narcs off the lot and protect the hookers from being arrested.

Sure enough, one of the trucks pulled out of his parking spot and blocked the detective unit from leaving with two hookers. A standoff ensued. Several drivers stood by the truck that was blocking the drive lane. The drivers demanded that the women be let loose. Both detectives stepped out of the unit, one with the shotgun. This only made the drivers angrier. They did not seem afraid of guns. Every cop there thought these drivers also had guns. This could become nasty.

Nasty like the time a pimp tried to free his hooker and exchanged gunfire with the cops. They chased each other across the lot and around trucks. That time no one was hurt. Two cars ended up with bullet holes and a pimp was taken into custody along with his woman.

Now the detective raised the shotgun level with his waist and calmly said, "Move that damn truck or I'll blow the radiator out."

The drivers kept coming, laughing at him. They took one more step and he racked a round into the chamber. When they took that next step a hole appeared in the radiator and the antifreeze ran onto the pavement.

The drivers got the message. They all scattered. They knew that the load they carried would be in a storage yard and they would be without a job when the company received the notice that the truck had a hole in the radiator and the driver was in jail.

The following week on Friday, Ray and Jack worked late and since their wives had already made other plans they decided to make a run to the truck stop to see what Friday nights were like there.

It was just about 7pm and the sun had been down for thirty minutes or so. The truck stop was fairly well lit except for the back area along the freeway. Driving through the lot in the plain unit, they did not see much action and the CB was silent. Then they noticed that along the back fence there was a car parked that looked out of place.

Jack hid the unit next to a truck and they walked over to see what was going on, since they could see movement in the car.

As they got closer Ray goes, "Uh, oh, that looks like Pug's car."

No one was visible from where they were, so they walked up to the car and then noticed two men in the front, one with his head in the other's lap. They must have heard the approach because the one sat up quick and the other pulled up his pants since they were down by his knees. It was too late to see if a sex act had been interrupted, but it sure looked that way. The man Pug was with did not have his erection covered before Ray saw him pulling up his pants.

Pug's face was white with fear when he saw who was standing there watching. His pants were down to his knees too. If he had an erection it had gone down faster than a dropped rock. He made the excuse that they had been drinking at the Magic Lamp during happy hour and parked here to rest. Then they fell asleep.

Asshole! Who did he think he was fooling?

Ray and Jack stepped back to discuss what to do. It was obvious that Pug was drunk, and he probably had been having a gay relationship. What could be done without getting into deep shit for busting the Deputy DA and prevent creating a hassle or problems for themselves? Yet they were not going to let him skate, they knew this was a God-given opportunity to settle the score.

"Got it," said Jack. "How about we make out a Field Interrogation on the gay friend and call Pug's wife to pick him up. We tell him this is what we have to do to protect his reputation and not arrest him for being drunk and giving blowjobs. If he leaves we will have to arrest him for drunk driving so we cannot just let him go."

They asked the other guy for his ID. He was a truck driver from Ohio. When they took him aside he confessed that he met Pug in the restroom at the truck stop. He did not go to any restaurant to drink and no he hadn't heard of the Magic Lamp.

Pug knew he was busted, that his lies were obvious, and there was nothing he could do to change anyone's mind. He had screwed over these guys and now it was payback time. He knew the adage that says, "Do not piss off the Good Humor man." That

75

referred to the day when the ice cream company named Good Humor Ice Cream sold ice cream on the street. When someone was nice or good to you it was a bad idea to screw with him, because the good humor would be gone and there would be hell to pay. He had pissed off two good humor cops. That was a bad idea, Pug.

Six months later Pug resigned from the DA's office, moved out of town and his wife filed for divorce. Good riddance!

Across the lot the other team was working hookers.

Billy Bob, called that because of his Alabama accent, and his partner were in a United Van Lines truck. This truck was being used for a few hours while the driver was treated to a meal. He hated hookers because they constantly knocked on truck doors and woke him up when he was trying to rest.

A curvy good looking black woman jumped up on the steps on the driver's side. Knocking on the window she said, "Hi honey, can I come up and sit with you?"

"Sure, come on in."

She jumped down, and went to the other side and climbed in. "Want to date?" she asked.

"What do you mean, date?" he asked. "Back home when we date we go ask the daddy if we can go out for something like sweet tea and a hamburg."

"No dummy that is not what I mean. I mean do you want sex, like a blow job or a fuck."

"Whoa! That sounds good but that is not a date back home. Does this cost money?"

"Of course it costs money! I don't screw strangers for free. It costs thirty bucks for head, forty for half and half."

Billy Bob reached for his wallet and put two twenties on the dash. As he did this she reached over and pulled down his zipper.

"Whoa, wait a minute," he said as he flipped out his badge. "I am a police officer and you are under arrest."

She laughed, "You are funny. Put the phony badge away. You're too stupid to be a cop."

Billy Bob laughed too, "Ya honey, that southern boy action gets them every time."

Chapter 16

Upland Police Department initiated an investigation of stolen cars that were being brought to an Upland chop shop. There they were dismantled and some of the parts sold to body shops while other parts and engines were reassembled and sold as salvaged cars. This was commonly referred to as a chop shop.

An informant identified the auto shop on East Arrow Highway as this chop shop. He was not the most reliable or trustworthy informant because he came forward with the information as a condition of receiving a light sentence for his own arrest on Grand Theft Auto. But who would know about a chop shop other than a car thief?

He bragged, "He tells me what kind of car he wants and I steal it for him."

Nevertheless, the information sounded not only plausible but likely since this shop often had lights on late at night. The graveyard shift patrolmen had checked out the shop a few times to see if everything was all right, but there was no response to their knock. The owner was called to come and check the shop, but he did not answer his phone. The officer then checked the building for signs of forced entry, but none were found.

Upland's detective, Carl Maury, passed the information to the California Highway Patrol's task force. The departments began a joint effort investigation. They did surveillance, photographing the visible cars that were stored in the building and in the adjoining fenced lot. They took photos of people who came and went during the normal working hours and after hours.

The shop had several signs that indicated chop shop activity. There were people working late at night but there was no response to knocking on the door. It was suspected that the nighttime workers parked inside the fence and stayed overnight until the shop opened in the morning, and then cars would leave.

The task force decided to do a highway patrol check on the site. They would do what was called a routine inspection to look at the vehicles that were being worked on and look at the document file for altered and salvaged vehicles.

Two officers from the CHP and one Upland detective conducted the inspection. They checked the vehicles that had their motors out and checked the engines that sat around to see if the

VIN numbers were intact and who they were registered to, they compared that information to the list of stolen cars.

When they opened the next file drawer, they discovered a folder that contained DMV forms. Among those forms were Vehicle Verification forms. These forms were to be filled out listing the new body or engine numbers in cars that had been salvaged. They took the engine and running gear from a totaled auto and placed them into a car body that had body damage that was inexpensive to repair, creating a new car from the reassembled parts.

These forms were intended to prevent an automobile from being registered as a legit vehicle if it contained stolen parts. Therefore each form had a signature line for law enforcement to sign. This form, when signed, verified that the VIN numbers had been checked and the numbers on the form coincided with the actual numbers on the engine, frame, and other places designed by the manufacturer. Qualified law personnel signed this form under the penalty of perjury. The perjury stipulation was removed several years later and is no longer required by the DMV.

Four Vehicle Verification forms were found in this folder that had been signed but not filled in with the vehicle description or VIN numbers. Sergeant Washburn of the Ontario Police Department had signed these blank forms.

The Upland detective who discovered the signed but blank forms had previously worked on the West End Regional Narcotics Task Force, with four Ontario detectives and others from Chino, Montclair and the San Bernardino Sheriff's Department. They all had maintained contact and information was passed back and forth to each agency. Carl Maury also became a regular visitor to the Canopy to meet old friends. He passed the information about the signed forms to his old buddy and partner on the task force, Ray, over drinks at the Canopy one day.

Ray approached the OPOA with this bit of news. Reports had been filed and they had been told that Sergeant Washburn had been interviewed, but there were no reports in the file and no enforcement action taken. It had been several months or more since the raid on the chop shop, so they wondered if this was being "swept under the rug" or was the system going to handle administrative staff the same as rank and file officers?

Another letter of inquiry was sent to the chief and copied to the city manager. This was done without letting the public or the officers know, thus preventing false accusations or misrepresentations of truth to cause any damage. After all, these signed blank forms enabled stolen cars or engines to be registered for license plates, and then never checked on again; that is why the signature was required *after* inspecting the serial numbers on assembled cars that are ready to sell.

Jack was called into Chief Brookings's office. Jack and Chuck, the vice president, waited for the invitation to sit, and when it was not given they took seats anyway. The chief was clearly upset, and he did not invite people to sit down when he was upset.

The chief said, "Why are you always making trouble and getting involved in what is not your business?"

Chuck replied, "Well, sir, the men have the opinion that justice is not happening in the department. They correctly or incorrectly think discipline for officers is stringent but for administration is lax. So when things come up that becomes public knowledge they are interested to know how fair discipline is. This is not personal; we just expect openness and clarity and we believe that crime and justice is our business."

Brookings's face burst into a glower as he became red from his neck to his eyebrows. "The matter was looked into and the decision is that this was foolish and an indiscretion. That is all you need to know," said the chief rising to his feet.

Jack and Chuck knew this meeting was over, so they left.

Two weeks went by. Chuck found an envelope that someone had pushed into his locker. It was not addressed and not signed. Enclosed was a copy of the report, written by Washburn, regarding the Vehicle Verification forms? There was also a copy of the letter written by Chief Deputy DA Pug O'Brien, to City Attorney Carlos Hoover, absolving the sergeant of serious wrong doing. Interesting! Someone in the upper echelon wanted to expose the "white wash."

He took the letters and called for a meeting of OPOA Board.

Six of the seven Board members made it to the meeting and heard Chuck read the report.

Earlier this year, exact month unknown, a friend for three years asked me to go with him to Texas to pick up two cars that he was going to bring to California. He was temporarily laid off from his regular employment and had time to work on these vehicles.

After he returned to California with the vehicles, he called me to request that I sign off the DMV forms for him, and to look at the new shop he was moving into. I responded with a visit to his small shop in Upland, had a cup of coffee and personally checked the VIN numbers on the only two vehicles in the shop. The VIN numbers on these vehicles were the same as the numbers on the certificates of ownership. A blank DMV form was stapled to these ownership certificates.

After assuring myself of the validity of the VIN numbers and the ownership certificates, I signed off the DMV forms, thinking at the time that these forms would be typed in by the DMV.

It has never been an uncommon practice to me, in dealing with people you trust, to sign blank forms. I recently signed a blank paper at Bank of America for a substantial loan. P.O.S.T. reimbursement forms that must be typed have for years been signed blank by myself and other officers. Additionally I had complete confidence in the integrity and honesty of my friend. I had absolutely no reason to believe anything illegal was occurring, or as a matter of fact, anything illegal was ever done!

Sergeant Washburn

This report was sent to the chief who hated it when an officer assumed something to be factual. When interviewing officers and they said they assumed something to be factual he would reply, "Do you know what assume means? When we assume, you make an ass out of you and me. Do not assume!"

O'Brien's report was read next.

The officer admitted that he signed certifications on two applications for registration of foreign vehicles without the information having been filled in over his signature, and then gave these forms to a friend. At the time, the form called for the officer to sign the certification under penalty of perjury. However unwise the officer's conduct, it cannot serve as a basis for criminal prosecution. Aside from that there are evidentiary problems because the application forms are no longer available as they are missing. Penal Code section 118 and Government Code 6203 both require that the information over the signature be false and that the certifier knew they were false. The undisputed evidence is that no information appeared and no information had been filled in over his signature when the documents were seized.

The same DA deputy and the same city attorney who were involved with the bookmaking investigation were asked to write legal opinions on stolen vehicles. The owner of the shop was arrested for possession of stolen auto parts.

Providing a signed blank form was aiding car theft, and the forms were there but the cars his friend had brought from Texas were not. Where did the cars he supposedly signed off on go?

The OPOA Board decided that this was not the mountain to die on. The odds made anything they did futile because all of the evidence was gone. Destroyed by whom? The only things remaining were the reports.

The department was willing to harbor a thief's accomplice! Why?

Chapter 17

It was shaping up to be a long day. Jack was in court all morning for testimony on a simple under the influence of heroin charge. It turned out to be a short trial, when the defense attorney made the rookie mistake of believing his client.

"Of course I was not under the influence. I stayed clean from when I last went to jail five months ago, man," was what Frankie told the attorney. "Officer Hillberg is prejudiced and picks on us Mexicans. They are going to fire his ass for being prejudiced."

So the attorney built his defense on the premise that his client was not a user and that the officer was lying.

When testimony began the deputy DA called Jack to the stand. The jury was seated and waited patiently for testimony to begin. They already heard the opening comments by both attorneys and were anticipating the testimony. They wondered if the officer really was a rogue officer that used his authority to railroad minorities as alleged by the defense attorney.

The stage was set with the background questions regarding where and when the contact was first made.

What caused the officer to suspect the defendant was using drugs or was under the influence?

Where did you first see the defendant?

"He was the passenger in a vehicle that was driving south on Bon View from Holt," Jack said. He continued, because he knew what the next question should be. "The right rear brake light was broken and not operating."

The defense attorney stood up. "Your Honor," he began, "This is a common ruse used by police officers to initiate contact. Before this officer testifies I want to take the officer under voire dire to determine his experience to qualify as an expert in drugs and narcotics use."

The judge responded in his slow and carefully enunciated way, "You are welcome to ask this officer any question you want to determine his expertise; however you should be aware that this officer has qualified as an expert in narcotics many times in this court, so if you have new questions or information you may ask them now."

"Thank you, your honor; I accept the court's previous determination."

The prosecuting attorney continued with the questions, establishing the probable cause for contacting the passenger in the vehicle.

"What drew your attention to the defendant?" he asked.

"It was a warm day, over 85 degrees and he was wearing a long sleeve Pendleton shirt. He kept looking away, avoiding eye contact with me and the driver. Most people want to see what is going on, but he was avoiding eye contact, looking out the window or down on the floor board. When I asked him for his ID he opened his door and attempted to run. I anticipated this as it frequently happens. I told him not to run because it would only mean he would go to jail tired and out of breath, but he ran anyway. I was already moving by the time he began to run. I caught up to him in about twenty feet, sir."

"What then, Officer?"

"I placed him in handcuffs, removed his wallet to get his ID, and ran a warrant check. The report came back with no warrant but that he had a record of heroin use. I, then, used my flashlight and pupil meter to check the dilation of his pupils."

"What did you observe?"

"I observed that his pupils were pinpointed, that is very small and did not change when the eye was in shade or in bright light."

"What did you do next?"

"I asked him if I could roll up his sleeve so I could inspect the veins in his arms for injection marks. I found numerous injection marks on the veins inside both elbows indicating recent usage of a needle injecting heroin."

Again the defense attorney rose to his feet.

"Your honor, I would like for this officer to inspect the defendant's arms, here in front of the jury, to verify whether he is capable of determining if injections have been made and to explain how he can tell if injection marks are from heroin or other injections or results of sparks from welding."

"Request granted," intoned the judge. "Have the defendant approach the witness stand."

The defendant slowly rose to his feet and walked to stand in front of the witness box even more slowly. He was looking back at his attorney when he gingerly rolled up a sleeve.

Jack was amazed. The arm had a track of injection marks, which indicated that the defendant was using heroin multiple times a day. The judge already anticipated this, so he ordered the defendant to roll up both sleeves.

Frankie was looking down and away. He knew he was in trouble and that his attorney was going to be pissed for having been lied to, and going to be even angrier at himself for believing an addict.

Jack described what he saw to the jury and the judge.

"Your Honor," he began, "the oldest of these marks are tiny brown scabs indicating injection from about two weeks ago. The injection of heroin causes a slight inflammation to the site, which then forms a scab over the injection site. The older the site is the smaller the scab until the inflammation is gone. The freshest sites have a circle of red inflammation and a scab has not formed as yet. The freshest marks have a tiny pinprick mark with no inflammation. The red inflammation gets larger for four days and then recedes as the scab forms. The marks on these arms indicate injections have been made twice a day and sometimes three times a day during the past fourteen days. This mark here," Jack pointed to the latest injection, "indicates an injection was made less than four hours ago. If you would like, I can check his pupils and confirm that he is under the influence of heroin now."

"You may return to your seat," said the judge.

"Anything further?" he asked the defense attorney.

Both attorneys stood and said they had no further questions. The closing arguments were short.

The judge told the officer to stand down and return to the prosecution table. He gave the jury instructions for their deliberation and for selection of a foreman.

The defense attorney was looking down. He wanted nothing to do with his client and was embarrassed before the remainder of those in the court room. Mercifully, the judge said nothing other than to excuse the attorneys and order them to be available for return when the jury reached the verdict.

The deputy DA and Jack went out for a cup of coffee. Neither one had ever seen a defendant expose himself so thoroughly in front of a judge and jury. One hour passed when they were called back to the court. The jury had returned a verdict.

As the jury walked in and took their seats they smiled at Jack and the DA. The defense was not even looking in their direction.

"Have you reached a verdict?" asked the judge.

"Yes, Your Honor," said the foreman. This was all quite formal, but that was how courts worked.

"What say you?" asked the judge.

The foreman looked down at his notes to be sure he said it just as the script said to do it. "We find the defendant guilty of Health and Safety Code section 11550."

It had taken the jury more time to select a foreman than it took to make a decision of guilt or innocence.

After court Jack helped Ray and the burglary teams serve a search warrant. They found drugs and a room full of stolen goods. By the time the reports were written it was way past dinnertime so they went to the Canopy.

It was time for more stories and tall tales.

Jack and Ray joined four patrolmen who had almost finished their Texas Burgers and were washing the fries down with a cold draft. Jan Van De Broek, aka Dutch, was there too. He came infrequently but was always welcome and was well respected. He fit in with the group, since he was the ultimate backup and was on the OPOA Board. He never had more than two drinks because the Board members were always watched. Staff wanted to find weak spots to use against them when a Board member represented officers that faced discipline proceedings.

"Hey, Dutch! What was that call about this afternoon where you called for an ambulance and back up without sirens? Something goofy?"

"It came in as a PC415 (peace disturbance) call on east Maitland. I expected to see a crowd and hear some boom box or Mariachi music. Instead there was no one around. It was almost ghostly. Nobody in any of the front yards and the street was empty. I pulled into the drive and stepped out onto the entry walk. Then I heard the music. It was a stuck record, a 45rpm going on and on, playing 'Onward Christian Soldiers,' over and over and over.

"The house's driveway side door was open, so I walked up and saw this dude sitting on a fruit crate with a twenty-two rifle standing on the floor, and he had the barrel in his mouth. The record player was next to him, stuck on this one phrase, 'with the cross of Jesus' so I backed away, hoping he had not seen me or realized that the police were there.

"I called for a backup and the ambulance, knowing somebody was going to the hospital. Hopefully it would be 'Mister Christian Soldier' going to the 5150 ward, and not to emergency. I went back to the door to see what he was up to. His hand was on the

86

trigger guard, not on the trigger, so that was good. He must have heard something, because he turned and saw me. Immediately his finger went to the trigger. Shit! What should I do now? I did not want to witness him blowing his brains out.

"There was no time to call SED [(Special Enforcement Detail), which was the precursor for today's SWAT] or a negotiator, it was up to me. So I took off my helmet to look less intimidating. I knew that was trouble for me, because I received a letter of reprimand for not having the helmet on during a traffic stop last month. I guess that goes along with being on the OPOA board.

"Anyway, I figured this guy is religious and had some problems with God. His mind was fixated on church music. So, I think it was a God thing, then I thought about the Sunday school song every kid learns in church, 'Jesus Loves Me.' You know I could not sing a song if my life depended on it. Well, now it was this dude's life that depended on what I did, so I started singing with my scratchy and off key voice, *'Jesus loves me this I know, for the Bible tells me so, little ones to him belong, I am weak but he is strong. Yes, Jesus loves me; Jesus loves me, for the Bible tells me so.'*

"You know, it worked. His hand went off the gun and he lifted his head to look at me. My gun was unstrapped and my hand was on it as I walked in and started the chorus of the song, *'Jesus loves me, yes, Jesus loves me.'* That was when I was close enough to touch him and take his rifle away.

"He looks at me with glazed eyes asking, 'Are you sure?'

"Yes, I know Jesus loves you and he wants you to get help from people who really care about you. Will you go?

"Right on time the ambulance arrived and the attendants were at the door. He got up and walked to the gurney the ambulance crew had set up on the driveway. They took him away to Patton State Hospital."

"You're a lucky man," they all said.

But Dutch knew it was a God thing and he was grateful.

Chapter 18

Jack was assigned to Narcotics and Ray moved to Burglary. As great partners did, they found ways and times to work together. Whenever either one needed help they would call each other first.

That was what happened when at 4:30 a phone call came that there were several prostitutes working the truck stop and knocking on the doors of the rooms at the motel next door. Jack's crew wanted to go home, so Ray said he would go. This was good, but also bad, because Jack was dressed in Levis and a dirty T-shirt but Ray was in a suit and tie.

"We will make it work. Let's go!" Ray said as he took off his tie but kept his suit coat on to cover his weapon and cuffs. Jack went to the motel office to talk to the clerk who called. She explained that drivers called the front desk to complain about being unable to get the sleep they needed due to the persistent knocking on the door. She gave them the keys to a vacant room on the back side of the motel, overlooking the truck parking area.

Jack and Ray went in a few minutes apart. They scattered some newspapers, food and soft drink cups around the room. They had no bags or extra clothes, they hoped the girls would not notice but stay focused on making thirty dollars.

They turned the TV on with the volume high enough that it could be heard by anyone who walked by outside. They waited. The blinds were closed so the hookers could not see in and notice Ray's suit.

Knock, knock. Someone was at the door. Ray ran to the bathroom to hide and waited to backup Jack when needed. Jack opened the door. The woman was not bad looking, which was somewhat unusual for most hookers, but she looked like she had a life of hard knocks. She did not know it but life was not getting better.

"Want to date?" she asked.

Jack stepped aside and she stepped into the room.

"Sure, how much?"

"Twenty for a blow and thirty for a straight."

"Okay with me."

"Let me use the bathroom to get ready. You can get ready while I'm gone, Okay?"

Jack agreed and reached for his belt, loosening it to let her know he was serious.

He heard a scream from the bathroom and the hooker came running out yelling, "There is a man in there!"

Ray came out right behind her, flashed his badge and told her she was busted. She was relieved to know they were the police because when she walked into the bathroom and saw the shoes and legs wearing suit pants under the shower curtain she thought she was going to be kidnapped and taken into captivity or severely molested and abused. She was almost glad to go to jail instead.

Before they could make a call for a police car to transport her to West End County Jail there was another knock on the door.

Ray took the hooker back into the bathroom and told her to keep quiet. She complied. This time there was a black woman there, dressed in hot pants and a top that only covered the tips of her breasts. She had more body hanging out of her clothes than inside.

"Hi honey, are you horny?" she asked.

"I wasn't but I sure am now," said Jack. "You are too hot to pass up."

"You got fifty bucks for Sugar, honey?"

This was too easy, so Jack negotiated with her for forty. The negotiations were just to make the hooker comfortable. He wanted her to think she was dealing with a thrifty trucker and not a cop. The deal was made. He went to the bed to take his badge and handcuffs from under the pillow. Before he got there she peeled off her top. This was good, because she would not run away with her boobs showing.

Seeing the badge she goes, "Oh shit, not again."

She was cuffed and a patrol unit was called to transport both of them.

Jack and Ray waited for more, but the news must have gotten out that the narcs were on site. Thirty minutes later they left too.

On the way out Jack' calls, "Hey Ray don't let your shoes stick out past the shower curtain next time."

Prostitution was a sad business that victimized the women more than the men. The men, or Johns, might get ripped off or even get a STD if they were stupid enough to engage in sex with a hooker without wearing a condom. But men who held power over them in some way forced many of these women into this life. The women, especially if they were young or naïve, were promised a great life and luxury.

The first month or two the pimp typically took them to fancy restaurants and bought them nice clothes. Then he needed to date his other girls or find new ones. By then the girls were trapped by the pimp. He would beat them if they threatened to leave; or he might introduce them to drugs that they could only get from him, making them virtual prisoners.

Others just had low self-esteem or not enough confidence to make a living by using their brains or getting training in some skill. Sex became the easy, or often the only, means they could see of earning a livelihood.

Ray arrested a typical young woman who needed to make ends meet and thought she had no way out except to sell her body. She lived in an apartment near the Thunderbird Bowling Alley, so she prowled that area for customers. She was a pretty blond and she had married before finishing high school. She became pregnant and had two children before she was nineteen. By this time she was twenty-two, her husband decided to move on with a woman he met at work.

She was left with no job, two small children, and not enough child support, which was not even paid some months. Her car broke down and she could not find the funds to pay to fix it. Her family was in another state and her relationship with them was strained. Where could she turn for help? Having sex was easy, and quick. Plus she would not have to leave her kids with a sitter.

The phone call came to the bureau. The girl was taking clients to her bedroom while the kids were home. "Something has to be done! This is really bad for kids," said the caller. "Here is her phone number."

Ray and Jack went to the bowling alley to create the background noise when they called her. "Hi! My name is Ray. My friend says you are real nice and provide a good time."

"What did your friend say about me? Who are you and what do you do for work?"

"I work construction and my friend is an accountant. Can we both come over?"

She gave Ray her address and said, "When you knock, wait a few so I can send my kids outside to play."

Ten minutes later Ray and Jack knocked on the door, and sure enough, a very nice petite blond opened the door. She ushered them in. Then she went to the sliding glass door, opened it and said, "Mommy is busy so be good and do not bother me, okay?"

Turning to the guys she said, "Who is first?"

Ray stepped up and she led him up the stairs to her bedroom.

"Got twenty five for a good time honey?" She said as she stepped real close and unbuttoned Ray's shirt.

Ray took the money from his wallet and put it on the dresser where she asked him to put it. For some reason prostitutes did not like to take money into their hands. Maybe then they could say the sex was for fun and the money was a kind tip from a friend. She stepped back after undoing Ray's belt, leaving him the task of removing his pants. She quickly unbuttoned her blouse and took off her bra. *Nice,* thought Ray. He pulled his badge from his pocket and told her to dress herself because she was under arrest.

They walked out of the bedroom and returned to the kitchen where Jack was waiting. Barely three minutes had expired. The hooker provided her driver's license and sat down at the table. She began to cry. Sobbing, she pled for mercy. She explained her circumstances and asked for time to make a phone call to her mother.

This was tough! Tough for her because she needed to reach out for help; thus exposing her secret life and tough on the detectives as they too had families. They thought about their sisters or daughters, hoping nothing like this ever happened in their lives. They wished they did not have to make this arrest, but children should not be exposed to seeing their mother take a variety of men into her house.

There was sadness all around. Her mother was going to post bail and come to help her with the children. Meanwhile, the children were brought to Child Protective Services and their mother was booked at West End.

"Shit, sometimes I hate this job. Well not the job, just the crap we see every day."

Chapter 19

The Narc Unit teamed up with detectives from neighboring jurisdictions to form a regional task force. Upland supplied two, Montclair one, Chino two, and the Sheriff's Department two; along with Ontario's three men and a supervisor it made a nice team.

Jack and Ray were chosen. They no longer reported to work at the police department. They met in a garage that was built back in the nineteen thirties. It had a half bath and they could enter off the alley. The comings and goings were not noticeable to the neighbors, and if it was necessary vehicles could exit two ways, on the street or the alley. Only the owner of the property knew who they were.

It was a great place to operate from. It provided security and removed the possibility of being seen at a police station. Two weeks after they set up shop Upland PD received a call from a neighbor. He said that some really scruffy men were hanging around this garage. "They drive beat up cars and motorcycles, drink beer and just hang around."

This was good. Our cover was secure and it was nice to have concerned and watchful citizens. The station assured the caller that the police were aware of this and were keeping an eye on the place.

When narcotics deals were set up, the plans were that the detectives from the other jurisdictions then the city the deal was going down in would make the contacts or buy the drugs to help eliminate the possibility that someone would be recognized. Before they went into a residence or other location to make a buy a record check was done on the house and occupants to see if anyone there was known by one of the team. Booking photos were used to view those who might be associated with the dealer to reduce the possibility of being recognized. This helped, but did not always work because sometimes other associates would be there that knew the detective.

That happened in Chino, which had been a difficult place to buy narcotics, especially heroin. Three times an informant set up a buy only to have the transaction fail because the dealer did not show up or the dealer told the narc that he knew nothing about any dope, so why would they come to him?

93

The Chino detective was called in to advise and help the team understand what was happening. Was someone tipping off the dealers? If so this could place the officers in extreme danger, depending upon who the dealer was. He assured the team that no one was tipping anyone off. This failure to finish the transaction was just a fluke and was probably caused by the action or demeanor of the buying officer.

A few weeks went by and another informant brought them information about a dealer who lived off the alley between Third and Fourth Streets, south of D Street. It was not far from the police station and located in the middle of Old Town, where houses were built back in the early 1920sand 30s.

This time the information was given to the sergeant. Nothing was mentioned to the Chino officers. The plan was to send the Chino detectives on surveillance in east Ontario while the remaining team set up the buy in Chino.

Jack was selected to make the purchase. He prepared his arm with a few pricks from a Bougainvillea, and created some old scar tissue with Super Glue. The Bougainvillea thorn's pricks created some inflammation that to a casual observer looked like injection marks.

There was no place nearby to set up surveillance where visual contact would be possible, so the backup team was two blocks away listening to transmission of the event on the wire.

The informant went in and came back with the dealer, who then proceeded to question Jack'. He asked to see his marks, which Jack showed him.

Then he said, "Come on in and we can fix together."

Jack knew that was not going to happen, so he says, "Hey, you can see that I am only shooting a few times a week. I am stretching this out for special times."

Armando went back into the house, and said he would be back.

Jack got back into his ride just as a police cruiser came south in the alley. Shit, this could get messy. He quickly took his .45 Semi-Auto out of his waist and hid it under the seat. The officer and his police reserve got out and asked for ID. Jack' had identification provided by the Department of Motor Vehicles that had a different name and address, so he was okay. A check for outstanding warrants and criminal information was made and came back negative. Of course! Thank you DMV.

94

The officer asked here' to roll up his sleeves. He refused saying, "You do not have any probable cause to search me."

This irritated the officer, who then slammed him against the car and did a pat down search. Since there was no hype kit or other paraphernalia or gun on his person, the officer questioned him about what he was doing there. Jack knew it looked suspicious to see a gringo in a Mexican neighborhood, but equal rights laws and political correctness prohibited mentioning the obvious. Of course it looked suspicious to have a grubby white guy in the alley behind a known dealer's house. He certainly was not a Mormon missionary making church calls. The cop asked for permission to search the car, which was denied. Jack did not want him to find the gun because then this dope buying operation would go downhill faster than a lead balloon. The cop was frustrated. He made some comments, but because he found nothing to follow upon he made out a Field Interrogation card and left.

Before Jack could get back into the car the house door opened and another Hispanic male came out. Jack recognized him as someone he arrested for being under the influence of heroin a few months before starting this assignment. Robert was the guy's first name. Jack did not let on that he knew him. Robert asked what the officers wanted and quizzed him extensively about what was said. When he thought the answers were satisfactory, he points a finger at him and goes, "I know you from someplace?"

Jack realized that this was why he asked all those questions. He suspected that something was wrong. Jack felt very hung out. If this guy figured out who he was there was going to be big trouble, and his gun was in the car. Back up was at least two minutes away, which was an eternity when a cop was in trouble.

Remembering this guy's arrest, Jack thought that he likely served his ninety days in San Bernardino County Jail. So he responded, "I don't know where we met. Were you in the County? I just got out a week ago."

"Yeah, that must be where I know you from."

God was near. Jack was relieved. He felt the sweat running down from his armpits. Staying cool he lounged against the car, sure that several pairs of eyes were still on him.

Robert went back into the house and the informant came out and gave Ken a balloon with heroin. Heroin was placed into small balloons, the kind kids played with. The amount was used as one dose. It was shaken down to the bottom of the balloon and then

tied off and rolled up into a small ball.
   Great! We were in!

Chapter 20

The phone in the garage rang. Only the participating departments had the number, so everyone wondered who they wanted.

Sergeant Bill Laski said, "Hey Jack, it's for you. Some guy says that your touch wants to see you. He will see you at Satan's Place at 8pm."

Jack groaned because that meant he couldn't get off work early and eat dinner with the family. His son played football on the JV team at Ontario High. At least he could watch the game from six to eight. If he was a few minutes late Cliff would just have time to drink another beer.

The game was tough and the score was tied at halftime, fourteen all. Jack loved going to his kids' events and always rooted them on. His kids said they always knew when he arrived because they could hear him yell encouragement. Of course, that is why he would yell loudly at the first opportunity so his kids would know he was there. It seemed they turned up the effort a little when they knew Dad was there. The third quarter came and the score was 21 to 17 in Ontario's favor. He hated to leave, but something told him that Cliff had something serious to say.

As he drove up Mountain Avenue he recalled the ribbing he got from the team for meeting at Satan's Place. It was a nude bar and it was near the motel were Clifford lived.

"Get your snitch to set up a meet where you can enjoy the view, huh?"

"You know that lots of Hells Angels hang out there. Sure you don't need a backup?"

Jack's stock answer was, "You know there is nothing in that bar that I want. I would rather be in my own house with my own woman."

He turned down Mission Boulevard and pulled into the parking area. It looked like there was not a big crowd, at least not yet, and there were no bikes. Good! He went in and found Cliff sitting on the far side at one of the tables made for two. He ordered two beers, one for him and the next one for Cliff, who would likely stay until he could barely stagger home. Jack figured to give him a few bucks so he would have lunch money the next day, but Cliff would probably just drink until the money was gone.

"Heard that you went to Chino to buy heroin," Cliff said.

Jack was stunned. How did he know that? Cliff knew amphetamine and coke users but not heroin. Jack did not admit anything. He just asked, "What do you know about that?"

"Dude at work was shooting his mouth off about it and it sounded like you when he described you. He got real afraid after the cops came and someone thought they knew you. After you dropped him off he went back and told them that the police had threatened him and made him take a narc there. He was protecting himself and did not want to lose his contact for dope. He says they have figured out just who you are and will kidnap and kill you when you go back tomorrow. You are going back tomorrow, that is the plan right?"

Shit, everything he said made sense and added up.

Thank you Lord for informants who look out for your welfare. What would he do now?

Every officer knew that when he worked with an informant there were risks. Some of them were flakier than Kellogg, while others were want-to-be cops; still others were working off an arrest. But all cops knew that the life and safety of his informant was the responsibility of the officer. He must do whatever he could to protect and assist the informant. The cop did not have to like him, but he was responsible for his welfare. If an informant was beat up or killed it was a huge weight for a police officer. When it happened he hoped it was the snitch's fault and not something he could have prevented.

Jack went to the Canopy to think through this information and decide what to do with it. He did not want to bring this home and worry the family. They already had lots of fear and tension because of his erratic schedule and the low-lives he dealt with and spent the biggest part of the day with.

Ray was at the Canopy too. He worked a search warrant and came afterward to unwind. It was great to get together and swap some stories. Two beers and some conversation about old times and fun things calmed him down. It was not every day one came face to face with the reality that his life could unexpectedly end. Most guys were not worried about the danger and death, but nobody wanted to be the victim of some low life hype. Dying as a hero was one thing, but as a victim of some scumbag crook was what they worked to prevent. Just as informants were his responsibility, it was also the informant's responsibility to keep the officer safe. When one of them did not do his part shit happened!

They worked on a plan.

Chapter 21

Ray related the latest event in his career, now both had to deal with death threats. The drug dealers and users in South Ontario were feeling the economic pinch in their trade and having their lives interrupted by spending ninety days in the county jail for being under the influence.

Like Ray was fond of saying, "Every hype is a thief; if you want to decrease the burglary rate put the hypes in jail. Works all the time."

Ray had an informant that called him for a meeting, and he wanted this meeting out of town. They met at Polly's in Norco. No heroin users from Ontario would be there, nor would anyone they might know from anywhere else. It was safe and out of the way.

The informant was afraid; his hands were shaking while he drank his coffee.

"What's up dude? Are you in trouble or what?"

"It's not me that is in trouble, it's you man! They like, put out a contract to kill you. I was there and they are going to know I snitched to you but I couldn't just let them do it. You've been good to me and always played straight. So I am telling you, watch out!"

Ray sat back in the booth, shocked, pissed, and wondering what to do. He said, "Who set this up?"

"Hey, a bunch of the dealers and guys got together and said 'we got to do something, we filed citizen complaints and picketed the city for discrimination but nothing is working. Ray and his buddy, Jack', keep busting us; every week two or three are busted.' They put up five thousand dollars and Meras said he would take care of you. By next week you are a dead man. He is fucking psychotic enough to do this too."

Ray told Jack about it the next day.

"Meras is a rotten cold-blooded douche bag! What are you going to do? Have you told the sergeant or captain yet?"

"No, I didn't tell anyone. You are the first to know. But I already took care of it," Ray answered. "Yesterday when I came back from the meeting with the informant I checked out a Patrol Unit and went looking for Meras. I went south and cruised the streets. His car was gone from his house so I figured I'd see him somewhere. And I did. He was driving down Campus from

Mission when I spotted him. He had two gang bangers with him. I lit up the reds and he pulled over."

"I walked up to the driver's window and scoped out the two dudes. They had been through the drill before. The guy in back had his hands on top of the front seat and the guy in front had his hands on the dash. Sure is nice to deal with well-trained crooks."

"Anyway, I walked up as Meras rolled down the window. When it was down I just reached in and grabbed him on both sides of head, getting a good handful of hair so it would hurt and keep his attention. Pulling his upper body out through the window, and then turning his head so he was looking up at me, I said, 'I hear you are planning to kill me, chump!'"

"He replied, 'Oh, not me Officer Follett I wouldn't do that.' He was half out of the car, panicking and sweating and feeling some pain; but I didn't care. It's my life he was hoping to end. I told him that he better make sure nothing ever happened to me, because every cop in the city would know it was him, and they would find a way to kill him. For good measure, I added, 'And whenever you see me make sure your hands are where I can see them, because if you put your hand in your pocket, even if it is to toss your dope, I will know you are going for a gun and will shoot you before your hand is out again. Remember, you are a dead man if something happens to me!' I threw him back into his car and left."

Jack sat back amazed, "Damn it Ray, you crazy?"

It all made sense. What was a cop supposed do when crooks made plans against him? Everyone knew it was against policy and not politically correct, but so what? He could not get a Restraining Order or have a bodyguard everywhere he went. This was part of the territory when he put on the badge; nobody warned him or advised him on what to expect or what to do. It was just him and the crook; no chief of police, no sergeant, judge or mayor or councilperson could help him. He had a choice: be a victim or be a survivor. To be a survivor he had to act or the target on his back just got brighter.

"You should have let me know and I would have gone with you. If those guys had their guns with them you could have been shot walking up to the car, man!"

"I know, I know! I thought about telling you. I knew you would insist on going along, to do this together, which is the way we are, always there for each other. But I did not want you to get

102

in trouble too, so I decided to do it alone. Besides, doing it alone put more fear in those assholes than if a bunch of guys did it together. This way if they file a citizen complaint it will be just me, and not you, in trouble. But thanks anyway, I appreciate your willingness to help."

Now Jack knew for sure what he would do with the informant who was setting him up the next day. Life sucked, but he had to do the hard stuff along with the easy.

Chapter 22

Jack called his sergeant to tell him the informant called and the buy in Chino was off. He said, "Robert Davila figured out who was coming to make the buy and the whole house was cleaned out; no dope, no sale. Oh, and I'll be in about ten. Worked late last night so I am taking the opportunity to see my family at breakfast and take care of family matters."

At 8:30 Jack called the informant. They chatted a few minutes. Jack was waiting for the informant to call off the buy. This was his opportunity to warn Jack, but there was no warning. The time for him to redeem himself passed. They agreed to meet in half an hour to get ready for the buy, get the team set, and the wire and equipment ready. They met at the usual spot, the parking lot of Ontario Christian High School. No one expected or looked for cops on that campus.

Jack was in a detective unit and met the informant as planned. The informant was apprehensive about getting into a police car instead of the old beaters they had been using, but he knew he had no choice.

"What is going on? Why are we in this car, where is the Chevy we've been using? We can't go anywhere in this without being burned," he grumbled.

Jack just smiled and told him not to worry; the Chevy was at the office for them. Mr. Snitch sat back relieved until he noticed that they were not headed to Upland. Instead, they turned on East Belmont and were approaching a known dealer's house. As they slowly drove by, Jack pointed at the house and acted like he was asking questions.

Then he drove down Park to Cherry, turned south and went to Sunkist east of Sultana, headed east and drove by two more dealers' places. By that time the informant was yelling, "What the hell are you doing? You just fried my ass, you son of a bitch. Get me out of here." He hit the floorboard, hiding from people on the street and front yards.

Jack stopped the car at Sunkist and Campus. Looking down at the cowering slime ball on the floorboard and said, "Get the hell out of my car! I looked after you and took care of you but you set me up."

"I am sorry man! I didn't want to. I was stuck. They

105

would've killed me later when they found out I introduced a cop. I didn't know what to do. Sorry man," he blubbered. "You can't put me out here. They will beat the hell out of me or kill me! Please?"

"Yeah, I am sorry too. Sorry I ever trusted your sorry ass. Now get out and remember never to screw over a cop."

Jack watched as he ran north on Campus, hoping to find help or a place to get away before someone spotted him. How long would he last before they caught him and did what dope dealers do to rats?

Justice is not always sweet but it was necessary. Jack could never allow an informant to tell his contacts and friends how he screwed over the police. If he did, survival for narcotic officers would be fleeting. Street justice was tough and sometimes brutal, but survival was paramount.

Chapter 23

At two o'clock in the morning the phone rang. Groggily, Jack reached for the phone. "What?" he grumbled into the phone. It was only three hours since he came home from a stake out.

It was the watch commander.

Jack sat up, groaned, and apologized, "Sorry sir, just tired and sleepy."

Lieutenant Meinders apologized too, for waking him up, but said he had an urgent call from a man who said he had been helping Jack. "He needs to talk to you right now. Says his name is Woody and that you will want to call him right now." He left the number and disconnected.

He patted his wife on the butt, "Just an informant in trouble honey. I'll call him and be right back."

He went to the kitchen to use the phone there. He hated these night calls. They disturbed sleep, but mostly caused a lot of tension for his wife and family. Last week a drunk called to threaten his life. It had taken alcohol to give him the courage to make a vengeance call because Jack had arrested him a month earlier. Not good for peaceful sleep.

He dialed the number on the rotary phone and it was picked up on the first ring. Woody was almost hysterical as he began to ramble on with a story about his wife being found dead. Los Angeles County Sheriff deputies found her lying alongside the 57 freeway, just north of Highway 60.

"She was strangled," he said. "They think it may be the freeway strangler. You got to be there for me! You are the only person I can trust."

Jack assured him that everything would be okay. He told him that the sheriffs were very good about investigating. They would surely clear him of suspicion. Jack promised they would meet tomorrow to go over personal items to help Woody while working with the investigators through this tough time.

He just wanted to go back to bed and sleep. Woody was a low life that was a master manipulator and liar. So far the information received from Woody had not produced very much. The only bust so far was for the sale of LSD, and that was a small- time crook that would not give up his source. It seemed like he was passing off the peripheral data and protecting his main sources of drugs and guys operating a suspected counterfeit money scheme.

Then Woody made a most untimely and unusual request; he asked Jack to serve as pallbearer at the funeral.

"Sure, I can do that for you, be glad to stand with you." He knew he would attend the funeral anyway, just to see who Woody's associates were. This made it real easy and would give him the opportunity to talk to some of Woody's friends. *Why was he thinking about funerals and who would be the pallbearers? Shouldn't he be grieving, not planning?*

Jack hung up the phone and then he placed a call to LASO San Dimas station. After he identified himself he asked for the deputy who was working the homicide.

"What's up? Why are you interested in this homicide?"

He explained that Woody had been an informant and that he called about his wife's death. Woody sounded strange on the phone. It sounded like he was very concerned about his wife's death, but it also sounded phony. Jack informed the deputy that Woody and his wife had not been getting along and had numerous fights and disagreements in the past few weeks.

"Frankly, I think Woody is your primary suspect."

He returned to bed. His wife snuggled up behind him and asked if everything was all right. He assured her all was well, and with a contented sigh she drifted off to sleep. Jack wished it was that easy for him. He knew that jerk had something to do with killing his wife and that Woody was trying to use him to deflect the attention.

He lay there thinking, recalling how he met Woody and what a scammer he was. It was about four weeks ago that the arrest report came across his desk with a note from the arresting officer attached, to let him know that, "This guy wants to talk, says he can help." He was busted for drag racing but when the car was impounded a pound of marijuana and a sawed off shotgun were found. He had a criminal history but never served more than eight months in the county jail, and he was on unsupervised probation.

Jack interviewed him the next day while he awaited arraignment. The possibility of Woody helping was discussed with the DA. The DA agreed to release Woody on OR and delay the arraignment to give time to see how good the information and help would be.

A few investigations were initiated, resulting in the arrests of a minor LSD dealer and another for selling baggies of marijuana from the KFC chicken franchise in Montclair. That one had been fun. Jack' went in to order some wings and told the dude, "I want to fly." He told Jack to meet him out back. The marijuana was kept in the toolbox of his pickup. After a quick exchange he was back inside selling chicken.

Jack had been in Woody's apartment in Pomona. He lived in an old brick building on North Park Avenue that was built back in the 1950s. He met the wife, a cute little blonde, who kept a neat house. She did not seem to be a match for the sleazy, unkempt husband she had.

They had a small spat during that visit. She brought it up. It seemed intentional because she was looking for support from Jack during their discussion about money and jobs. The rent was late and she did not want to move again.

Jack and Woody left to buy groceries that Jack paid for out of his own pocket.

"Dumb bitch won't help! She expects me to do everything," Woody muttered as they went down the stairs. "I just wanted her to do a couple of tricks, not regular or anything. What's so hard about giving a few blowjobs to help pay the rent?"

With disgust dripping from every word Jack asked, "You want your wife to hustle herself? Are you fucking crazy?"

The next morning Jack went to work at 10am.He loved staying home in the morning to make breakfast for his wife and kids, and then see the kids off to the school bus. Then he would leave for work. It was one of the few perks for working on the Narcotics Task Force.

There was a note to call the LASO deputy that was investigating the homicide. Information was not detailed, because only the investigators of the Freeway Killer knew the details. But this homicide was a copycat killing done by someone who knew something about the Freeway Killer's means of death but the trademark was not there on this one.

It was agreed that Jack would attend the funeral service as a pallbearer and keep in touch. The graveside service was held at Crest Lawn in Norco.

Jack met Woody for lunch at the In-N-Out on Indian Hill. Woody seemed light-hearted and not at all concerned about being implicated. He was sure his wife was the victim of the serial killer.

109

He said his finances should pick up soon because he expected an insurance settlement. He asked for a few hundred bucks to help him get through this short time.

Jack asked him how he was so sure that money would be coming to him. Woody responded with the information that she had a small life insurance policy with him as the beneficiary, and that her father also had a life insurance policy on her with Woody as the beneficiary. She and Woody had been trying to start a family and her father wanted to be sure his grandkids would be taken care of. They left lunch with the promise that Jack would be at the cemetery for the graveside service. There was no other service, since neither of them nor neither of their parents had religion.

The service was short. A person wearing a clerical collar made some comforting comments about an afterlife. The only people who wept were her father and mother. Everyone else just talked and drank a few beers. Jack tried to fit in. He wore Dockers and a polo shirt, but was still the best-dressed person there. He gave his condolences to everyone he met, and then he left, promising Woody that he would stay in touch.

The next day he received a call from Debbie's mother, Woody's mother-in-law. She was crying when she made her request, "Debbie trusted you and thought you did not believe very much of his bull, so may I talk to you?"

They met at Bob's Big Boy that afternoon. She related the turmoil that had come to the family when Debbie and Woody got together and then married. Woody tried to use her in his schemes to sell drugs and bilk people out of money. She had no knowledge of any counterfeiting, but said that Woody had not held a job in years but always seemed to come up with cash. When he was arrested things got worse. He tried to balance his crime life with working off the arrest. She and her husband had become increasingly worried and tried to talk Debbie into leaving and coming to live with them. When she decided to stay they changed the beneficiary on the insurance policies. There would be no money for Woody from insurance. They had received a call from Debbie the day before she died, she was crying, saying that Woody was forcing her to become a prostitute to keep them in the apartment and have money for dope. Debbie promised to leave that night and come home, but she never made it.

Jack passed this information on to LASO. The next day

Woody was arrested and booked for first-degree homicide. During the interrogation he broke down and wept. He admitted to being overcome with rage that Debbie was not willing to do her part to bring in money.

"She was good looking, dumb bitch. She could have made us a lot of money."

The trial was short and the sentence offered no mercy for Woody. He got life without the possibility of parole.

Two years later he hung himself with his bed sheet. Good riddance.

Chapter 24

1980

Thursday morning the bureau sergeant was holding briefing. The detectives straggled in, some with a cup of coffee and others waiting to go out for a cup and breakfast of a donut. Donuts were the energy food for those on the run. Even guys who did not like sweets learned to eat donuts while they worked patrol. It was quick and most often free, because the donut shops liked the security provided by cops coming in during those early morning hours while the world slept; early morning traffic was mostly cops, crazies and those who were part of the commuters rushing to work. They needed something to eat on their way to work.

The sergeant waited to begin. He didn't say anything until the room became quiet. As he stood waiting it became apparent to the guys that something was up, so suddenly the noise stopped and everyone looked at the sergeant.

He cleared his throat, looked up at the assembled men and when he had their attention he began, "I think we have some good news. Mueller has been spotted." He did not need to explain who he was talking about, that name was burned into the minds and hearts of everyone. "The FBI found the cabin where Mueller had been hiding out, about thirty miles or so from Sandy Point, Idaho. They tracked him to the cabin and exchanged gunfire with him. That is the latest. We will keep you informed of the events as they become known."

Relief swept over the room. Everyone was happy that this saga was coming to an end. Most hoped that Mueller would die in the gun fight, and also hoped and prayed that Mueller would be the only one to die. Short prayers were said for the safety of the FBI agents and sheriff deputies. No such prayers were offered for Mueller. Prayers for him asked for a bullet to find him, maybe in the head, just like Ricky. Some wished they could be there to deliver the fatal shot, while others were content and happy that somebody else would do it. The cops had no desire to kill anyone; they just wanted justice for Ricky. Justice that would leave Mueller dead and in hell for what he did to Ricky and the entire police family.

It had been months since the escape. Nothing had been heard

about him since, so everyone had settled back into the routine of life and work. No one expected him to return to Ontario. In prison he had affiliated with the white supremacy gang and probably had contacts with them. It was suspected that this group assisted in his escape, and certainly that they were hiding and protecting him somewhere. Finding him in Idaho made sense.

About noon the news was on the radio that Mueller was hiding in the cabin. The FBI had surrounded it, with the assistance of the local sheriff's department. It was a standoff. No shots were being fired. The negotiator was attempting to arrange surrender.

Tension was evident on the faces of everyone at the station and in each unit. Work was disrupting the thoughts and hopes of each officer. They realized that they should not let this distract them from what they were doing or they could land up doing what Ricky did, letting the distractions interfere with safety.

The majority of the street cops were hoping for swift death and justice. The administration was concerned about repercussions and wanted to keep complaints and investigations away, so they were hoping for success in the negotiations.

No more news came during that day. Everyone went home and turned on the TV to catch any late news about what the FBI was doing in Idaho.

The next morning came and there was no new information. Those who were close to Ricky and those who hoped for swift justice were discussing the FBI tactics.

Why wait so long?

Shoot some teargas or flash bang the place!

When he shows himself shoot him!

Simple! Just get this done! A capture and new trial would not bring any justice. It would just cost huge amounts of money, and would prolong the agony for the survivors.

Around ten in the morning the police radio broadcasted that the standoff was over. Everyone in the cabin was dead, either from gunfire or when the place burned to the ground. Such a remote location made it impossible for fire trucks to do anything except prevent wild fires and make it safe to go through the rubble.

A sigh of relief came from the entire PD. It must have been heard throughout the city, because every police officer let a sigh at the same time.

In spite of the fact that everyone waited for and desired Mueller's death, there was no joy or happiness. No real cop ever

114

really liked death. It was just part of justice. Besides, the pain of missing Ricky overrode the justice God brought to Mueller.

It turned out that no one else was injured because Mueller was alone in the cabin. He initiated the shootout. He probably felt trapped and committed suicide by cop. No law enforcement personnel were hurt. God was taking care of business, setting up judgment day.

Chapter 25

A larger than usual crowd of cops was gathered at the Canopy. It was a real mixture of uniform and Bureau personnel. Mueller's death had affected the men and women more than they professed it had. The conversations started off in hushed tones and voices that showed there was strong emotion in the room. The FBI standoff and death of Mueller came up as people spoke in hushed voices as they traded the bits of news they heard about the final hours.

How did he ever manage to escape?

How did he manage to hide for six months after the escape?

One of the dicks recalled having contacts with Mueller when he was a teenager. Then he was a petty thief and general asshole. The family lived in a singlewide trailer in a rundown trailer park next to the Green Lantern Bar on East Holt. The parents were alcoholic but caused no trouble that resulted in police action.

"Those bars on east Holt have always been a problem," said another, interrupting the story. "I remember one night the Hessians rolled into town and took over the Nite Lite, just down the street from the Green Lantern. There must have been fifty of them. The lot was packed with bikes and anyone with any sense left when these guys showed up. The barmaid wished she had left or could have closed the doors to keep those greasy dirty guys out.

"She called the PD when she realized that these guys stopped paying for the beer they were drinking. They had started urinating on the barroom floor because both the men's and women's bathrooms were full."

Jack continued, "When she went to the back room for another keg she made a quick call for help, which she had to deny when she was confronted when we got there. Ray was with me when we arrived. We walked in and saw the place had standing room only and it was crowded from wall to wall. They were all wearing their colors on their denim jackets and wearing Levis that had not been washed for months, if ever. The smell was pretty bad. Anyway, these guys moved aside to let us get to the bar and then came together again, leaving us feeling trapped.

"When we arrived at the bar, the barmaid, who was a German girl who was married to a US Army soldier talked to us.

"She looked frightened and denied that she had placed the

117

call to the police. The guy next to me spoke up, 'We are not causing any problems are we?' His voice sounded threatening, matching the scowl on his face.

"I looked at him and realized he was the club president. 'Let the lady speak.' I told him.

'Up yours!' he said. 'There is no problem here and you guys should just get your ass out and leave us good citizens alone.

'This is not good,' said Jack. 'A good citizen would let me talk to her if I wanted.

"Meanwhile he looked for the entrance to the back of the bar. The bikers had it blocked. He put his hand on the bar and began to leap over it. Before he got a foot off the floor the president's hand was on his shoulder pushing him back down.

"'I told you to get the hell out of here, now you are interfering with us. We will just have to kick you out.' Raising his voice, he yelled at the gang. All of them were focused on what was happening at the bar. He shouted, 'Let's kick some ass!'

"Oh, shit! We were in deep trouble! There were at least fifteen guys between us and the door, and the total odds were about fifty against two. Not good.

"We each placed our hands on our .357s and we both put our backs against the bar. The president saw this and said, 'You cannot shoot us all, and we will stomp your guts out before you can pull that trigger twice.'

"Ray barked, 'Just back off. No one needs to die or get hurt, but you are going to die with me asshole.'

"The gang crowded closer. It was almost impossible to move. We were not sure we could even draw our weapons with the pressure on both sides.

"Just then the door opened with a crash as it slammed against the wall. There was room for the door to swing because the men were all crowded around us. All eyes turned to the door.

"It was Jeff McInnis standing there. Not saying a word, he just racked a shell into his sawed-off shotgun. That was the sweetest sound I have ever heard, knowing the best help we had was at the door in good hands.

"It was not so sweet for the Hessians; for them it was a terrifying sound. They knew those double ought (OO buckshot) do a lot of damage to one's innards. Wisdom took over their bravado and without a word spoken they shuffled out, got on their rides, and headed back to Whittier."

118

"Let me finish what I was saying," said the detective who had started his story earlier. "The Mueller kid had been caught shoplifting a number of times. When he was little it was candy and food items, but these thefts were always handled by counseling and releasing him. His only arrest had been for stealing a tape recorder that he planned to sell. It seemed that he started smoking marijuana and needed the funds to buy dope."

The detective went on with his tale, of how Mueller's attitude changed from being a surly brat to a conniving weaseling liar who smoked dope to cope with life. Moving from the trailer to a house on Nocta did not change his attitude; moving from trailer trash to Okie Flats was not a big step up.

He had never vented his anger in any violent manner. There were no fights or family disturbances of the peace. He was just a messed up kid that grew up into a messed-up young man who had no values or goals. He drifted through life and no one would have suspected he would someday become violent, killing over drugs and then killing a policeman. Even when he went to prison, no one suspected he would become violent and get into a shootout with the FBI. Sure, he had been in some prison fights over smokes and establishing the pecking order in the cellblock. But that was it.

Chapter 26

Jack Hillberg was reassigned to graveyard patrol. He was classified as an Agent II, more commonly known as corporal or detective; a corporal was assigned to patrol as a training officer and a detective was assigned to the bureau as an investigator. This assignment was a first. Not only was the classification a first for Ontario PD, but they also never had a corporal assigned to graveyard shift until now.

Jack figured it was just part of "career development", an executive plan to mold officers into who the chief wanted them to become. This term was used mostly for those who somehow rubbed the Brass wrong or did something that was not against written policy but that stretched the rules far enough to tick off the chief, or to cause the officer to be perceived a maverick or potential problem.

Jack had done two things that were known to upset the chief or cause questions by a city councilman. One came from his role as president of the Ontario Police Officers Association (OPOA). The other was his long list of narcotic arrests. He had more arrests of those who were under the influence of heroin or driving under the influence of heroin than the combined number of arrests for those offences in the rest of the department.

The lone Hispanic on the city council had received complaints that too many of "his people" were being arrested. His reputation was that he was not really a councilman for the city. He was a councilman for his friends and his ethnic group. He viewed all police officers as prejudiced, biased and intolerant while viewing himself as the only person who was totally objective.

Jack's opinion was that every addict who was arrested saved ten houses from being the victims of burglary. He had a great record of convictions. He was a court-recognized expert in narcotics and had never lost a court case for someone under the influence of heroin or other drugs.

The heat was on the chief, so he put pressure on the street cops. A decision the chief made was poorly thought out causing it to backfire when the OPOA filed a grievance. It was not Jack's fault the chief made this big mistake and then stubbornly refused to change when it was brought to his attention and explained to him. The problem was that it was Jack, serving in his role as president of the association, who had brought the mistake to the chief's attention. Chief Brookings did not like it when officers stood up to him, so he reacted in his common bullheaded way.

The issue was that the officers could use more training. It was a good idea with the right goal in mind. But getting them to attend special classes was difficult to coordinate and most officers did not want to spend part of a day off sitting in class. So Chief Brookings decided to do the training in fifteen-minute segments. The fifteen minutes would be added to the pre-shift briefing. It was simple to him-just add fifteen minutes to briefing. Then the shift would be informed of current trends, actions and training to help them be efficient, aware of safety, and up to date on community awareness and policy matters.

However, there was one slight problem. Adding time to the workday was a "meet and confer" item under labor rules. The contract the city had with Safety Personnel, including OPOA, was for eight hours of shift duty and fifteen minutes for briefing. Adding an hour and thirty minutes to a work week required agreement by the OPOA members.

It was Jack's role, as OPOA President, to meet with the chief regarding this change. He was reluctant to do it. The vast majority of the officers wanted the training and thought the chief was on the right track, but they did not want to have the extra work time forced on them without some type of remuneration. Compensatory time or some flex in schedules would help ease the transition.

Jack and Vice President Chuck Coffman talked with the chief's secretary for a few minutes while they waited for the Chief to welcome them in for a meeting about it. It was his standard procedure to keep OPOA officers waiting fifteen minutes.

Chuck grinned, "Fifteen minutes again?"

The secretary did not reply. He saw her roll her eyes while she directed them to sit and wait. It was a game they played. They kept their eyes on the clock or their watches to see whether the rule was in place today. Sure enough, almost exactly fifteen minutes passed when the phone rang and the secretary told them they could go in.

Jack and Chuck extended their hands for a shake and greeted the chief warmly. The chief hesitated to shake their hands and had a semi-scowl on his face. He did not invite them to sit. Jack realized that the meeting was not going to be a warm exchange of ideas and camaraderie.

Jack thought back to the first time he visited this office. Gerber Finley was chief then and was doing the final interview in Jack's hiring process. Chief Finley had been very personable. He asked several questions about Jack's family. All of the questions were designed to show the character and morals of the home. At the end of the interview he asked whether Jack attended a church. When Jack said he sometimes went to a church in Upland with his parents, the chief was pleased, but added, "If you ever want or need a church, you should visit mine. It is right at Euclid and 'I' Street."

Now Jack and Chuck stood there awkwardly, shifting their feet, waiting for the chief to speak. It appeared that he was not going to, so Jack cleared his throat and began. "Chief, the OPOA Board met and discussed the training time that has been added to briefing."

The chief said nothing. He just waited for them to continue, as his eyes narrowed and brow wrinkled.

Jack plunged ahead, "We like the training, sir, but the Board feels that this is a "meet and confer" item. We would like to schedule a time to meet and confer to discuss the change in working conditions, sir?"

"I really do not care what the Board feels. This is not a "meet and confer" item. Do not tell me what I can or cannot do," he growled through clenched teeth. His neck was growing redder as he spoke, with the red creeping up higher and higher.

"Excuse me, sir, but it *is* a "meet and confer" item," replied Chuck. Jack was grateful that he was not alone and that Chuck helped by speaking up.

Jack opened his file folder and withdrew a sheet of paper, which he extended to the chief. "Sir, here is a letter from our attorney, explaining the reasons that it is a "meet and confer" item and extending our desire to discuss this with the purpose of reaching a mutual agreement."

Brookings did not take the proffered letter, so Jack laid it on the desk.

"Anything else gentlemen?" asked Chief Brookings. "If not, I have a busy day." He pointed them to the door.

Jack and Chuck said nothing as they walked out, waiting until they were outside to speak. Experience taught them that the walls had ears. Someone was always listening or that area of the station had listening devices. Shooting off your mouth too soon would come back to bite you.

Once they were out in the rear parking area they looked at each other.

Chuck said, "What is he so worked up about? Does he have that much of an authority complex?"

Jack wrote a report on the meeting and deposited it in each Board member's mailbox. He scheduled a meeting for the next week in the conference room. He knew he would change the site a day before the Board meeting, for fear the meeting would be recorded or at least monitored. They would end up meeting at the Elks Lodge.

The Board was disappointed in the chief's response. They were caught in a situation where they were legally right but only wanted to be heard. They did not have any plans to be demanding or retaliatory. Now the chief had thrown down the glove, so to speak, forcing his will. The association was not looking for confrontation. They didn't want to make anyone look bad. Now what? It was now very difficult to save face, an important factor for guys, especially for cops.

"We tried. He did not want to hear us and even refused to read the lawyer's opinion. Hell, he wouldn't even let us sit down to discuss any part of it."

"He is choosing to be obstinate, not us. But he blames us."

They were not ready or willing to capitulate. Brookings had shown his hand in several autocratic decisions, many of which the administrative staff opposed if the scuttlebutt was correct. No one liked the Agent II ranking, especially the detectives. Now the badge said Agent II, which caused a lot of questions from victims and suspects. A badge that said detective was clear and simple; everyone knew the role and the authority.

Jack liked to keep things clean, simple and direct. Playing politics and games was not his forte. However, when the attorney suggested that this was a golden opportunity and prime circumstance to prove a point, everyone agreed.

They decided that one more letter would be written with a request (demand, in labor terms) to meet and confer regarding the extension of briefing time. When this was rejected, as expected, a claim would be filed for the overtime pay of one hour and thirty minutes per week for each officer, at the hourly rate at the lowest pay scale. The lowest pay scale was selected because this was not about money or hurting the city; it was about following the contract.

As expected, the chief and city manager turned it down and the claim was filed for eight weeks of overtime, to be extended until an agreement was made or the briefing time was returned to fifteen minutes instead of the half hour that included the training.

When the claim was presented, Chief Brookings, the city manager, and the city council rejected it. They all wanted to show support for the chief, but sometimes being pigheaded gets costly. Costly not just in money, but also in morale. This was not a mountain to die on, why stand tough on a losing battle? Didn't they check with a labor law attorney?

Another month went by before the hearing that was scheduled with an arbitrator in the department conference room.

Those in attendance included Chief Brookings, the assistant city manager, Jack Hillberg, Chuck Coffman, and attorney Chuck Silverman.

The assistant city manager opened the presentation by explaining the need for training, complimenting the efficient manner in which the chief inaugurated the training, and describing the great benefit this training had for the department and the city.

The arbitrator waited for the city manager to conclude. Then he held his hand, palm out toward the OPOA, indicating that they should wait. He stated, "I have two questions. Did this training change the hours of work for the officers? And if so, was this negotiated?"

The chief wanted to defend himself and not leave it to the city manager. He said, "They come in fifteen minutes earlier. They are always there anyway, just hanging around, so I wanted to make constructive use of the time. We, that is, the city and I, agreed that it did not require negotiations."

"During this time of loitering around before briefing was everyone always there and were they free to come and go until briefing started?" asked the arbitrator.

Jack and Chuck sat back. They did not say anything and thought things were going quite well.

The arbitrator leaned forward and said, "Gentlemen it seems we have a clear case of overstepping authority and avoiding labor law. The only question left is how do you want to settle this?"

Chuck was grinning but Jack poked him with his elbow. Now was not a good time to gloat. It was time to come together and resolve this. As Jack had said earlier, "If we can save their face, we should do it, winning is enough satisfaction. No sense in damaging relationships further."

His Board derided him often about that statement, because he was the only one who felt it was important for the opponent to save face.

The city never cared about saving OPOA's face.

"So what," queried Jack, "we will save the other side's face anyway. It is the honorable thing to do no matter what anyone else does. Why would we want to be like them?"

Being president of the OPOA put Jack in cross hairs with the chief. There were consequences to pay for that. Here he was, having his career developed and he knew this would probably not be the last time.

Working graveyard was not so bad. The action was great and there was time at the end of the shift to get reports done. The only overtime worked was testifying in court. That was the worst part, working all night, getting a nap, and then appearing in court most of a day.

Chapter 27

Jack was cruising east on Belmont Street. A known heroin dealer lived a few houses west of Bon View and Jack had made a number of arrests in this neighborhood for people being under the influence, possession of a hype kit, and the occasional possession of narcotics.

He had a keen ability to spot hypes. The way they dressed, the way they walked, the look of their skin, hair and eyes, were all telltale signs of heroin users. Jack looked for all of that as he scanned the streets patrolling his beat. He loved it when he was driving behind users. They always gave themselves away by how they drove and how the passengers acted. He might not know who they were but he could smell hype from a block away.

He noticed that there were men in a parked vehicle. They ducked down just as his ride came up through a dip and his headlights were full on their car so he could plainly see two guys duck down. Not thinking about the other reason his career was being developed. He pulled in behind the 54 Chevy. Putting the spotlight on the driver's mirror, he walked over on the passenger side.

He had called in the check and expected a back up to roll in soon since he was a one-man unit. There was no one on graveyard shift to train yet. Maybe next week he would have a trainee to show the ropes to.

He asked all three men in the car for their IDs. The driver and front passenger took out their wallets and handed over their driver's licenses. The man in the right rear seat was a big dude. As he reached into his rear pocket he opened the door and took off running west. Jack took off after him, leaving the other two in the car and his police car there with the door open and engine running. The shotgun was still locked in place, fortunately.

Four houses over the runner opened the three-foot high chain-link gate, and ran to the front door. It was not locked. It was also not his house, as the cops found out later. He opened it and ran in, slamming the door behind him.

Jack hit the door with his shoulder just as it latched. The jamb splintered and the door swung open, striking the runner's heel. It was dark inside. The only light came through the venetian blinds from the streetlight, which was not much. Jack saw the shape of the runner directly in front of him. Jack pushed hard into his back to knock him down just as he reached the coffee table.

The coffee table crashed to the floor, all four legs collapsing, the candy dish and flower vase flew sideways into the wall sending glass fragments flying. Jack landed on top and placed a knee in the back of his neck. He reached for his handcuffs. The runner moaned and then began to yell, "Kill the motherfucker! Somebody kill him!"

Jack reached for his gun instead and yelled, "It is the police. Call the police station! I am the police, call the police station."

A door opened and an old man looked out to see what was happening in his living room. It had been only five seconds since they crashed through the door, but Jack was wondering where his back-up was and if he was going to get out of this place alive. It was not the best of neighborhoods.

The bedroom door slammed shut. Jack wondered if any other doors were going to open and what would come from behind them. He yelled again, "Call the police."

He left his holster unsnapped, took out the cuffs, and cuffed the runner. The dude was big, over two hundred and twenty pounds, and it was difficult to get him on his feet. Jack could not get out of there fast enough.

Paulie Garcia had outstanding warrants for burglary and under the influence of heroin. He struggled and kicked while Jack was trying to get him out of the house.

Jack turned on the light as he backed out the door. He wanted to be able to see anyone who might come into the living room. The room was a mess. The coffee table was flat on the floor, all four legs busted and sticking out the sides. The pole lamp next to the sofa was broken, along with the glass vase and dish that had been on the table. The love seat was lying on its back and a sitting chair fell over with a broken leg. Jack had no idea how all this got busted up when he was always on top of Paulie, who was on top of the coffee table. There must have been legs and arms flailing around knocking things over and clearing off end tables.

When he hit the sidewalk he spotted the backup unit cruising down the street toward him, apparently looking for him and not knowing where he went. Those were the days of no cell phones, no GPS, and no radios, other than the huge hand-held radios. That radio was lying on the sidewalk where Jack dropped it when he went through the gate.

Jack found the driver's licenses he dropped, gave them back to the two men who were still waiting in their car, and thanked them for staying and cooperating. He released them without doing warrant checks or checking to see if they were heroin addicts-a reward for being cooperative.

The sergeant went to the house to view the damage and apologize to the owner, telling him the process for making a claim with the city for damages.

Everyone was relieved with the outcome. No one was hurt except Paulie, who had a few bruises on his face from when he and the table hit the floor, and on his forearms from where he scraped the broken table. No one tried to shoot Jack, although no one called the police either.

A few days later Councilman Rojas called for an investigation of Jack Hillberg, claiming racial discrimination.

Damn! A guy did his job, risked his life, and the reason was because he hated Mexicans? Come on, get real!

Chapter 28

Councilman Rojas met with the chief of police and the city manager to discuss the future of Jack Hillberg in Ontario PD. Councilman Rojas demanded that he be fired, or at least suspended without pay during the investigation he had called for. If suspension without pay was approved this investigation would become a long drawn-out affair intended to ruin Hillberg's life. It would result in financial ruin for Jack and give no incentive for the investigation to be done in a reasonable time.

The City Attorney Carlos Hoover was consulted, wisely, and the plan was to do a complete investigation of all Jack's arrests, citations and relationships in the department, but there was no suspension at this time.

Internal Affairs went to work. Jack was not sure what the motive or plan was. Would this be an objective check? If so, he had no problems. But if this was going to be a railroad, life was going to be tough and miserable.

He had seen career development mess up attitudes, relationships, home lives, and the careers of those it was supposedly improving. He was not sure just what he would say when he got home. He stopped at his pastor's house first for some encouragement.

When he got home at 9am the kids were already gone to school, which was good. Jack did not want the kids to be bothered with his troubles. They had enough fears about daddy being gone all night working. As soon as he walked in the door his wife, Gail, saw that something was wrong.

"What's up, babe?" she asked.

"Same shit different day."

"Okay, what now?"

"Well, the department is doing an investigation to see if I am prejudiced. It seems like one councilman is on the warpath."

Jack proceeded to tell her about the investigation. He made sure she knew he was not suspended or anything.

"You know it will come out all right. Everyone who knows you realizes that you don't have a prejudiced bone in your body. You treat everybody, rich or poor, brown, black or oddball the same, just as an equal, so don't worry."

"Yeah, that is easy to say, but these guys are going to dig and

131

dig. You never know what somebody is going to say or how facts will be twisted. They can make up a lot of stuff," replied Jack.

Then he headed for bed. He knew he needed sleep but was also aware that it would not come easy this morning.

Days went by and he heard nothing.

Then one night he needed a backup for a disturbance of the peace call. Raphael, one of the Mexican officers rolled up to assist. When the notes for the report were taken and they were ready to leave, Raphael said, "Hey, I want you to know that all of us are behind you. The captain interviewed me and all of the other Hispanic and black officers. We all met and wrote a letter, which we all signed, to support you and say that you have been the best training officer we have, and that you treat us better than almost everyone else. Oh, by the way, the black officers are doing the same thing. IA may not like those letters but we decided to make a stand. It is going to be difficult for them to screw you over. Hang in there, buddy." He slapped Jack on the shoulder, which is as close as macho cops get to hugging each other.

Jack had tears in his eyes when he thanked Raphael. He never expected these guys to go out on the limb for him. For the first time in weeks he smiled with some semblance of confidence.

The next week at briefing, the Sergeant said, "Jack, see the watch commander before going in the field."

Jack waited for the shift to head out, and for the guys who were coming off duty to clear the area, before he went to see the WC.

"Sit down, Jack," he said. He did not look happy, so Jack feared the worst. The lieutenant could see the dread on Jack's face. He said, "It is not bad, just not as good as I wish. The investigation is going to clear you, but it is unofficial for now. I will give you some of the details, which you did not hear from me, okay? That is why I am telling you instead of you getting official word from the chief. He will not be giving you these details.

"They counted every citation you have written since you started here and every arrest you made over the past seven years. The interesting fact is that even though you worked Beat Two and Beat Three most of those years and the population is predominately minority, over 70%, less than half, 48.6% of your cites and busts are of the minority. That is the good news. Oh yeah, and also, the guy whose house you busted up chasing somebody came to your defense. He said you did what was right.

132

He did not know the guy who broke in. He says, 'who knows what that guy might have done to his family if you hadn't been so fast and took care of business,'" reported the WC with a smile. He is grateful and claims, *"Hombre esta loco o muy macho"* meaning he thinks you are gutsy or nuts.

"However, the bad news is that the city council has been getting a lot of pressure from La Raza and other leaders in the Chicano Movement. They claim this investigation is a whitewash and now claim the entire department is prejudiced and is protecting you and others," he went on. "They want an outside agency to conduct the investigation."

"That is bullshit and they know it," complained Jack. "Isn't it time for somebody to have some balls and do what is right?"

"I am sorry, Jack. You are an excellent officer, you work hard and mostly stay in the rules, but politics is now driving this. The mayor is up for election in nine months and so are two councilmen, they want votes and need to keep away from controversy," explained the lieutenant.

"Yeah, and I get to ride the hot seat," muttered Jack. "Who or what agency is going to be asked to do this investigation?"

"A letter has already been sent to the Department of Justice in Sacramento. They want the Attorney General's Office to conduct this investigation. They have asked specifically to send a minority person," replied the WC.

"Shit, how long is this going to take?" asked Jack.

"You know how government works. This is going to take months. They are slow and they will want to look like they did a thorough job," replied WC. "They will be sure this is not seen as a whitewash. This report will be detailed and that takes time."

Jack got up and started out the door. He was angry and troubled.

But before he got to the door the WC said, "It gets worse, Jack. This week is your last week on patrol. When you return from your days off the chief has a special assignment for you. You are to see him at the end of your shift, before you go home."

"Shit," he muttered to himself.

The entire shift he drove around in a fog, thinking about all the bad things that could happen and likely would happen. He knew the chief was somewhat helpless, but damn, it would be nice if he had the guts to stand up for what was right. Jack was lost in his thoughts and he almost ran a stop sign, a sign he had stopped at hundreds of times while he was on patrol. Shaking, he realized that he needed to snap out of this funk or he might do something really stupid or dangerous.

He realized what was likely going on in Ricky's head the week he was murdered. He was waiting for the axe to fall for crashing his unit. Not knowing just what the future held, his head was somewhere else, going over what discipline he would face. The anxiety of not knowing kept him from staying focused on the job and it had cost his life.

Chapter 29

Jack returned to the station a little before the end of shift. He wanted to get this meeting with the chief over with. Since when did it take a direct meeting with the chief of police to handle a change in assignment? This must be something special or controversial else the watch commander or sergeant would have handed out the next assignment.

He recalled the first time he was called into the chief's office. He was a rookie, just finished with his year of probation. He received the call to 10-19, report to the station. That time he had walked into Chief Finley's office without any guilt or doubt, until he saw who was already sitting there across from the chief.

It was the man he had arrested two nights earlier for drunk driving. A set of crutches were standing next to his chair. They eyeballed each other but nothing was said. The chief watched this initial contact.

"Sit down, officer," he said, and with a wave of his hand he indicated the chair set there for him. "This man claims you beat him up and hurt his leg. Would you explain what happened?"

"Well, Chief, I spotted this car going east on Holt from Mountain Avenue. It wandered across two lanes and back. After I saw it bounce off the curb I lighted him up and he stopped right in the middle of the lane. While I called in the stop this man opened his door and got out into the traffic, which was very light at the time. He did not stand up, just slid face down out of the car onto the pavement."

The chief sat up, putting his elbows on the desk. He had not expected this story.

I thought, *Sir, if you had read the arrest report you would know this stuff,* but said nothing. Continuing with the story, I told him about the difficulty I had arresting this man. He was too drunk to stand or walk. With great difficulty, my partner and I got him into the unit.

The chief looked at the man with new interest, realizing how difficult it would be to place handcuffs on him and then pour a six-foot-eight man who weighed two hundred and sixty pounds into an Olds Cutlass' rear seat.

Jack continued, "My partner got into the back seat with him and I drove to West End to book this man. In route to jail he began

135

yelling and thrashing around and my partner could not control him."

"This man," Jack said pointing at the man sitting there, "put his foot onto the back of my seat and tried to kick me, sir."

The chief leaned forward some more, looking at both of us to watch the reaction and to grasp the intensity of the situation being related.

Jack thought, *well here goes, this is where the dude gets hurt.* He realized that all eyes were on him and the chief was waiting expectantly.

"When his foot grazed my ear I thought that was enough. We would crash if he managed to deliver a solid kick to my head. That, sir, was when I took out my flat sap and smacked it on his shin."

"How often did you hit his shin," asked the chief.

"I don't know sir. I hit his shin as many times as it took for him to pull his foot off the seat and put it back on the rear floor, where it belonged."

Looking at the complainant with a somber expression, the chief asked, "Is this true?"

His faced was flushed as he confessed that he had no recollection of the events. "I was too drunk to remember it all," he muttered. "I just knew that I was hurt and it must have happened when I was arrested and they used too much force on me."

Jack loved the next scene.

The chief stood up and said, "You mean you came to complain about this officer when it was you that was drunk, and put yourself and this officer in danger? This officer saved your life and likely someone else's too."

Stuttering and embarrassed, the man got up. "I am sorry. I did not realize what happened. I realize now that it was my fault and I apologize." He took his crutches and left, glad to get out.

The chief reached out his hand and shook Jack's hand as he said, "Well done, officer. That worked out rather well."

Back in those days there was no Internal Affairs. The desk sergeant or watch commander took citizen's complaints and turned them over to the chief to follow up on unless they managed to settle the complaint without needing to involve the chief. When the chief called you in you expected a fair hearing and never wanted or needed a representative. It was understood that if you had screwed up you would be disciplined. You might get a letter of reprimand, some time off without pay, or when you really screwed up, termination. It was pretty clear what to expect. Each officer knew when he had done wrong. What you did not want to do was lie to the chief, if you did big trouble would dump all over you!

Now politics affected everything. Votes were more important than justice or fairness. Officers were upset when someone searched their lockers or their personal vehicles, and resented the pressure voting blocs put on the politicians, who then put pressure on the chief. Chief Finley had been there for decades and was so well respected by the citizens and by City Hall that he was not swayed by pressure.

Times changed. There were new rules, a new chief, a new mayor and a new council. It was dangerous to go to the chief's office without representation unless you knew what the topic of discussion was going to be.

Jack knew that this visit to Chief Brookings was not going to work out that well. Times were different. Now the Community Relations Committee reviewed discipline and citizen complaints. The race-related issues were really the only things they cared about. Other policy violations were not as important to them unless they involved an officer the committee did not like, which was usually whatever officer was working the southeast beat. The only way to survive working the barrio with no complaints was to write no citations and make no arrests unless ordered to.

Jack hung up the keys to his unit, and then went down to the locker room to store his briefcase, clipboard and gear. Turning, he saw that the watch commander followed him down.

"You okay?" he asked.

Jack looked at him quizzically, "I do not know. Am I okay?"

"You'll be all right. You just need to get past this shit and it will work out, trust me. We are behind you."

"Thanks man, I appreciate that and appreciate you, but is the chief going to sacrifice me? That is what I am afraid of," replied Jack.

"Don't think he will or can do that, so stay cool," counseled the lieutenant.

They both left the locker room by different exits; the WC went back to his office and Jack went up the back exterior stairs to the chief's office. There was no one in the outer office. The secretary was not at her desk, but the adjoining door was open. As

137

the outer door closed he heard the chief call out, "Come in, officer."

It was just the two of them. No secretary, no Internal Affairs, no supervisor, nobody. Jack was nervous, so he asked, "Should I have a representative with me, sir?"

"No, no," responded Chief Brookings. "This is not a disciplinary hearing, just a change in assignment that will benefit you and the department."

Another career development assignment, thought Jack. He felt a tingle up his back because he knew he was going to get screwed but there would be nothing he could do about it.

With half a smile the chief moved a pile of books and folders to the front of the desk and motioned to a seat. Jack kept his face impassive, waiting. Waiting to hear what this pile of folders had to do with his future and how this would be explained as beneficial to all.

"This department," the chief began, "has grown and changed tremendously in the past ten years. We have grown in size, so we moved from the old station to this new one here on Cherry Street. We have nearly doubled in manpower and there are many changes in the laws. Therefore, we realize that our Policy and Procedure Manual needs to be updated and revised."

First Jack thought he should say nothing and just wait to see what was coming next. But Jack blurted out, "That may be the thing to do, but what has that got to do with me being here?"

"Well, Jack," continued the chief, "we think you are just the right man to tackle this project. You have a way with words, you do a good job writing for the association newsletter, the 'Cop Out,' and as president of the Association you would need to review it anyway."

"But sir, I do not have a BA degree and am only part way in my AA degree. I have no administrative experience," he replied, and hastily added. "But whatever you say, sir." Jack realized that the chief's facial expression had changed and the red was creeping up his neck. He had that hard look on his face.

"These," he indicated, pointing at the stack of material on his desk, "are our current manual and copies of policy and procedure manuals from the cities of Cypress, Long Beach, and Compton, all of which have been revised recently. I regret that there is not an office available for you to use. There will be a table and typewriter set up for you in a corner of the briefing room in the basement.

138

Also there is not a secretary available to type this up, but we are confident you can do this and do it well."

"Is there a time line on this, sir?" asked Jack.

"No, we know this is a lengthy project so will not pressure you to complete it soon. Just take your time and work on it. Oh, and you will have Saturday and Sunday as days off. This will be nice for you and your family. Let me know if there is anything you need," he said as he got up and handed the stack to Jack.

How nice of them to be so considerate of my family. Jack wanted to puke, but kept a straight face, picked up the stack of books, and walked out.

What a pile of crap! They needed a new policy manual and the best choice was a street cop who worked as a training officer or detective. No typist, no schedule, no office, no guidelines. It was a means to calm Councilman Rojas and keep an eye on him and keep him off the street while the AG office did their investigation. Jack would not be aware of who was doing the investigation or who was being contacted for interviews while sitting in the basement. It was a real nice well-crafted plan to isolate him from all the police activities and limit his interaction with his peers.

Monday morning at 8am Jack was sitting at the table in the basement briefing room. The table was not designed for typing, so he placed a cushion on his chair to raise himself to the correct height for typing and to make the work more comfortable. He smiled to himself as he realized that neither the chief nor Councilman Rojas had any knowledge that he was actually a pretty good typist. Arrest reports were hand printed and case reports were recorded on tapes for clerical staff to type. It was forbidden for an officer to use typist's desks, so officers never typed their reports.

When he had transferred to Chaffey High School from his school in Fresno he was forced to take a typing class to fill out the needed credits. Now this class was going to bear fruit. It would not take nearly as long as they hoped.

He knew he might as well make the best of this and do a good job. There was no way this was going to bring more troubles. Well, at least not trouble for insubordination or lack of work ethics. He could not get in trouble for writing the policy manual in the manner that would help the OPOA.

First, he read the entire manual to get a gist for what it said,

139

how it was written and to understand the various sections and goals. Next, he took each manual and made copies of each section. Then he made a folder for each of the sections, thereby breaking down the work into manageable segments. Then he took the manuals from the other cities and broke them down into similar segments and combined them into the folders.

It did not take long for his typing skill to return and improve. No one came to see how he was progressing and there were no progress reports to make. He was correct in his thoughts. They were isolating him in a cave, and it might as well have been Siberia or Africa. Only his friends and the OPOA Board came to see him.

If he needed a phone he used the wall phone and stood up to make notes. Not that he used the phone a lot, but he did seek advice from the Association attorney regarding the manual. Any other items he needed to talk to Silverman about were addressed on pay phones or phones in the detective bureau, because everyone suspected that this wall phone was monitored.

OPOA had installed a gym or workout room next to the locker room in the basement. It had free weights, benches, floor pads, and stations with multiple options to work on weights without the need of a spotter. This gym was free of charge to all active and retired officers. Only men worked out because the department had only one female police officer and two more were being hired. There was no female locker room.

Three times a week retired Chief Finley worked out there. Chief Finley did not venture into the briefing room, but whenever Jack came through on his way to the rest room or his locker they would engage in conversation and small talk.

The second week of confinement to the basement, Chief Finley stopped Jack. "I know it is not my business, but I heard you are having a bad time. Really sorry about that, but hang in there, it will turn out for you."

Then he paused and asked, "You are still walking with God, right? Remember when I hired you I told you that you needed God to be able to put up with what you see on the streets and what would happen to you? This is one of those times."

"Yes sir, I am, and I am confident in my future. Thanks for asking."

The subpoena to testify in court gave Jack opportunities to get out and see the sun. He hated being in a room with no

140

windows or outside exposure. He was to testify on a burglary case that was expected to take three days of testimony. For three days he sat with Fogelman, Deputy DA, as the investigative officer.

During a break he went outside to talk to the deputy DA and enjoy the fresh air. A man dressed in a nice, but not expensive, black suit came out of the DA's building. Jack had seen him there the day before too, talking to the front counter clerks at the court.

The deputy DA noticed him too, and said, "Have you met Trey Mikulec? He is the AG's investigator that is investigating you."

"So they sent a black guy to check me out? Has he talked to you already?"

"He interviewed everyone in the office that has worked directly with you and he talked to each judge in the West End courts. I think he is doing a good job and will not let anyone railroad you. He is very objective and professional."

"I wonder if he will talk to me too. What do you think?"

"No, I think he will get a clear picture of who you are and how professional you are, and see how well you relate to minorities. You will be fine."

"Thanks, Joe. I needed that encouragement. It is the pits, literally, to be holed up doing crap work in the basement. You know and I know they will never use what I put together."

Joe shrugged, "I know, sorry does not help, but hang in there."

Six weeks went by and the manual was finished. The revisions reflected the new laws and included the department policies that had been attached but not included. Concepts, rules and many ideas from Compton, Cypress and Long Beach were included. Jack added an entire new section on race relations. There was a new index, glossary and cross-reference.

At 10am Jack called the chief's secretary to ask for an appointment to see the chief to show him what Jack called "my progress in the work."

"He will see you right after lunch, at 1:15"

Jack went to lunch with several friends and Board members. He swore them to secrecy, at least until after the meeting, telling them that the manual was finished.

They all were surprised. "How did you do it so fast?" they asked.

"I worked hard at it, so I can get back on the streets. I like what I wrote and you will too, I put some things in that reflect the Association's views, but my bet is that this project will never be read and certainly not used."

Jack was one hundred percent correct. He delivered the manuscript to the chief, who was surprised it was complete. He asked no questions about how it got done or what was in it. He placed it on his side credenza, and said, "Thanks."

Jack waited.

The chief looked up with a questioning look.

"What's next, sir? When will the review be done so I can incorporate those items into the second draft?" He knew that since no one would read his work, there would be no second draft.

The chief paused and seemed to be at a loss for what to say. He quickly regrouped and replied, "Report to the bureau captain Monday morning for your next assignment."

"Thank you, sir, hope you like the manual," Jack replied and happily walked out. He survived another step in career development.

Chapter 30

Six months passed since the city council asked the attorney general to review bias complaints and investigate Jack Hillberg. Jack had no idea what happened or what was about to happen. The investigator had been seen around town at City Hall and a few times at the police station and the courts. It was rumored that he visited the fire department and the Chicano House.

Everyone seemed to be sworn to silence. No one talked about being interviewed and the administration was unusually silent. Jack was assigned to narcotics again, so he was growing a goatee and had his hair styled in an Afro.

The African-American community was not interviewed regarding any bias. It was known that Jack was well respected there. The church pastors liked him, and even Charlie Bratton liked him and invited him to parties at his house.

Charlie Bratton was an often-arrested African-American. His rap sheet was several pages long, consisting mostly of thefts of metals, receiving stolen property, illegal burning, and Fish & Game violations. Jack had arrested Charlie for the warrant that charged him with Fish & Game violations.

Jack goes, "Hey, Charlie, what did you do to have Fish & Game hunt you down?"

"I was fishing at Salton Sea with too many poles, Jack," he replied.

"How many poles where you using?"

"Fourteen. I was fishing for my family," he laughed.

Jack laughed too, "Fourteen poles and just you in the boat?" That was crazy. But that was Charlie.

On the way to West End Jail Jack swung by Charlie's house so he could pick up enough money to post bail and arrange to have someone come to pick him up.

Jack was just happy to be working again after his stint in the basement.

On a Tuesday Jack happened to meet Captain Gruber as he came out the back door of the police station. Captain Gruber pulled Jack aside.

"Looks like you are going to be cleared, but do not say anything. Just thought you had a right to know. It is on the agenda for the council tonight." Then he walked away.

Jack was elated! The pressure of living in a glass bowl was about to end. Life had been tough. Everyone in town knew about the allegations and the investigation, because each time something new evolved it was on the front page of the Daily Report newspaper:

"Officer Hillberg Investigated"

"Officer Hillberg Reassigned"

"Attorney General to Investigate Hillberg"

The headlines screamed his name. The newspaper was fairly objective in reporting the news, and almost always printed both sides of an issue. However, having his name in the limelight created lots of pressure for Jack. People he did not even know would come and make comments, most of them supportive.

One of the supportive people represented a group Jack did not want to be affiliated with; they called themselves the Minutemen. They sent a representative to invite Jack into membership. The pamphlets and information he gave Jack confirmed his conviction to stay away. The material was anti-Semitic, anti-minority and promoted hatred and racial bias.

That was not for Jack! The OPOA lawyers were Jewish and his neighbor was Jewish, and he had the utmost respect for them. Besides, what other race or ethnic group contributed more advancement to the welfare of mankind? Jack thought about how many Jews had earned the Nobel Prize, in a wide variety of areas, more than any other race or ethnic group.

Lots of people called Jack and left messages or letters of support. This helped Jack to deal with the uncertainty and the thought that the world was after him. Almost every time he was in a restaurant, coffee shop or business someone asked him how it was going and made encouraging comments and well wishes.

That was all very nice and appreciated, but Jack was the one that carried the burden and lived with the fear that his future and reputation were in the hands of politically motivated people who demonstrated little acumen for justice or backbone for just doing what was right.

Jack called some of his friends to tell them he was going to the council meeting that night and to ask if they would go with him. Jack', Ray, Jeff, Pete and others were happy to go.

The officers did not come into the chambers at the same time, but Jack' staked out the next to back row for them to sit together.

The city attorney saw them and looked surprised. He got the

mayor's attention. The mayor looked over and kept a poker face but nudged Councilman Rojas. Rojas looked up and his face darkened into a deep scowl. He looked pissed.

There was nothing on the posted agenda regarding the AG report, so they were wondering what the officers knew or thought they knew. The meeting went through the posted agenda, and then called for a recess. One of the councilmen, Merriam, came to Jack during the recess. The association supported him in his past two runs for office, so he liked policemen and appreciated their support.

"What are you guys doing here? It would be best if you were not here," he told Jack.

"We just stopped in to see what's happening, just in case something came up that we might be interested in."

"Yeah, sure," he said. "Just stay cool, okay?"

The meeting started again. Many people that had been in the audience were gone. Just the gadfly and regular attendees were there, along with the officers, until the door opened and in came another interested party.

Raul Padilla and the head of the Chicano House walked in together.

Interesting! Did they know what was coming up? Were they invited, or did they just wander in too, like the officers did.

Padilla had an interesting background. He had been removed from the Council Chambers a number of times for disrupting meetings with rants and shouts about La Raza, and hatred for anything law-enforcement related.

Two of the officers who were there and Jack had all arrested him in the past. He was found guilty on every arrest, yet he attended city functions to proclaim his innocence and the prejudice of all police officers, from the chief to the newest foot beat officer. His hatred for all things law-enforcement, and particularly hatred for Jack, brought him there.

The arrest Jack made started with a call regarding a peace disturbance at 1900 S. Campus. Four Hispanic males made themselves obnoxious at the house of the lady who called the police. They were all asked for identification. Two produced their IDs and two said they had no ID with them. That led to more questioning, and the discovery that one with ID and one without ID were illegal aliens. In those days, when illegal aliens were identified they were turned over to the Border Patrol and eventually returned to Mexico or some other South American nation.

When Raul was asked if he was a citizen he cleared his throat and spat a beer and saliva goober in Jack's face. He should not have done that. Jack was easy going but being spat upon was something he took serious offense at. Jack never in his entire career threw a first punch, but the second one was always his and he made it count. Being spit on was that first punch.

Jack did not believe what had just happened. He put his hand to his face to confirm that the spittle was real. Jack's left hook knocked Raul to the ground, and by the time he hit the ground Jack was on him, turning him over onto his stomach and cuffing him.

Jack stood him up and told him, "You dumb shit! I may not like what I have to do and you may not like what is happening, but that is no reason to be stupid."

And thus began years of hatred and harassment by Padilla.

Now here they both were at this meeting.

The mayor and the city attorney looked worried and put the AG's report off until last. It was after eleven when it was finally brought up.

The city attorney calmly reported, "I have here a letter from the Attorney General's office. It is regarding the investigation done on our behalf regarding the complaint of bias and prejudicial actions by one of our officers. I would like to summarize this letter, unless you would like to have it read in its entirety, Mayor. It is two pages long."

"Please give us a synopsis and summary of the results," responded the mayor.

"The report says, 'After three months of research and interviewing citizens, court personnel and interested parties, the AG's office finds nothing to indicate improper procedures or prejudices or biased behavior.' Here is a copy of the letter for you all to read," said the city attorney while he handed out the copies.

Councilman Rojas was livid. He began to stand up, but sat back down and shouted, "This is a travesty and a whitewash. We all know that where there is smoke there must be a fire. I do not know who worked to cover up this investigation, but I will find out!"

Silence covered the chambers. The officers wanted to stand up and cheer but were wise enough to keep calm.

146

Raul stood up but did not say anything right away because Jorge was pulling on his sleeve, trying to make him sit down. But he would not be stopped. "Basta," he shouted. "The pigs always win! We want justice!" He was pulled down and he stayed seated and quiet, although he muttered to those near him.

Rojas broke the silence. He was visibly angry. "I move that we turn this matter over to the county Grand Jury for investigation and that Officer Hillberg be suspended without pay until the investigation is adjudicated."

There was no second to the motion because the city attorney spoke up. "We may request the Grand Jury to investigate this matter, but we will not be able to suspend Officer Hillberg without pay. We may suspend with pay if you desire."

"Motion to refer this matter to the county Grand Jury," intoned Rojas.

There was a second and the motion passed three to two, without comments.

Everyone left the chamber. The officers waited to allow Raul and Jorge to go first. They did not trust them enough to let them be behind them.

The council and city staff all left via the back door, so they did not have to face or be confronted by the public.

"Can you believe that? They have absolutely no *huevos*. What a bunch of eunuchs!" muttered Pete.

"Let's go to the Canopy. See you there."

They all headed out.

Chapter 31

The Canopy was nearly full. It was a good night for business and a good night for the wayward-minded to pick up on a groupie. There were four women, good-looking women; two at the bar and two at a table. They could have their pick of men if they were trading on their looks. But they were there for some short-term fun with a uniform or badge. Maybe some of them hoped this would result in security for a longer time.

Bedding down with a cop was safe, at least as far as having to be concerned with steady income, living a drug-free life, no STD's and being responsible. But then they never saw the houses cops lived in or whether their bank accounts were as flush as they were told. Some of the women looked up and appraised the guys as they came in and others were circumspect in checking out the new arrivals.

The look on the guys' faces warded off the groupies. These guys were not on the prowl. They exchanged greetings with several officers and detectives, but the cops chose to sit at their own table, rehash the events at the council meeting, and speculate on the future.

The cops ordered their beer; they had Foster's on draft, which was the favorite of many. Good Australian beer, eh mate?

Then the speculation began.

"What do you think the Grand Jury will do? How long will this take?" asked Jack. "You know this has been going on for seven or eight months already. I am tired of not knowing and waiting for somebody to decide my fate. Do you know that AG investigator never even interviewed me? At least he came to the right conclusion."

Ray, who was studying law at La Verne School of Law, responded. "That investigator did not need to talk to you. He could be more objective by checking you out with all the people you have contact with. He knows who is biased or a bullshitter. I hear that all of the judges spoke well of you. You have some great support there. They see cops, victims and suspects every day, giving them the opportunity to become good judges of character." Then he laughed, "If he interviewed you it might have messed up his good impression of you."

"Hey, hey just kidding old buddy. Sorry, I know this has

become a major pain and worry," added Jeff.

"Thanks guys. I know you are there for me. It is my sweetheart that I worry about. She is on the outside looking in. She sees and hears what is happening to me and it upsets her, but she is helpless to do anything. I know she cries a lot when I'm gone. The kids have asked me why mommy cries. I asked them when mommy cries. Sometimes she is just sitting by the table with her head down crying. The kids think it is their fault but it is not. She is worried for the family and me. The uncertainty is killing her. Sure wish somebody would man up and end this charade. I am so tired of them playing politics with my life."

Just then a union representative for the Kaiser Steel workers came to their table.

"Hey, Cal, how are you?"

"Great, guys, what are you grumbling about? What's up?" asked Cal.

Ray proceeded to tell about the night's events, and told him about the council meeting and the referral of the investigation to the Grand Jury.

"No shit," laughed Cal. "I just got onto the Grand Jury a few months ago, so I will check up on it." Placing his hand on Jack's shoulder, he said, "Don't worry. I'm sure we will take care of this. Several people on the jury know you. They will not be swayed by someone's hatred of law enforcement. It will work out."

The way the Grand Jury worked was that they received complaints from citizens or government agencies regarding crimes, torts or malfeasance of office. They chose whether to take the case or not. When a case was taken the results were secret. None of the testimony or research became public unless there was an indictment or it was written into the Final Report. The Final Report contained only the items that investigations uncovered and needed attention. When no problems were found they might say nothing or they might simply inform the complainant that they found no cause to prosecute. The accused was not notified.

Feeling relieved from Cal's informed advice, they all sat back, tossed down the beer, and ordered the second round.

Stories began to flow. It was time to forget the problems and focus on the oddities and ridiculous stuff of everyday police work.

"Hey, Ray, tell us about your famous bust. Or should we say the infamous case of arresting a bride and groom on their wedding day. Just how did you do that?"

150

Everyone leaned forward as Ray began his tale. "My partner and I were cruising east on Holt from Euclid when we both smelled the strong aroma of marijuana. We thought it came from the car in front of us. The car turned north on Sultana, went past the police and fire stations, and pulled up in front of a house just off the corner of El Morado.

"The aroma continued, so we knew we had the right car. Smoke came out when they opened the doors, so we knew they were all smoking. They were all laughing and giggling as they ran into the house.

"'What the hell,' says my partner, 'let's go see.'

"We got to the door about the same time as some of the stragglers. The front door was open and we saw that it was a wedding party. The bride was dressed in her white gown and the groom was wearing his tuxedo. Thirty or so people were milling around the room. What caught our eyes was the bag of grass on the coffee table and the groom passing a joint to the bride like it was wedding cake. There it was a felony right in front of us. We had to make the bust," related Ray.

"You didn't bust them at their own wedding? Really?"

"Yeah, we took the entire wedding party, groom, bride, best man and maid of honor. They were all smoking dope so we took them. The booking officer had a cow when we marched the bride into West End while she still wore her wedding gown. But they all got booked for possession of marijuana."

Dick said, "You are going to need forgiveness for screwing up the wedding night, Ray."

"Talk about forgiveness! My partner wanted to get married again. He divorced his first wife and now found another lady he wanted to marry. Being a good Catholic he wanted a church wedding," related Jack.'

"We were in the Bureau and had completed an interview at West End. While we headed back to the station, Will asked me to stop at the church so he could talk to the priest. We pulled in at St. George's. It was midmorning and things were slow. Will jumped out and I waited in the unit to answer any calls.

'Confess all your sins or he won't absolve you,' I warned him.

"Will laughed, 'No kidding, I'll keep it short.' He walked to the open church doors.

"Barely five minutes went by and we got a call to go see the

151

deputy DA about a case we filed the day before. Will had his walkie-talkie with him, so I figured he would be out soon.

"The walkie-talkies, or bricks, as they were commonly known, were the huge and heavy radios that the officers used on the foot beat and whenever they were out of the unit. The body was hard plastic, three inches wide, two inches deep and eight inches tall, plus a six-inch antenna. They weighed nearly four pounds. They were great when they were needed but far too cumbersome to carry, especially on foot pursuit. When cops were on a foot chase the officers hoped they had a partner who would pick up the radio when it was dropped, along with any other gear that was hindering a good run.

"Will was in the confessional when the call came, and was just telling the priest about the misery he experienced in his first marriage. He was about to rat out his ex for infidelity to make himself look okay when the call came. 'Oops, sorry Father, I have to go, can I come back in about an hour?' he asked.

'Ah, you are a police officer. Yes, for you I will be here until noon,' said the voice on the other side.

"An hour and a half later we were back. It was 11:55, so we barely made it. The Father was there and Will finished his story about his wife and said that since he didn't want to embarrass her they had a quick divorce so she could be with her lover. He did not tell the Father about his own skirt chasing and contribution to the breakup. That was all ending anyway because he found his next true love.

"Will never did say what atonement or stuff he needed to do, but he did get the absolution he wanted. 'Bless you Father. You are a policeman's friend.'"

Feeling better and relaxed, they downed the beers and headed for home. One of the groupies said, "Lucky women they go home to! I wish I had one of them."

Chapter 32

By the time Jack got home his funk returned. He went to bed, but tossed and turned while he thought about all of the possible scenarios for his future.

He got up at five thirty, tired and restless. He quietly got out of bed so he would not disturb Gail. He took his sweats and running shoes to the kitchen to put them on. Going out the back door and using his side-yard gate, he went for a run. Leaving the rear door unlocked did not concern Jack. His dog slept on the patio next to the door.

Baron was a Great Dane Boxer mix and was very protective of the kids and house. Jack loved this dog in spite of the mischief he got into. Just the week before Baron decided to inspect under the bed in the master bedroom. There he found a wire that he decided to chew on. It was the electric blanket wire, much to his dismay. The cost of a new cord was worth the spectacle of watching the bed being bounced and shaken as Baron tried to get away from the shocks. The bed actually moved over six inches or so as he tried to extract himself.

Jack went for a four-mile run through Carbon Canyon. The ups and downs of the hills helped stress his lungs and heart, which was what he wanted to help take his thoughts off the current events.

Afterward, soaked in sweat, he came in the back door. Gail was sitting at the table drinking coffee. He saw that the expression on her face was fearful. She attempted to hide that.

Smiling she asked, "Are you okay?"

"No, I am not sure just how I feel. Puzzled and angry mostly, I guess."

"What happened last night? You didn't wake me so I guess that means bad news."

"Both good and some sort of bad. The Attorney General's report supposedly says I am okay and that the complaint was unfounded."

"That's good. What's wrong with that? That ends this mess right?" But looking at Jack's face she knew she was wrong. "Okay, what did they do?"

Jack sat down and slumped in the chair. His face became dark, angry and concerned. "They apparently did not want to hear the truth. They were expecting, or even wanting and hoping to hear that I am a racist asshole and an out of control cop."

"So what did they do? They have already done two investigations and both clear you of doing wrong. What do they want?"

"They are a gutless bunch of politicians. Rojas has them afraid of their own shadows. He refused to accept the report and made a motion to send the investigation to the county Grand Jury. They are determined to find a way to hang me. It has become a vendetta against the police department and I am the ball they kick around."

Gail got up, walked over to Jack, and sat on his lap as she hugged him. He knew she was really concerned and really loved him, because there was not much she hated more than sweat.

"What now, honey?"

"We wait some more. It has been seven months. I am not sure how much more I can handle."

As the wait dragged on, the pressure and angst continued to build for Jack. He started to withdraw from social contact. He stopped going to the Canopy, where he had enjoyed stopping once or twice a month after a difficult day. Now he wouldn't go for fear he would turn to alcohol. And frankly, he was tired of talking about the investigation.

A month went by. He did not really expect any results this soon, but the waiting was getting heavier. Jack stopped going to church. The people were nice and very supportive but he did not want to answer the questions his friends and pastor asked. He had no answers and was tired of talking about it.

"Pray," he was told. "You just need to pray, and then God will make it all right. Prayer will give you confidence in your future."

Jack began to hate adages and pious sayings. If he heard one more person say, "Let go and Let God," he was going to puke and throw a tantrum.

The only other worse thing was the advice to "Pray harder." What did that mean? To pray harder? Did God wait until you were totally desperate? Or, was God measuring your angst or sincerity? Furthermore, why was the person in pain at fault and required to pray harder? Maybe it should be the spiritual leaders or those who portray themselves as spiritual to do the hard prayers. Jesus never required a person to pray harder. He had compassion and touched people, healing and helping them. Was it too much to expect those spiritual leaders to demonstrate the compassion of the Jesus they taught?

"Shit," thought Jack. It really was one of his favorite words, at least lately. Being raised on a dairy farm that word was used in everyday talk. After all you walked in it, washed it off the cows, spread it on the pasture and it got onto your clothes. Shit was something to deal with. Now he used that word because the whole affair smelled and it was everywhere around him. It seemed like he was stuck in a huge pile of it. Along with the pressure of the investigation, the lengthy duration was increasing the pressure on his shoulders all because he was not praying hard enough.

What did praying hard mean or look like? As far as he knew, his wife was the only person "praying hard" besides himself.

It had been eight months of this. Maybe God didn't care.

So doubt crept in.

Work became just a routine. He did what he was told, helping his partners. It was all mundane and just an exercise to get through. His mind was always off somewhere, mostly worried about his future and even more worried about Gail. She did not deserve any of this. She was a good Minnesota girl who probably thought she should have stayed there. Jack would not blame her if she did feel that way; he just hoped she would stay and not go back. He didn't want her to leave him over all this senseless garbage.

Jack drove slower, knowing his attention was not always where it should be. He was hesitant at work, afraid to make mistakes. He thought that even the smallest screw up would result in discipline. He watched his mirror to see who was following him, knowing he was under the microscope.

Paranoia was added to doubt.

Two more months went by. Still there was nothing from the Grand Jury or from Cal.

Gail tried to help as much as she could. She was loving and kind. The kids were too young to realize what pain dad was going through, but they knew something was wrong. Often they would crawl onto his lap after dinner and cuddle. They needed assurance that everything was okay. Jack tried.

When he was alone he mulled things over. He had some great employers before he went into law enforcement. He had bosses that looked after the welfare of their employees. One employer came to the construction site one day, drove up to Jack, opened the door to his pickup, and said, "Jump in."

As they drove away his boss said, "Jack, when this building is done there is not enough work to keep you. I am really sorry about that. However, I am going to introduce you to your new boss. This guy just picked up six month's worth of work and wants to meet you." How many bosses were there who took that kind of interest in employees?

He continued to be in turmoil about how the city was handling his complaint. If he did good and worked hard to earn his pay shouldn't the city, or at least the chief, support him? Shouldn't they make decisions about what was right and what was wrong? This was law enforcement, right? Where justice was the goal? Politics sure makes a difference when it comes to how employees are treated.

Why did Jack feel like he was being fed to the wolves?

Where were the real men? The men who said, "Opinions or expediency be damned, I am doing what is right?"

Jack knew he was being naïve. Justice was not the goal. Political gain was the driving force.

Despair set in.

It was Sunday morning. Breakfast was finished. Gail told the kids to get ready for Sunday school and church. Jack had missed several Sundays by then. She looked at him as if to ask if he was going with her and the kids.

Jack spoke up before she could ask, "I am going to do TV church today."

A tear formed in Gail's eye but she quickly turned away, hoping Jack did not see it. But he did see it and it hurt that he could do nothing to help her. It was just like that for him. There was nobody that could help him. He was all alone. No matter what anyone said, they could not know his pain or help carry it and he felt helpless and hopeless in future and helpless in watching Gail deal with her pain.

When he was alone he began to think. He realized that he had to make a choice. He needed to come to a conclusion about things.

Jack turned on the TV. Maybe there was a church program that would feed his soul. Rex Humbard was coming on. Jack liked Rex's messages and his reliance on scripture for teaching. Rex Humbard was preaching at his church in Akron, Ohio. Jack saw him as a true man of God who made the Bible understandable to

156

his audience. He was talking about God's presence and goodness reaching out to everyone.

"Sure," mused Jack, "I sure don't feel Him, and I am not sure anymore if He even exists."

He turned off the TV and again began to process his thoughts. Jack was a realist and he was analytically pragmatic, so he began the process of looking at what he had always believed to see if it held water, as he liked to think about logic.

His faith in God was shaken. He wanted to figure out if the religious things he was taught were true or if they were figments of theologians' imaginations, used to enslave minds. Rex Humbard had just said something about God creating the heavens and the earth. Was that true? Or could evolution and the Big Bang Theory be correct? Jack didn't know. How could anyone really know for sure? Smarter, more educated people had debates about it and they could not prove it to each other either.

"What should I believe?" mused Jack. "All right, let's say that evolution might possibly be correct," he decided.

He remembered that Humbard also mentioned that the Bible was God's word. Jack thought about what he was taught about the Bible. That it was written by God and infallible. Others said it was a collection of writings that man assembled and declared to be God's writings. They claimed it was contradictory and made up solely by theologians.

Again, Jack thought, people much wiser and more educated than him debated these things, and they had not been able to sway each other with their logic. So, maybe the Bible was just a collection of historical writings that had spiritual truths, but was it really God's word for mankind? Not necessarily.

Jack was not feeling any better. He had not made any real or solid discovery, or come to any rock-solid conclusions. Humbard talked about God. His church preached God. His family and many friends encouraged him to trust God. They kept telling him to pray to God.

"Well," mused Jack, "is there really a God?"

He had not experienced God for a long time. He felt that his prayers were just going into empty space. He stopped praying in the normal or accepted manner of prayer. Closing his eyes, bowing his head, or kneeling were not and had not been part of his life for several months. His soul cried out. His heart and mind searched for answers from God, but nothing happened.

157

At least not yet.

His thoughts took him to question how he could know if God existed. God was not visible to the eye. People might say, "God told me," but no one had heard the audible voice of God. Sure, the Bible talked about men hearing God speak and about angels who brought messages from God, but no one had seen angels either, at least not like the ones in the Bible, with wings and everything.

Maybe atheists were correct. Maybe God was a figure used by people to control and enslave minds. Good and evil just existed in the hearts and minds of mankind. When people died, that was it. There was no heaven and no hell. Could that be?

Somehow that did not seem correct, but why was it not correct? Just because God was not visible, did that make Him less real? There were lots of things that were not visible that we knew were real: radio and micro waves, the wind, warmth, and energy.

God must be a spirit as the Bible said, and the only way to realize He was real was to see what he did and to feel His presence.

Had Jack ever felt His presence?

Jack went back in time to remember important events in his life. He recalled praying to God as a four year old, when he was afraid that an American bomber would bomb his house because the Nazi army had anti-aircraft guns and munitions trucks on the family farm. He remembered the staunch faith of his father as he helped the underground movement to aid the Jews who were escaping to freedom and avoiding the death camps.

He recalled the day his mother was dying from cancer. She was in a coma for days. Then just hours before dying, she said with joy, "I see the angels." Then she smiled as she drifted off into eternity.

What about the time when a drug dealer put a .45 Automatic to Jack's head and asked if he was a cop? What made him put the gun down, even though he still would not sell any speed?

What about all of the times the experience of God's nearness and love was so real that Jack was in awe that God loved him?

Then Jack realized that he knew God was real, he could not deny that it was God who had answered his prayer when the bomber came over and all those other things were not mere coincidences. And yes, God did create the heavens and the earth, and yes, God did write the Bible to bring life and guidance to the reader.

158

Jack was back! Rex Humbard's words of faith had initiated the thinking Jack needed to do to bring him through the turmoil of life. He was grateful God had brought Humbard to guide his thoughts when his own pastor and elders had been unable to offer realistic advice or help.

This torment he was in was going to end and there would be victory in justice. He would be vindicated.

It was another month before notice came that the Grand Jury had completed their investigation. Cal called and told Jack that he had been cleared, but to keep it silent. How could he not shout it out and go around with a huge smile on a happy face?

It was a good thing it was Tuesday and the council was meeting that night. The only person Jack told about Cal's phone call was Gail. He left work early to go home to tell her. They cried on each other's shoulders in relief. Then they thanked God for seeing them through.

Jack did not attend the council meeting, but several friends and Association representatives did attend. When the Grand Jury report was presented there was silence. The audience was stunned and the council was at a loss. They had no idea what they should do.

"Motion to receive the report? We do not accept or reject the report, we just receive it." Seconded and passed. They did not have the sense of justice or fair play to acknowledge the truth. Political expediency ruled.

The whole police department and the association knew that it was over. The dark cloud no longer hung over Jack's head. Everyone could breathe easy now.

But was it over?

How did they go back to normal?

Was trust of the administration and government damaged beyond repair?

How long would it take for the pain and fear to go away?

Chapter 33

July 1976

Ricky Augustino applied to the Los Angeles Sheriff's Office (LASO).He had become disillusioned with the prospect of making a career at Ontario PD. He and his wife, Carly, just bought a house on South Oaks Avenue, with a large lot where the kids could play and have pets. The oldest, Marcus, was twelve and had been dreaming of raising a goat and maybe a horse.

"Huh, please dad?"

Ricky realized that he would pay his dues working the jail for his initial assignment, but he hoped that would be short because of his field experience. Then maybe he could be assigned to the San Dimas substation, which would make his life wonderful.

Change was coming. Four officers were enrolled in law school-two made it and became defense attorneys. The other two failed the bar. One of them stayed but the other moved back to Wyoming to work on the family ranch.

Six officers applied to the Los Angeles Sheriff's Office. They preferred to work for Los Angeles Police Department, for Chief Gates, as opposed to working for Sheriff Block. The deciding factor was the retirement plan. The Sheriff's Office was with the Public Employees Retirement System, while LAPD had its own retirement system.

Ricky passed the oral exam and his background check was in process. This was the risky part, when a cop wanted to keep the transfer a secret. LASO was accommodating to this concern. They did all of the personal checks first, and checked with the employer near the end of the process.

Ricky worked swing shift traffic. He got a call: TC with injuries. He was the second unit to respond. The first unit was closer, so ran Code 3. Ricky was going to get there as soon as possible.

There was only one legal way for a police car to exceed the speed limit, and that was with a red light and siren. Yet every victim expected the officer to be there immediately when they needed help or they were in trouble. So every police officer learned that driving faster than the limit was expected. Every minute was precious when violent crimes were happening or people were injured in traffic collisions. Speeding was the norm. Just be very alert and careful. Not getting there was worse than getting there late. That was what the training officer taught each recruit.

Ricky was driving as fast as he thought was safe. The amount over the posted limit was up for discussion and investigation. Going south on Euclid, he slowed for each signal but rolled through. He had his flashing ambers on in the rear to give the observers notice that he was hurrying on a call.

"Son of a," is all he got to say before he crashed into a Toyota Supra. Ricky saw it coming from the left, barely slowing for the stop sign. Ricky slammed on the brakes but had almost no time before he broadsided the car. He left less than three feet of skid marks before the unit crashed into the passenger side.

The driver of the Supra jumped out and ran away immediately after he came to a stop. Ricky hit the end of the seatbelt. His helmet flew off, hit the steering wheel, and bounced back, hitting him a glancing blow to the top of his head. Regaining his senses, he quickly called in the collision and then bailed out of the unit to check on the other car. He saw the driver sprint away, but checked on the passenger before he got back on the radio.

The passenger was a young woman. She was slumped over onto the driver's seat and fell off the seat, with her legs on the floor on her side of the car. The only visible blood was a small laceration on her head, where she likely hit her door window. She did not seem to be breathing. Her chest was still. He placed his finger on her throat, feeling for a pulse. There was no pulse.

His head sagged as the reality hit him. He was involved in a fatal crash. Damn it!

Panting, he ran back to his unit to call an ambulance and to give a description of the driver, who was now out of sight.

A thousand thoughts ran through his mind as he raced back to the Supra and began CPR on the woman, hoping against hope that he could bring her back.

"Breathe, damn it, breathe," he muttered.

He continued to work on her, listening to the sirens that were coming in his direction. He prayed they would get there in time to do something or perform a miracle.

The ambulance took the passenger away, headed to San Antonio Community Hospital. Everyone realized she was dead but the procedure was to go to the nearest hospital so a doctor could make that determination. It was also a convenient way to avoid waiting for the coroner.

If Ontario Hospital was still open they would have gone there; it was only a few blocks away. Ontario Hospital did not have a good reputation amongst the officers. Most officers included a warning when they broke in a new partner. The warning went something like this, "Do not take me to Ontario Hospital, no matter how badly I am injured, because if I survive I will kill you!"

The traffic collision investigator was called out. He and the sergeant carefully measured the location of everything. They now knew the exact distance from the respective curbs for each item that came off the cars. The location and length of skid marks were all properly measured, photographed and recorded.

The force of the impact would be determined by calculating the damage to the metal and skid marks from any tire that left them. Hopefully that would determine culpability in the crash.

The driver of the Toyota was found walking as he turned south off G Street onto Laurel. He denied that he was the driver. He was brought back to the scene and identified by Ricky. When he was questioned he denied doing anything wrong.

"Hey, I stopped at the sign, man. No, I did not see any cars coming. How fast was that cop going?"

"Why did you run, if you did nothing wrong?"

Silence.

"Come on, I will find out anyway. It will just take longer. What were you running for?"

"I don't have a driver's license, man. The court took it away."

"Why?"

"Too many traffic tickets and I got busted for drinking."

"Drunk driving?"

"Yeah."

"Did you know your friend is probably dying?"

"I am not saying anything more till I have an attorney."

The driver clammed up. Apparently he had been through these hoops before. He was transported to West End Substation and booked for hit and run, a felony due to the injury or death.

Dietz Towing took the Toyota Supra and the patrol car away and then cleaned the street.

Ricky was taken to the station for an interview and to write his report of the entire incident. His mind was going crazy with

163

concern for the family of the deceased person. His compassion for others was well known, but the traffic investigator wanted the report right away. Ricky asked for some time to gather his thoughts and clear his head, actually, his heart, of the memory of trying to revive the lady. Ricky was mourning.

His second concern was getting the report correct. The city manager had put pressure on the chief to cut down on the expenses, especially repairs to patrol cars. He carefully tried to recall his speed and driving tactics prior to the crash, as well as his actions when he saw the car go through the stop sign. All of that would be analyzed and evaluated, so he wanted to be right and not fudge very much, or he would be in even deeper trouble.

He was not given the measurements, photos or details of the crash from the investigators. He had to rely on memory. This caused him concern. Why? Was this a test of his honesty or was someone looking to hang him? Helping him with the factual evidence could help him write a report that would help the city if a lawsuit was filed. What's up?

Briefing the next day included a short spiel on safe driving. There was no mention of Ricky's TC, but the notice was there. Blame was going to land some place and everyone thought Ricky was going to be disciplined.

The waiting began. When would the investigation be completed? The investigator was at the scene several days of the week and for three weeks he was there during the time span of the crash. He had the radar unit and took the high and average speeds of vehicles that traveled through that area.

LASO placed Ricky's employment application on hold. They wanted to see the outcome of the investigation before they hired a new officer.

Two weeks went by, and then three and four weeks elapsed. There was no decision yet.

Ricky was worried.

Ricky asked the OPOA to represent him and to check on the status of the investigation. Maybe he could find out what the process would be regarding Ricky.

Jack and Ray made an appointment with the chief and requested that IA or the traffic bureau captain be there. When the meeting took place they were in the chief's office. They suspected the meeting was held there so recordings could easily be made. They had learned to be cautious with what was said in the chief's office.

After the pleasantries were exchanged with the chief and IA officer they got down to the purpose of the call.

"We are interested in the status of the investigation of Ricky's TC. Is discipline being considered? If so, what is the plan for hearings and meetings?"

"I will not be questioned about what my plans are, and furthermore I resent being judged on what is being done to prevent the soaring costs of damage to city equipment. Two police cars have been totaled within one year. This must stop, and I will do what it takes," grumbled the chief, his voice rising as he talked.

"That is a legitimate concern, sir. It is not as if we like crashing cars and having officers injured or causing expense and liability for the city. We are also concerned about the stress it causes, and prefer discipline to be handed out fairly and with minimal delay, sort of like the courts guarantee of the right to a speedy trial," replied Jack.

"It takes time to access the value and the liability, and we are working on it. Be assured that we will handle each incident fairly and properly."

Jack was upset and let his passion override his good sense. "Sure! Like the discipline that was done when the captain crashed his car into the parked car after he left a poker party drunk? Oh, I am sorry. We do not know he was drunk because no tests were given, but everyone knows he drank more than a six-pack while he played poker. And what about the officer who was chasing rabbits at Whispering Lakes Golf course and got stuck in the mud when he drove into the lake? He didn't get disciplined, even though he was out of service for four hours having the car towed and washed. In fact, he was promoted to sergeant two months later.

"Now do you understand why we are concerned with what is happening to Ricky with his TC?"

Chapter 34

East Nocta Street was commonly referred to as Okie Flats. A mixture of people and races lived there. The old timers were either moving out or when they went to retirement or care facilities their children sold their houses; Investors bought these older homes as rental units for the working class.

Many of the residents worked at Kaiser Steel or Sunkist Orange, or labored at construction sites. The houses were wood sided with redwood siding, long before stucco became the popular and less expensive material for siding houses. They had one bathroom, where the value was in the eagle claw tubs. They were modest homes with two and sometimes three bedrooms. The concept of a master bedroom was not yet in vogue then.

The garages were detached and built for one car. The cars were smaller when these garages were built, so now they were used for storage. The lawn equipment, bikes, used toys, and other junk was just piled up in the garage. Pickups and cars were in the driveways or parked on the front lawn. Each yard had a front yard tree, under which the families sat during hot days and evenings of Southern California summers. There was no air conditioning. Some might have a swamp cooler to keep damp air circulating while the residents tried to sleep.

The kitchen was where food was made on the old gas range. Most people ate in the kitchen too, in the old days. Before families took their food to the living room and ate while they watched TV. The refrigerators were all small. Many of these houses were built when ice boxes were still in use or the first gas refrigerators, built by Servel, which could hold one ice cube tray and a few frozen items.

Having children became a burden. No longer did the family unit work together to achieve the status of middle class. Now the focus was on what the parents could or would do for the children. That created stress to increase the income of the wage earner. When the income did not increase the pressure to spend money like everyone else at school or in the neighborhood became too much. It would take a few beers at the Green Lantern, or Nite Lite at Holt and Corona or sometimes it was best or cheaper to be with some friends and drink beer in their front yards for a while in order to make life tolerable to go home.

The Mueller family home was there. They had three vehicles: a pickup and two cars that were parked wherever there was space. Beer cans littered the yard, dropped where they were emptied in the shade of the huge elm tree. The tree needed pruning and cleaning up, just like the yard did. The beer cans were collected once a week to redeem for enough cash to buy another case of whatever was on sale at Torley's Market.

The three Mueller kids grew up there. They went to Berlyn Elementary, Vina Danks Junior High and Ontario High School. When they became teenagers they exerted their independence from parental authority and were allowed to experiment with life and fend for themselves. The parents were not in favor of this but lacked the fortitude and ability to fight these changes.

Henk began to wander the neighborhood. He was a likeable kid and played with several friends on Nocta or Elma, the next street over. He hated coming home for supper for fear that his father would be drunk or wishing he was drunk. The bickering was only slightly worse than the hostile silence. It was best to stay away.

Staying away did not make for a happy life. As he grew older, his friend's older brother introduced him to marijuana. After coughing and getting over the watery eyes he found that he liked the way he felt after a few drags. He did not want to drink beer, like his dad and mom, so this was a good choice. Smoking dope once or twice was a nice break from life, and doing it once a week worked when his friends had some to share.

Henk dropped out of school. He hated to study. He hated it when people told him what to do. So he started hanging out with other dropouts. They talked about what a bitch life was, and bragged about the great jobs they were going to get and then they would make more money than their dads made. These jobs never came, so they smoked more dope and created bigger dreams. Parents stopped giving them money, telling them to get jobs and earn their own money, since they wanted to be independent.

Henk started shoplifting items he could sell to people he knew. Then he heard that Garth at G&G Auto would buy whatever anyone brought to him. It was safer than going to a pawn shop, so Henk and his friends brought stuff to Garth and sold it for fifteen cents on the dollar, also better than the local pawn shop that paid barely ten cents on the dollar.

Chapter 35

The regional taskforce had an informant who told them about places that sold stolen goods. These places included G&G Auto, Campus Bar & Grill, and a rest home that would take groceries, especially meats.

Ray went to White Front Department Store on Mountain and Fifth St. to talk to the manager. This store was experiencing a high amount of shoplifting and had become active in prosecuting the thieves. The softer touch had not worked out well for them. Ray talked about it with the manager and explained that the cops needed items to use as bait while they were investigating those who bought stolen property.

"Sure, I will donate used TVs or other appliances, if that will help?"

"How about new stuff, if we bring it back?"

"I'll do whatever I can. I am sick of these druggies lifting things. Just bring the TV back undamaged. Otherwise I could give you returned TVs and appliances that are near new but have slight damage."

The next day Jack, who was back in the bureau, went with Ray to begin investigating the places that bought stolen property. They began with a used color TV.

Jack did some concrete work on his time off to help pay his children's tuition, so he often wore his construction clothes when he met crooks. Shaking some saw dust or brushing cement dust off your clothes while you dealt with a crook was highly assuring to the crook. After all, what cop worked in cement or cutting lumber?

Jack had his sandy blond hair in an afro and he had a small goatee which was in need of trimming. Their cover looked good.

They drove to the rear of G & G, off the alley. Garth was in his office talking on the phone. He heard the car, looked up, and held his hand up to motion that they should wait. Soon he came out to the 58 Ford they had borrowed from Citrus Ford.

This was the first time they came there, so Garth was cautious.

"What can I help you with? Looking for a car?" he smirked. It was obvious they were not looking for a car to buy. If they were, they would have pulled up in the front and they would have been out of the car looking at the rows of cars along Holt.

169

Jack grinned back. "No, we might have something for you though."

"What?"

"A TV."

"Let me see it. What makes you think I want a TV?"

Jack just smiled, "A friend said you are in the market. Are you? If not, no problem."

"Let's see it."

Ray got out and opened the trunk, showing Garth the TV and a tape recorder.

"Is it used? Where did you get it? Is the recorder for sale too?"

"Yeah it is used. It was my mother's, but she died last week. The recorder is okay."

"Thirty bucks for both."

"You ripping me off?" said Jack. "Give me fifty."

"Back up to the shop. I'll give you forty. It's you that probably ripped off your mother."

The deal was done and they now had the bait and were ready to set the hook.

They waited a few days to go back to Garth. Meanwhile, they went to King Cole Market to get some meat to sell to Sanders at the retirement home.

Ray gave the manager the spiel about needing meat to sell to a fence. The manager was more than happy to help. "I know we have meat stolen all the time and it bothers me, but I understand when people need to eat. Stealing and selling it pisses me off. Sure, I'll help."

Ten pounds of steak and two chuck roasts later, they walked out and went to make a call on Mr. Sanders. This was not as easy as G & G. How would they get past the receptionist? They had an idea of what Mr. Sanders looked like and they had the meat. "Here goes," said Ray.

They walked in the front door and the receptionist looked up. A hint of a frown crossed her face as she saw the slovenly, dirty dress of the two cops.

"May I help you?"

"Mr. Sanders is expecting us," said Ray and he began walking toward what looked like the main office.

"Sure," she replied, and waved them toward the office. "He is there now. You just got here in time."

170

They both smiled inwardly, glad that the bluff or bravado worked. They entered the office and closed the door. Mr. Sanders looked up, surprised.

"Do I know you?"

"Not yet, but we have some really nice beef you would like to know."

"Who told you I liked good beef?"

"A friend of yours and mine," Jack looked around, hesitant to say more.

"Who?"

"Jose."

"There are lots of Jose's in town."

"Well, this is the one who brings you beef for your freezer."

The greed was visible in his eyes as he rose from his chair, "Okay, let's see what you have." Sanders walked them to the door. "I don't have much time. I'm having lunch with the city manager."

He was dressed in a fine one-thousand-dollar suit and shiny wingtip shoes. Ray and Jeff wondered if they were also stolen items, since they knew a shoplifter who stole suits and haberdashery to order. Just state your size and color and next week, presto a new set of clothes.

They went out the side door and to the same 58 Ford, opened the trunk and showed him the packages of meat.

"Twenty dollars."

"There is over a hundred bucks worth there. How about twenty-five?"

"Deal, Next time bring roasts or hamburger. I use that more often."

"Roasts are harder to hide."

"So, just do it. It pays better."

They drove away. Once they were around the corner they gave each other a high five. "Greedy bastard isn't he? He probably gets paid by the State or County and then uses stolen meat. Maybe he did pay for them fine duds himself."

Jack called Citrus Ford to tell them they needed the car for at least another week so they could complete at least one or two more sales before they switched cars.

Two days later they were back at White Front. This time they got two eight-track players, a boom box radio, and two boxes of chocolates.

They went to Campus Bar & Grill. The bartender they were

171

looking for was named Spencer. They sat at the bar and ordered a draft Bud, not sure if this bartender was the man they wanted. They waited. Hopefully someone would call him by name or else Ray would just go for it.

"I remember this corner really well. Sometimes I have dreams about it," commented Jack as he sipped his beer.

"Dreams or nightmares?

"Probably right, nightmares."

"What did you do, get into a big fight or something?"

"No, it was a long time ago, probably six years or so, when I drive down Campus it all comes back. I was assigned to Traffic for the week. That was bad enough. I hate writing tickets, and working TCs is a pain in the ass."

"So, what happened?"

"Hang on to your hat, man. I was coming south on Campus. I came across the tracks and saw the light at Holt turn green. I was maybe three hundred feet from the intersection when the first car was in the middle and a pickup truck came from the east and T-boned it, spinning it around one hundred eighty degrees. It was now facing south and the pickup landed up at this corner against the light pole."

"I flipped on the bubble gum and rear window lights, called in the TC and asked for an ambulance, expecting serious injuries. Then we had only seat belts and not a shoulder harness or child car seat that strapped us in."

"Just as I got to the rear bumper the driver came out with a baby in her hands. She was looking down at it and began to sob. She saw me and thrust the baby into my hands. 'My baby, my baby! She's dead,' she sobbed and fell to her knees. I had no idea what she expected of me. I'm no miracle worker, not even a paramedic.

"There I was in the middle of the intersection with traffic stopped four ways. People were getting out of their cars and running around, and I was holding a dead baby. She was cute, like all babies. Maybe two months old, but lifeless. There was no blood, but the head was lying sideways. Her eyes were closed and she was not breathing.

"I never felt more helpless in my whole life. I wanted to weep. Fact is tears did run down."

"What did you do?"

"I knelt down next to the mother, who was sitting against the

172

rear tire weeping, and asked her to give mouth to mouth to the baby until the fire fighter's med unit came. I figured this would give her hope and keep her from losing it until help arrived. I hugged her and told her to hang on while I checked on the other injuries.

"Luckily, we were only three or four blocks from the fire station and PD, so help was there by the time I checked on the other driver. He was lying against his steering wheel with a gash across his forehead. He was awake, so I grabbed my handkerchief and told him to press downward to close the gash, and then hold there on his wound to stop the flow of blood.

"Just then the medics arrived with two units, so we got the mess under control.

"The memory of the dead baby in my hands, that is tough. The shooting victims and suicide deaths don't bother me like that one does. Not even the guy who blew his brains all over his bedroom wall bothered me like this. Maybe it was because the baby probably died in my arms."

He turned away to hide the tears that welled up in his eyes. Then he gruffly said, "Enough of that. We better pay attention to what's happening here."

There were only three patrons. One was at the bar and two were playing pool. Obviously they were regulars; evident by the way they joked and talked to each other.

One of the pool players called out, "Hey, Spence, bring us another pitcher."

"Coming up," he yelled back as he began filling the pitcher.

Waiting for Spencer to come back, Jack gave Ray the nod to go ahead. The door opened hard against the wall. Everyone looked to see who these drunks were. Jack ducked his head and covered the left side of his face with his hand. He leaned over to Ray and whispered, "We are screwed. Don't look, but I busted that dude three months ago and just testified at the prelim. Let's go!"

They got up and left, walking toward the restroom area where the back door was.

Behind them they heard shouting, "What the fuck are the cops doing here? Do you know these guys are narcs?"

Jack and Ray hastened their retreat. They did not want to have a confrontation or battle with anyone. Maybe if they just got out these guys wouldn't remember what they looked like. This new guy had been busted for burglary and possession of heroin, and they found a loaded gun under the seat of his car. His name was Jerry Hancock and he was known as Crazy Jerry. He was a real screw-up. He had a long term on again and off again affair with the wife of a Hell's Angel. The husband and Jerry had fought over her for years, shooting at each other numerous times over this woman. She must make really "good stew".

Jack kept an eye on the mirror, as he headed out, to see if Jerry was armed and to see what the others were doing. The man at the bar moved to the end of the bar, keeping his eyes on what was happening. The pool players were standing there, one with the cue stick turned around like a club. He watched them leave but did not move.

The bartender ran behind the bar next to the register. Jack figured he had a gun there, intended for self-protection. But now?

Safely outside, they flattened themselves with their backs against the wall. Ray pulled his 9 millimeter, holding it against his leg, waiting to see if anyone came out after them. They waited a full minute before Jack got into the car and backed it out. His .45 was lying on his lap. When he had the car aimed for the driveway, Ray jumped in and turned west on Holt.

A block away they looked at each other. Jack was the first to speak, "I thought that son-of-a bitch was in jail."

"Sure did not expect to run into that crazy bastard. Who knows what he would have done if we hadn't got our butts out of there."

They continued west to Laddie's. Jack pulled in and they went in to get a coffee and a coke and to take some time to cool off and figure out what happened and to decide what to do next. This was not the first time an operation failed or fell apart because of something unexpected. You had to expect or plan for the unexpected. That was a good reason not to drink booze before or during work.

"You know, someday Jerry is going to succeed in killing someone or get himself killed. Maybe Trixie's husband will learn to be a better shot. Then we'll be rid of two idiots."

"Now that we are here, we have stuff to sell. How about going to see Garth? He is only a few blocks from here; might as well get something done today."

They both threw their cups into the trash from a distance, checking to see if their hands and nerves were steady. Both hit the can cleanly. They looked at each other and said, "Good to go," and headed out.

Three blocks down the road they again pulled into the alley behind G & G Auto Sales. Garth was sitting at his desk watching TV. When he heard them drive up he turned his chair to see who it was. He got up and walked to the passenger door, which was the side closest to him.

"Hey boys, what you got for me?"

"Just some small stuff, I'll show you," Ray reached over and took the keys. He got out and opened the trunk, showing the 8 tracks, boom box and chocolates.

"You can have one of the chocolates. The other is for my mama. Two were as easy to take as one, so whatever you want."

"Thinking about your mother or a woman when you're out ripping off a store?"

"My mom, she ain't feeling well."

"Ain't you just the best son? Forty bucks."

Ray threw the keys to Jack and they drove to the shop. Garth walked along, handed over two twenties and took everything, including both boxes of chocolates.

The next morning after briefing, the group got together to discuss what they had been doing and to agree on where they were going that day.

Sergeant Laski advised, "You better wrap up Sanders today. No telling what info is out there from your visit to the Campus. Crazy Jerry could be spreading the word you guys are working PC496 violations. Get one more sale to Sanders and then go see the DA for search warrants on both places. I'll get a team alerted to serve them this afternoon."

"You are pushing us, man. We need to get some beef and then make the sale. Then write reports and get the DA on board."

"I'll get the DA started with the info we have on the first sales. Get a lot of beef this time to make that sale look really good. That creep is playing footsie with the politicians while ripping off the system. I heard he pulled papers to run for the School Board."

"Either he thinks he is above the law or he is making himself look so respectable that no one will see he's a crook. He is going to be surprised."

"Sarge, if we take a lot of meat to Sanders it would be good to spend a few bucks, say two or three hundred, okay?"

"Right, see what Avery at King Cole will donate and buy the rest."

Two hours later they were loaded and ready to go. Jack took out the business card he picked up on their last visit, dropped a dime in the pay phone and called Sanders. His call was forwarded to Sanders' office.

"Jack, Jose's friend here, got the hamburger and roasts you asked for."

"When can you be here? I am leaving in an hour?"

"Be there in twenty minutes max."

"Park on the side street, where you were before, I will come out."

"Greedy bastard is hooked," said Jeff. "Let's reel him in."

Twenty minutes later they pulled up on Belmont near the side door. They stayed in the car, waiting and watching.

The wait was short. The side door opened and they saw Mr. Sanders come over toward them.

"You gonna need help carrying this man. We got over a hundred pounds, probably a hundred and fifty." said Ray as he popped the trunk.

"You boys did good! How did you get this much?"

"It was so easy. We saw Manning's Meat truck on Holt and figured he was going to our favorite store. When he went inside with his second loaded cart we knew we had enough time to grab what we wanted. So we grabbed the sixty-pound boxes of hamburger. When he went in the third time we took two boxes of roasts. Cool, huh?"

The three of them were standing there looking at the meat. Jack began to scratch himself on the arms and then on his hair, looking around nervously. Sanders observed this and a flicker of a smile crossed his face. He figured he had a doper that was in bad need of a fix. So he took out five twenty-dollar bills, thinking the need was great so they would not argue about the amount.

Ray acted pissed, "Come on, that is worth twice that much!"

But Jack reached out to take the money.

Ray grabbed Jeff's hand, "Wait, wait, hold on a minute!"

Sanders pulled another twenty from his pocket and handed it to Jack. "Keep it down! You want to have the neighborhood hear? Quiet down or we won't be able to do business."

Jack grabbed the money and they each carried a box into the building. Sanders told them to put it on the floor just inside the door. Ray insisted on being helpful and followed Sanders to the kitchen. He watched the beef go into the freezer.

The door was open for just a few seconds but Ray noticed that most of the meat was in assorted sizes and packages and had a variety of labels. He could not read all the labels, but recognized the Von's and Alpha Beta labels, it sure looked like the meat came from lots of stores. He knew they were not the only source for meat. Good info for the search warrants.

Jack continued his act of needing a fix, calling Ray to hurry. They could leave in a hurry without causing any alarm.

They got in the car and pulled the hand-held radio from under the seat, turned it on, and notified dispatch that they were in route to the DA's office. Sergeant Laski was already there. He also had a deputy DA busy writing the warrants. He provided the names, address and descriptions of both places to be searched. All that was needed were the details about what happened, what the warrant would describe to search and what items to look for.

Forty minutes later they had Judge Gallo's signature and best wishes.

Both sites were relatively small and did not have a lot of people to worry about. They planned to serve the warrants at both places simultaneously. Two officers and two detectives would go to G & G and three officers and two detectives would go to Sanders' retirement home.

Jack took Jack' and went to G & G, and Ray took Ken and went to see Mr. Sanders.

This time when Jeff went to G & G he pulled in the front entrance. As he walked to the front door Garth looked up. "Hey Jack, what's up?"

When he spied the officers and Jack', his face paled and chin dropped, "I'm busted aren't I?"

"Yep, you screwed up."

Jack read the Miranda rights. Garth said he understood and agreed to talk.

They took Garth with them to the shop and loaded up a pickup with stereos, TVs, a wall air conditioner and other items including the eight tracks. The boom box was gone.

"Where is the boom box?"

"Sold it an hour ago to a black kid, made a few bucks and he left happy. His momma won't be happy with the noise, but so what, not my problem."

Jack said, "Garth can I ask you a question?"

"Sure, what?"

177

"Your wife's name is Adelle, so where does the G & G come from?"

Garth dropped his head in embarrassment. Then, looking up, he confessed, "When I started this auto sales shop I was active in church with my wife. I figured that God helped me start this business, so I named it Garth and God Auto Sales, G & G."

"God is not too happy with you now is He?"

"No, I really screwed up. Saw an easy way to make a few bucks and got greedy. I am sorry."

"You are going to have some time to talk to God and get right with Him; then figure out how to clean up your life."

"Yes, sir, I plan to. God is not happy with me and neither am I."

Meanwhile Ray and the team were at Sanders. There was only one office person there, besides the maid and two women who cared for the residents. Sanders was gone for the day.

The office was searched for official receipts of purchases of food items and meat. The kitchen was searched for meat and other food items that might indicate multiple sources of food. The freezer had meat from seven different grocery stores, all varieties, sizes and cuts of beef and pork. They took photos and the product was removed.

The meat was taken to Ontario Frozen Food Locker on West California Street. The sergeant made arrangements for a secure locker that could be used to keep evidence and not have it tampered with. A padlock was placed on the locker and Ray kept the keys.

The next morning the front page of the Daily Report told the story of Mr. Sanders. "Candidate for School Board turns himself in on warrant for his arrest for allegedly buying stolen property. He claims innocence, and that he was set up by Gestapo methods. He was only helping friends, and he had no idea they were using him and lying to him."

After he was held to answer at the preliminary hearing he made a plea bargain with the court and ended his candidacy for office.

Nothing was mentioned about G & G Auto.

178

Chapter 36

This time it Ray who was selected for "career development." He was assigned to swing shift patrol. He liked having Sunday and Monday off. The schedule gave him family time on weekends and time for fishing or odd jobs on Mondays. He knew that was not considered when they gave him this duty assignment. He was to be the training officer for a new hire, an ex-Marine named Michael Chavez.

Mike was still a youngster. He was barely twenty-two years old and seemed eager to be on the street mingling with the bad guys. The Tuesday through Saturday schedule provided the most action and opportunity to expose Mike to a wide variety of circumstances.

It was Ray's job to settle him down, teach him safety and to teach him to avoid using the badge to push the public around. There was no future for badge-heavy cops. He needed to know how to survive on the beat. Being cocky would get him and his partner hurt.

One thing Ray would work on was to overcome some of the stress training the academy used. He despised the use of stress in the academies likening it to hazing done by fraternities at colleges. The stress and demeaning tactics were mostly done by policemen that had been bullies on the street, now at the academy they could act tough and treat helpless trainees as they tried to do when on the street. There is no use or need to treat future peace officers disrespectfully. How can degrading them, humiliating them and harassing them give them the proper self-respect and control to handle the streets? Ray wanted the rookie to see the citizens, whether they were lawbreakers or victims, as real people; people who had real needs and real feelings. Ray would teach why law enforcement was best served by treating everyone with respect and dignity, whenever it was possible. If you want respect you need to give respect.

Ray knew that some people were just scumbags and only responded when they were treated as scumbags, but learning to treat people with dignity was worth doing anyway. Sure, he had been in several fights and sometimes he needed to take people down to control them or cuff them. His policy for training was to use only necessary force. Once an arrestee was cuffed or under

179

control there would be no hitting or spraying of Mace, and kicking was never allowed.

This particular night they were assigned to Beat Five, which included the area from Euclid west to Benson. Benson was the border with Montclair. The south border was the railroad tracks and the north border was I Street.

Ray and Mike left the basement briefing room and went upstairs to check out car keys and hand held radios.

"Have you had a tour of the station? If not, let me show you around. This place is so much nicer and roomier than the old station."

"Yeah, I have seen this station. Where was the old one?"

"It was next to the tracks on Lemon, right behind City Hall. It was cramped and musty and there was no place to park your own car. This place on Cherry is so much better. You've seen the jail cells, interview rooms and the big parking lot."

"I like it here a lot."

They went to the parking area behind the PD and next to the fire department. They looked at two firemen who were playing table tennis and two others who were polishing the valves on the water truck.

"Those guys got it made. They work three days a week, eat, sleep and play and get paid for it. But they are cool and I love it when I see them coming to do first-aid at traffic collisions and family fights. You can get a good cup of java there too."

They got in the car and Ray checked the shotgun, mileage and gas gauges, writing his findings on his work log sheet.

"Before we go out on the street we need to get a few things straight. Not everything you need to know is taught in the academy."

"First, my name is Ray, not sir."

"Second thing, I drive until I know you are ready."

"Third, if someone gets the drop on us and tells you to drop your gun or he will shoot me, do not drop your gun. If you do we will both end up dead, so take your best shot and maybe one of us will live."

"I do not want to undo academy training, and you may have heard this before, but this is what I practice. Never pull your gun unless you need to use it. It is not a scare tactic, and misuse will get someone hurt that probably did not need to be hurt, including you."

180

"Furthermore, you do not shoot someone just because he has a knife or a stick. That is what a baton or Mace is for. Also, do not shoot just because you "think" someone has a gun. Even creeps do not deserve to die just because you are afraid. Control your fear, stay cool and shoot when you need to, not just when you think you may legally do it. It is damn difficult to undo a killing. Having said that, remember that if a crook is worth shooting once he is worth shooting twice."

"We do things above board here. Use the force you need. Take a suspect down and cuff him. This is not a boxing match and there is no such thing as a fair fight. If someone decides to fight a cop it will most likely be a life or death struggle, so you must win."

"Like I said, we do it straight here. We do not lie, do not write false reports, and do not cover up. However, we are here to protect and take care of each other. I am going to tell you about a real incident that exemplifies the extreme of what we do not do."

"My partner, Jack, and I went to North Las Vegas to locate a witness of a homicide. Our goal was to find him and convince him to return with us to testify at the trial, which was starting in two days.

"We contacted the PD to let them know we were going to be in town and why. They were great. They invited us to meet at the PD and we discussed where we thought the witness was staying, which was in a low-income project. They suggested that they accompany us because this was an area with lots of violence, drug sales and was hostile to law enforcement.

"We welcomed their advice and assistance. We were both pleased until one of the detectives removed a short barrel revolver from his bottom desk drawer. It was wrapped in a handkerchief. Carefully, he made sure it stayed wrapped when he placed it into his jacket pocket. Noticing our looks, he said, 'just in case we shoot someone and need this to place under the body.'

"No one in our PD has a throw-away gun. We will be careful to not shoot someone who has no gun. Got it?"

"Fourth, if I get injured do not take me to Ontario Community Hospital. You will take me to San Antonio Hospital no matter what anyone says. If you do take me to Ontario Hospital I will kill you if I survive."

"What is wrong with Ontario Hospital? I thought it was a good place?" the rookie asked.

"The hospital is good; it is the Emergency Room that has problems. For a while it was mandated that we had to alternate taking our emergency victims there and to SACH. But sometimes they had only nurses on duty and the doctor was on call. I took a TC injury there and the poor dude almost died. It took over forty minutes for the doctor to arrive. That is shit emergency work."

"Oh, I almost forgot. Many of the dangerous people we run into are loaded up on drugs or have psychiatric problems. The drug users bring trouble upon themselves but the nut cases are victims of their brains. Do what it takes to control them but always remember that they are people who need help, and do not take out your anger or vengeance on them. They each have a mother who loves them, and wishes she could help them."

"Okay, got it."

"Fifth, use trash cans. This car is not a dump and we do not throw anything onto the street, except my tobacco juice. Got it?"

"Yes, sir, um, sorry, Ray."

"Sixth, there are places that give us free food and drinks. Always insist on paying. If they refuse to take your money, leave a large tip for the food. Free coffee and day old donuts are okay."

"One more thing and this is probably the most critical of all. Academies like to talk about 'the thin blue line' making it seem that it is the cops against the world. The reality is that we stand between the ten percent who are bad people to protect the ninety percent who are good people. That ninety percent is what makes the world a good place and they like cops and respect what we do. Therefore, always remember to treat people with respect so they will be there for you in your hour of need."

After the instructions, they left the parking lot and drove to Cherry Avenue, and then south to Holt, where they headed west.

"Ontario one-zero-five. Family 415. Neighbor calling that man is beating on the woman next door to 918."

"10-4," said Ray as he replaced the mike.

"Next call you handle the radio."

"Yes, sir."

Ray looked at Mike and scowled but said nothing as he sped off to the call.

They found the house next door to the caller, a one-story stucco bungalow. There were two cars on the driveway and one on what used to be a lawn. Now it was bare dirt, packed down from

182

the cars, and there were patches of dry Bermuda grass.

Both of them walked to the front door. As they got to the door but before they could knock, they heard the sound of a person choking. It sounded like a woman was trying to breathe but was being choked. Ray grabbed the doorknob to enter, but it was locked. Mike, realizing the urgency, took off, running to the back of the house.

The sound of a struggle continued. Jack heard a woman's voice call for help. Her words were cut off by more choking noises. Ray decided not to wait for Mike. He stepped back and kicked the door right next to the knob.

The sound of breaking wood filled the air. The door swung in and crashed into Mike, who was just reaching to open the door. Mike staggered back, holding his wrist. Ray saw a man on top of a woman. She was sprawled across the couch and one of her feet was on the floor. The man had both hands around her throat, and was squeezing and shaking her up and down. She was gurgling and her face was blue.

Ray and Mike rushed to the sofa. Jack grabbed the man by the hair, jerking him back hard. Mike grabbed for the man's hands but missed, as the guy let go of the woman's throat and reached for the hand that was lifting him up and throwing him onto the floor.

"See if she is all right or if she needs an ambulance," said Ray as he rolled the man onto his stomach and cuffed him.

"Real tough guy, aren't you? Like beating on women? Let's go Mr. Tough guy. You're busted." He marched the guy to the police car and locked him in the back seat. Just then Beat 101 pulled up.

"Watch this guy while I go take statements."

Ray went back inside to see how Mike and the victim were doing. She was sitting on the sofa, softly crying.

"Need a doctor?"

"No, I am okay now. Are you taking him to jail?"

"Yes ma'am, sure are. He won't bother you for some time."

Tears started streaming down her cheeks and her shoulders began to shake. Sobbing, she asked, "Do you have to arrest him? He really didn't mean to hurt me. I'm sure everything will be alright now that he is cooled off. It was my fault anyway."

"Your fault? What do you mean your fault? The dude was choking you to death!"

"I spilled some of his beer when I was bringing it to him. I should have been more careful. What am I going to do without him? We've been together for fifteen years."

"Leave, which is what you will do. It will only get worse."

"He is all I got. I don't have family, no kids, and no job. Please let him go! I need him!"

"How about we get you a place to go, where you will be safe and taken care of? You can go to the House of Ruth. They will provide shelter and help you get on your feet."

"Really? You can help me get there and they will take me in?"

"Sure, just get your stuff together. I'll reserve a bed for you and get someone to ride over with you. You do have a car, right?"

Mike and Ray finished taking notes for the report and left. They took the suspect to West End Jail and booked him.

The week went by with mostly routine traffic stops, a few citations, and TC reports. Mike started driving, alternating days with Jack.

On West Holt there was a nude bar. It used to be called Villa Nicola but the name changed to Villa Theater when ABC took the liquor license away because of the nude dancing. Now they showed porn movies, had nude dancers, and served nonalcoholic beverages. Wally Linza was the new owner.

Wally always welcomed the beat cops who stopped in. He liked the security because it kept clients from getting too rowdy, and lots of the cops liked to stop in to get a peek at the bare boobs. Ray would visit with Wally in his small office and bullshit about life and some cop stories Wally liked to hear.

Wednesday night was quiet. Mike was driving and suggests, "Got time to take a look see if Wally has any nice pussy up there tonight?"

Ray couldn't care less. He shrugged his shoulders, "You kids just got to keep looking and dreaming, don't you?"

Mike parked the unit by the front door. Mike walked in and stood against the wall, checking out the blonde. She was not a real blonde. She was flirting with a customer, trying to earn a ten-dollar tip.

Ray walked to the back toward the office. The barmaid yelled at him, "You can't go in there."

Ray looked at her, frowned, and said, "Sure I can. Wally said to stop in anytime."

He did not see her face turning pale as he opened the office door.

Wally looked up, turned ashen white, and started to shake. "What the fuck, I told the barmaid to keep everybody out?"

"You should've locked the door dummy. You told me I could drop in any time. I didn't know you had special times that you did not want to see anyone."

Ray saw a pile of little white pills and a bunch of aluminum foil rolls on the desk. Wally was rolling Benzedrine pills, into rolls.

"What are you doing, Wally? Skimming money on a nude bar is not enough. Now you're dealing dope too? Shit, you know I got to bust you, you dumb ass."

After the booking report and logging in all the evidence it was the end of shift.

Ray said, "I am going to the Canopy, want to come along?"

Mike knew that he was making progress being accepted if he was invited to the Canopy. "Sure, can't stay long, but I would love to have a beer. I hear the burgers are really good too."

They sat at a table with a couple of detectives. They shared the story of today. Four thousand pills was a pretty good bust for a patrolman.

"Those nude bars are places to stay away from. Too easy to get in trouble there," said one.

The other replied, "No kidding! I thought I was in trouble when I stopped at Satan's Place. It was about a year ago, when I was in patrol and did a bar check there. I no more than walked in, stood against the wall just checking out the crowd, when the dancer, a cute young thing, put on this see -through top. She stood at the edge of the stage and yelled, 'Are you married honey?' Then she jumped off the stage, ran up to me and jumped up. She locked her arms around my neck and her legs around my waist. There I was, in uniform in front of a bunch of drunks and leering old farts, with this chick hanging on me, kissing me, and saying, 'This feels good honey.'"

"I could not get out of there fast enough. The whole place was laughing and clapping."

While they ate Texas Burgers and drank Foster's, Ray gave Mike more sage advice. "This is a cool place and good things can happen here, but do not make this a regular thing or you will be finding trouble. Keep your nose clean, keep your wife, and ignore the broads that hang out here. And don't get drunk."

The very next night this advice was played out as sound counsel.

They were assigned Beat Two. It was the southwest quadrant of the city and included everything west of Euclid and south of the railroad tracks. It was a large beat and had lots of open space. Armstrong Nursery grew roses and alfalfa on a huge portion of the quadrant, and there were small ranchettes, with chickens, horses and orange groves. There was a commercial sector along Mission Boulevard and Euclid Avenue. De Anza Park had its problems with drug dealers, who committed executions in the restrooms and had fights in the parking areas there.

On Mission Boulevard at Oaks Avenue there was the other nude bar, Satan's Place. Ray had some fun memories of events there, like the night the Hells Angels were there causing trouble. They chose Satan's Place to do one step in their initiation process of earning wings. The inductee was to perform cunnilingus on the dancer on the stage. If the dancer put up a fight one of the molls would take the stage and do it.

A wise bartender got wind of the plans and called the police. He told the bikers they could do it after hours when the doors were locked, but their rule was to do it in public, so it had to be during open hours. Ray and three others had herded the Angels out of town.

One night Ray thought he would introduce Mike to Satan's, since they had a good bust at the Villa. They had not yet called out a bar check, but just pulled into the parking area. As they pulled in, Mike thought he saw a black and white out in back of the parking area. He drove toward the back and saw that it was an Ontario police car. It was the sergeant's car.

There was a woman with her legs up on the hood of the car, and the sergeant was having sex with her. His pants and gun belt were on the ground at his feet.

Ray doused his headlights and backed out. "Shit!" He looked at Mike. "You didn't see a thing."

"Right, I wasn't even here."

"Do you think he saw us?"

"Not sure. I do think he knows that some cops saw him, but he can only suspect it is us because it is our beat."

Ray grabbed the mike, "Ontario 1-O-2, checking open door at Ontario Christian High School."

"There, that will give us the explanation of not being here. Now he can worry without getting us involved."

They sped off south to be at the school in case another unit responded and did not find them there.

"He is probably freaking out, wondering what we saw and if we are going to snitch him off."

"It serves him right. He should have a heart attack, the dumb shit, doing something like that on duty, and with a low life dancer at that."

As they drove away Jack used the time as a learning moment.

"Sarge is not the only screw up this department has or had. We had a new guy and the second week on the foot beat he made a hooker give him head in the alley behind the Orange Hotel. Dumb shit! She snitched him off and the next day he was gone."

"Just because somebody has rank does not mean they are smart, wise or good cops. It just might be that they have been careful and have not been caught yet, or did not get snitched on."

"You have to live with yourself, so do the honorable thing and keep your nose clean."

"Are we going to report this?"

"No. He has been treading on thin ice for some time. Trust me, he is going to do something stupid that will get him fired or demoted, and we won't have to be the bad guys."

"Besides, there are different rules for rank and for street cops."

"What do you mean different rules for rank and street cops?"

"When you have rank there is a lot of leeway or flexibility in discipline."

Ray told him the story about the gun that was missing from the evidence locker, the blank DMV forms, and the time the captain who was on call for the weekend had crashed a detective car going home from a poker party. He had been very drunk, but no sobriety tests were given and nothing was done about the damaged unit, not even a letter of reprimand.

Chapter 37

It was 9am and Jack was the only detective in the station when the phone rang in the bureau. The secretary was at the printer and the other dicks were getting coffee and donuts at Bert's. Sergeant Porter was in a staff meeting. Jack was at his desk catching up on reading the stack of reports that came that Monday morning.

Weekends brought lots of reports and incidents that seldom occurred on weekdays. Seems when families are home together or at least away from their work schedules, they contrived or found time to do strange, cruel and unseemly things.

That was what the phone call was about; some cruel and unseemly thing. A mother had lost control over the weekend. She had too much to drink and wanted more time with her boyfriend, who spent weekends at her house. She started feeling sorry for herself. Her boyfriend was not committed to her and the kids interfered with the time she and her lover had to be together, so she took out her frustration and anger on her children. They had become a nuisance and a bother to her, limiting her time for leisure and sex. She had to go to bed early to be able to take care of them in the morning, when she was tired and really wanted to sleep. She lost control, again, on Sunday. That was what started the entire mess, and resulted in the phone call Jack was taking.

Jack wanted to ignore the call. He wondered why he should be so lucky as to be the one there to answer the phone. But duty called, so he picked it up. The caller sounded like an elderly lady. She wanted a detective, not a patrol officer. She wanted an immediate investigation, and therefore called the bureau. Surely an older, more seasoned officer could respond and do what is needed or take a report.

She did not want a report; it was action she was looking for.

Her first question was, "Do you have children?"

"Yes ma'am, I sure do a boy and a girl."

He heard her sigh with relief, "Good! Then you will understand."

She went on to relate the reason for the call. She had started working in her front yard flower garden when a little boy and an even littler girl came walking down the sidewalk. The boy asked her if she had any work he could do because his sister was hungry.

189

"This was when I realized that something was wrong, so I invited them in for breakfast. They are eating now so it gives me time to call you. They must be lost or runaways. They are gobbling the food like they haven't eaten in a week. They are so young and so skinny."

"I will be right there," Jack did not want to pass this off to patrol. His gut was telling him that something was screwed up and he should get there before these kids walked away. They were in a safe place now and that was where he wanted to talk to them. Besides, having a plain-clothes officer come would not be as scary for these kids as a uniformed officer might be.

The caller lived on J Street near Campus, not far from the station. It took less than ten minutes to grab a car and get there. When he pulled up he saw a thin little boy pulling weeds alongside an elderly lady. Sitting on the front porch steps was an even thinner and younger girl, holding a glass of milk.

"You just got to love grandmas," thought Jack. "God bless the little old ladies."

She stood up when he approached, smiled, and reached to shake his hand. "Thank you for coming. I told this nice boy that a nice policeman was coming to talk to them and help them. He has quite an interesting story for you."

Jack sat down on the porch step next to the little girl, and said, "Hi, What is your name?"

She looked at him and smiled but did not respond.

The boy had stopped pulling weeds and walked over to them.

"She cannot hear very well, you must talk loud to her," he instructed. He stopped and stood in front of them.

"Well, okay, I will talk louder. Do you want to sit here with me for a minute and tell me about yourself? What is your name and what is your sister's name? She is your sister, right?"

"Sure, my name is Danny and my sister is Lisa."

"How old are you?"

"I am almost eleven and my sister just had her birthday two weeks ago, she is eight."

"Where to you live?"

"We live on La Deney."

"Why are you here this morning, young man?"

Danny lowered his head and did not answer.

"It is okay, you can tell me."

Looking shyly back at Jack, he stuck both hands into his

pockets, shuffled his feet, and backed up a step, like he was thinking about running. He looked at Lisa with a sorrowful, sad questioning look on his face.

It was obvious that they knew how to communicate together. She looked back at him and smiled. "Go ahead, you can tell him."

With his head down as if he was ashamed he started his tale. "We ran away from home and I wanted to find some work so I could take care of my sister. She was hungry and I hoped to be able to buy her a candy bar and later some breakfast," he said, pointing at Lisa.

"Can I take you home?"

"No!" they both exclaimed at the same time.

Jack looked at both of them with questioning eyes, and he saw the fear in the faces of both children. "Why do you not want to go home?"

"Our mom will beat us. She was mad at us. We cannot go home now."

"Would you come with me to the police station, so I can help you?"

They again looked at each other, and then both nodded their heads, slowly, "Will we have to stay there?"

"No, you will not have to stay there. I want to hear your story and find a way to help you."

"Okay." They each took hold of one of his hands.

Jack thanked the lady and promised to let her know what happened. They walked to his car together.

Hand in hand, they walked into the station and went to his desk. Danny and Lisa took off their sweaters since it was warm inside. When Lisa had her sweater off, Ray noticed a bulge under her blouse and took notice that she was even thinner than he first thought. She was actually gaunt.

"What is that?" he asked, pointing to the bulge.

Danny replied, "That is her hearing aid battery. She has bad ears and needs that box to be able to hear."

"Danny, would you like to tell me why you ran away from home?"

After looking at Lisa for her consent, he began his narrative.

"Our mom was mad again yesterday. When her boyfriend left she drank some more beer and started yelling at us, and then beat both of us. I guess that fight with her boyfriend caused it, but she blamed us for him leaving. We tried to make her happy, but she

191

got madder and madder. She yelled at us, screaming, 'I hate you!'"

"She hit Lisa with the broom stick on her back and her legs. When I told her to stop she hit me too." He pointed to a red welt on his shoulder as he pulled back his shirt to expose his back.

"Where else has she hit you?"

"On the back of my head and on my back and legs."

"Does this happen often? Does she hit both of you at other times?"

"Yes," they both said. "Almost every week, but this time was worse. When she is this angry she makes us sleep on a rug in the garage. But this time she let Lisa sleep in her own bed and I was sent to the garage. It is cold and dirty there."

"What did you do then?"

When we were going to bed I told Lisa that at three o'clock I would come to wake her up and we would run away together. I told her she needed to get her clothes ready, and I promised to take care of her, so she would never be beaten again."

"At three o'clock I got up and got my sister dressed. We took sweaters because it was cold, and we left. We were real quiet, so mommy would not hear us."

"What were you going to do?"

"I am real good at working. I do lots of chores at home, so I planned to find work so I could buy food for Lisa and me. Then I wanted to get enough money to buy a present for Mommy."

Stunned he asked, "What? You want to buy a present for your mom? Why?"

"I thought that if I bought her something it would make her happy and make her love me."

Jack turned his face away as he wiped the tears that were welling up in his eyes. *Damn it, how could someone mistreat sweet kids like these?* Turning back to them, he told them that they would stay here in this office for a while because he was going to talk to their mom.

Jack grabbed Ray and they drove to the house on La Deney to interview Danny and Lisa's mother. Ray observed Jack's somber face, "What's up, man this stuff happens every day, don't let it get to you."

"That boy wanting to buy his mom something so she would love him, really got to me, man."

"Yeah, pretty heart wrenching stuff."

"It hit home for me. It reminded me of all the attempts to do things for my mom, hoping to make her like me or love me. Seems nothing ever did, I picked her flowers, learned how to crochet, and learned how to cook and clean the kitchen but nothing worked. This poor kid still has hope, but it will not work for him either."

"It is a shitty world we work in."

Her story was another sad tale of human depravity. She was raised in Topeka, Kansas, by a mother who hated her. Her father, who was a truck driver was gone most of the time and was afraid to interfere with what the mother was doing. She was beaten with willow switches and had her hair or ears pulled daily. "I hate you, I wish you never were born," was shouted at her daily. It brought pain and anguish that she had never gotten over, and now she was passing the same pain and anguish onto her children. Her mother had been meaner to her than to her brother, just like she was doing to Danny and Lisa.

Jack and Ray took photos of the dump she called home, and then drove away.

"Damn it, somebody has to break this mold. Danny and Lisa need a chance to survive and be somebody."

They drove to the county office of Child Protective Services to present this case in person. Jack offered to take custody of the kids until the courts could decide what to do. After all, he and Gail had been licensed as a foster home for years but had no foster kids at that time. The last child they had was a boy who had also been beaten and neglected. Jack grimaced as he recalled the day Phillip left. It was the first time Phillip had shown any emotion. He began to cry because he was leaving and going to be with his mother.

Sergeant Porter would not approve Jack taking temporary custody. It was a bad idea to mix work with emotions.

"Bullshit," said Jack. "Who wouldn't be happy to provide for a boy who is looking after his sister, and his goal in life is to buy the mother who beats him a present so she can be happy."

You just had to love kids like that.

Child Protective Services said they needed a court order or the mother's permission to do anything with these kids other than to place them in Juvenile Hall.

Two weeks later the kids were released to the mother, who beat them again the first day. It was a week later, when the beatings were discovered. Lisa told her teacher she had slept in the garage and was hungry because mommy was sleeping and they did not have breakfast.

Chapter 38

Spring 1974

"Rock Concert Planned at Ontario Motor Speedway," screamed the headlines in the Daily Report.

The Speedway was in financial trouble. Races were few and far between and the National Drags were moving to Pomona. The government bonds were not being paid and the private investors were losing equity and receiving no dividends. The Speedway worked quietly with the city manager behind the scenes to make a plan to bring in revenue; enough revenue to keep the ailing track operating for another year.

Woodstock was recent history. It had been a great event for promoters, music aficionados and pot smokers, but a disaster for law enforcement and the local community. All of the problems at Woodstock would be addressed and fixed. This would be a great success and bring millions of dollars of revenue to the business community. At least that was what the official press releases touted.

Safety was the worrisome issue: safety for concert goers, for the public, for traffic coming and going, and for police officers working traffic and crowd control. How do you handle the three hundred thousand people that were expected to attend?

A city ordinance was passed to assure safety. There would be one police officer per one thousand attendees to provide ample security. The manpower would come from volunteer officers who were recruited from surrounding agencies. The OPD staff would work twelve-hour shifts with days off cancelled.

Cal Jam was discussed at briefings, at the coffee shops, and at the Canopy. Most cops expressed apprehension about having three hundred thousand dope smokers, beer drinkers and drug users wandering the streets of Ontario for the days before and after the event. Lots of questions and expressions of uncertainty were shared, most of which the OPOA brought to the attention of those who were planning the event.

How would crowd control be handled?

Would drugs be confiscated or arrests made for possession or for sales?

What about overdoses of drugs and alcohol?

195

All of the questions and uncertainty were discussed and plans were made. Event Staff would handle security inside the venue. They would hire college football players, wrestlers and others who the concertgoers would respect. No uniformed police would be inside the venue and no arrests would be made inside the venue or in view of the crowd. The concern was that making arrests and having uniformed officers inside would incite the crowd and cause a riot.

The City of Ontario was creating a two-day environment for drug users to openly use and break moral, Health & Safety, and Penal Code standards.

The VW vans and old buses started arriving a week before the jam began. The parking lot had a cluster of old cars and buses. The country roads that were lined with eucalyptus trees were now lined with encampments, as well as any shady spot that was not near housing developments.

At the onset, the patrol officers cruised these areas to check up on how many were camping and to create a presence of law enforcement. Soon it became apparent that cruising by these encampments was dangerous. Dangerous to the campers, because they were negligent in safety for themselves and safety for anyone on the street. Litter and debris narrowed traffic lanes and police who passed by were yelled at and taunted.

Farmers were afraid to call the police, but were tired of the mess, the nudity, and the toilet habits. The campers openly performed their bodily functions whenever and wherever they wanted to, because they had no toilet facilities. Some used the toilets in the dairy barns and used the hoses for washing cows to clean themselves.

Jack and Ray were leaving court after testifying on a drug case when the call came for them to respond to an encampment at Archibald and Guasti Road. The freeway, Interstate 10 (I-10), was hectic with traffic. It was too early in the day for commuter jams. These were mostly music lovers headed to Cal Jam.

Suddenly the cars in the lane on the right slowed down, and brake lights came on everywhere. Bang! The Pinto and two cars ahead in the number three lane crashed into the car in front. The old 54 Chevy behind it swerved to the left and crashed into the Pinto, causing it to swerve to the right. This was lucky as now they were pushed to the shoulder.

Ray turned on the rear amber lights and pulled in behind the

Pinto. Jack was calling in to have the CHP dispatched when the Pinto burst into flames. Ray was already out of his unit. He ran to the Pinto and opened the passenger door. Jack dropped the mike and ran to the driver's door. The driver was slumped over the wheel. Quickly he pulled her out and away from the car.

Ray opened the other door so front seat passenger jumped out. Ray shoved the seat up and began to pull the rear passengers out. The first one was safe and not injured. The second, middle, passenger had blood running from what appeared to be a broken nose. Her blouse was on fire and they quickly doused the fire. The third passenger was not injured but her hair and clothes were in flames. Jack grabbed her and ripped off the burning sweater, then used his hands to smother the burning hair. Breathless, they all gathered a safe distance from the car, now engulfed in flames.

"You guys all right? Can you wait for the highway patrol? We have got to get going. We are on an emergency call," said Ray.

"Sure, thanks," they said while Ray and Jack ran to their unit.

The other cars in this collision failed to stop and were long gone, lost in traffic. After determining that these people were safe and would not need further attention, Ray said, "Let's get the hell out of here, before we get in trouble for stopping."

"We just saved three or more lives! Why would we get in trouble for that?"

"You know they told us to do only what we were told and to let everything else go. We weren't to get involved with Jam issues. I am not taking chances. We are not reporting that we were even here. I do not trust them. Make the call seem like we saw this in passing."

Jack understood Ray's fear of discipline. Therefore, he made the radio call without mentioning that they had stopped and helped.

Laughing, he turned to Ray, "You know they give medals at the awards banquet for what you just did."

"So what! Awards and medals don't really mean shit."

They had their call to take care of and then had to head home to change into grubbies and prepare to work inside the event.

197

Chapter 39

Fortunately, there was a gate near the bummer tents where they could enter the Raceway infield, because the crowds at the entrance gates were backed up hundreds of people deep. The press of the crowd that wanted entry nearly pushed the newly-constructed chain link fence over. That was the intent. Many were trying to push the fence down to gain entry without paying.

A quick thinking employee backed a truck up against the inside of the fence to stabilize it, ending the fence pushing. Once the concert started, the reality hit that this fence was keeping these crazies inside the area, and its purpose was not just to keep nonpaying people out.

Jack and Ray hooked up with Jack and Bob, bought a coke, and went to the area at the rear of the crowd to talk about what they could or should do. This crowd was growing and growing. The stage looked small and the performers were mere midgets from where they sat on the grass.

The aroma of grass, and not the kind your lawn is made of, but marijuana, filled the air. The people kept coming. The crowd was past the area where the cops were, although it had not swelled to the side fences.

Each team had a radio with a remote mike. It did not take long to realize that this radio made the attendees look at them and think they were cops. It was not good to be one of four cops inside a fence with three hundred thousand dope smoking rock fans. Especially since most of them were using drugs of some kind or drinking alcohol, and had the paranoia that was so common for people who used marijuana.

They agreed that it was impossible and very foolish to attempt any law enforcement. The best they could do was take some notes and photos to create a realistic report of life inside a rock concert, and to assist with finding and treating those who overdosed on drugs. Maybe they could save a life or two.

"Overdose? You really think anyone will overdose?" asked Ray in his classic police cynical voice.

The others knew he was cynical, but they also realized that the practical side of being there was the reality that among the drug users there were those who were too young and inexperienced. They could and would overdose.

They wondered if parents would allow their children to be there if they knew about the depravity and substance abuse. What about the politicians? Did they care about sacrificing morals and safety when this much money was at stake?

They agreed to meet every hour at the rear of the crowd. It did not take long to realize that this would not be possible, because it was extremely difficult to maneuver through the people who were lying around, walking or standing. Everywhere they went there were people smoking dope. Within an hour the haze over the crowd looked like the brown layer of air that covered the Los Angeles basin on hot summer days. When planes flew into LAX or cars drove south on Interstate 5 through the Grapevine, this layer of smog was enough to cause one to think about turning around and going back to clean air. The haze over this crowd was like that, except it did not make the eyes water and chest restrict with difficulty breathing. This haze made your head feel light. Just being there brought a mild high. All four cops had their first experience being under the influence of marijuana.

Ray said, "I guess I can still say I never used drugs or smoked marijuana, but I cannot say I have not been under the influence. Whoopee!" he giggled. Everybody laughed, realizing he was just goofing off.

"Look at that," said Jack' as he pointed at the roll-off trash dumpster, sitting along the fence. Three young women were climbing out. They were holding their pants and underwear in their hands. Others were climbing into the dumpster. They were using this dumpster for a toilet because the lines at the Port-O-Potties were backed up for a half hour wait or more.

The guys were urinating against the chain-link fence; others were squatting and pulling up grass to wipe themselves. Bob was going to take a photo but Jack' punched him, "You crazy dude! They'll kick our ass if you take a picture."

That is how it was. Very few photos would be taken for fear they would be attacked. None of the four wanted to get beat up by a crowd of dopers. The possibility of needing to use a gun to defend themselves for taking a photo did not make sense.

"If only we could take pictures of all we see," thought Jack'. "Look at the LSD, Quaaludes, grass, heroin and speed being used," he muttered to himself.

The closer they got to the stage, the denser the crowd was. Few even looked at anybody who was around them. They did not

200

care who saw them roll joints or light hash pipes.

Ray was watching the stage. They were close enough to be able to see the facial features of the singing groups. Black Sabbath was on stage, and Emerson, Lake and Palmer were next. The lineup was impressive. Besides the opportunity to behave as you wished, the bands were a great attraction. Other performers included Rare Earth, the Eagles, Earth Wind & Fire, Seals and Croft, Deep Purple, and Black Oaks Arkansas.

Ray stumbled over someone who was lying on the grass with a group that sat cross-legged while sharing some dope.

"Watch where you're going, asshole!" the guys yelled as he quickly gathered up what he had dropped.

Jack' helped Ray up and watched the dude and his friends. They were picking up bindles of dope, balloons of heroin and a syringe. The guy next to him was unfazed as he continued to inject heroin into the inside of his elbow. The next guy had his arm tied off already. He was looking past the dirty handkerchief at his vein already dreaming about how good this was going to be when he got his fix.

They quickly made their retreat and stood back behind a group of girls to watch these guys as they finished shooting up. There were six guys and two women. All were dressed like hippies. Their hair was long and unwashed. Like their clothes, they could all use some soap and water. They were probably with one of the groups that were camped out in the vineyards without water or facilities.

Two of the guys were nodding off and just rolled over on their sides, sleeping in the euphoria of their highs. The others were drowsy but awake.

"Really enjoying the music," said Jack. "Is getting loaded part of the fun of why they come here, knowing it is safe from being busted?"

They made their way to the side of the crowd but realized that was where the portable potties were, so they turned away. Trying to get out of this crowd and get some fresh air away from the odors of overflowing toilets and smoke, they decided to check in with Jack'and Bob.

They heard screaming in front of them. This was different than the screams for whichever band was performing. They realized something was wrong. Sure enough, a girl was holding her boyfriend, shaking him, and crying, "Wake up, wake up!"

201

They grabbed the guy and told the girl to follow them to the Bummer Tent. Pushing, shoving, and yelling at people to get out of the way, they rushed him forward. The crowd opened for them willingly. They all knew how dangerous an overdose could be.

They arrived at the tent and turned the guy over to the medics. Ray jabbed Jack, "Look, there is Jack' and Bob." They were coming in the tent from the other side.

They were holding up a girl that could not walk. Blood was running down her cheek from a small cut. She was as filthy as if she had been rolling around in the dirt. She actually had been, because she had gotten into a fight with another girl. Luckily, the cut was from a piece of glass and not a knife.

The tent had twenty beds and about that many medics and nurses. Most of the beds had someone on them, receiving treatment or being monitored for overdoses. Two ambulances were loading patients for a ride to the hospital.

Bob was talking to a nurse who came to assist the girl he brought in. "What are they hauling off?" he said, nodding toward the ambulances.

"Probably another DOA. These kids are coming in here really messed up. They are mixing drugs and taking things they cannot even identify. It is a mess in here." She turned to tend to the wound. "This is the least of our problems," she said while she washed the wound.

They left the tent and called in for someone to bring them lunch. They had spent six hours watching depravity and inhaling smoke. They made their way to the fence that was well past the portable toilets and the crowd. Out there they only had to avoid tripping over two couples that were having sex. They were either so drugged out or so into achieving an orgasm that they did not notice people walking by.

"Six more hours," moaned Ray, "Six more hours of watching this crap. How many have you seen urinating or defecating in public, screwing their hearts out, shooting up or toking up, or just sitting there in the nude like zombies?"

"What a free for all! The mayor and council should be here to see this degenerate mess. They will get these nice reports that officially say how great it was, and that the entertainment was excellent, which it is. They will hear that it was a safe environment with minimal problems and no arrests," responded Jack.

"No arrests, no shit! How many jails would we need to book

202

and house every crime we saw today? Besides, if we tried to make arrests there would be a police funeral. These people are fanatical and would never let us get away with hauling anyone off. The chief was smart. He put four of us here, knowing we could not and would not stick our necks out. And the report will be that the police were in the crowd and did not arrest anyone or take any enforcement action."

Ray continued with, "Yeah it was safe, too. I bet the records show that nobody died here today. I know that at least six people were dead when they left here in the ambulance."

The truth was that at least thirteen people that came from the Speedway arrived at the local hospitals DOA. Officially, no one died at the concert. The death reports listed DOA at San Antonio Hospital or Kaiser Hospital. There was just a rise in deaths at the hospitals that was coincidental to Cal Jam.

The guys outside the venue were also having problems. Cars were abandoned along the freeway because getting to the parking area was impossible. Good sense was not present. They just left their cars on the freeway, close enough to the event that they didn't have to walk too far. Other cars were parked in vineyards, on ranches, and on farms. Towing companies had a great day, or at least a busy day, clearing the roadways and private properties. Many of the cars were never claimed and ended up being sold for storage fees. How did these great minds get back home?

Chapter 40

October 1978

Henk and three buds were sitting on the floor passing a joint. It had been an afternoon of drinking, smoking and mixing in some speed.

"Man, I am really fucked up," said the only Mexican in the group.

The others just grunted and looked at him. They watched his head sag and his eyes roll back. A foolish smile or grin crossed his face. "Look at all the colors man," he said. He closed his eyes as if he was dreaming and then did fall into a deep sleep.

A few hours later they started to return to some form of reality.

"I am hungry, got the munchies bad. Let's get some burgers and a coke," said Henk.

Slowly, they got to their feet. Each one checked their pockets for more dope and for money.

"Shit," said Henk, "I am empty."

They all came up empty or just some change, not enough to buy eats. Staring stupidly at each other, they tried to think about what to do. The after effects of being drunk and high most of the day had their brains scrambled. Reason or logic had not been part of their lives for a long time. They had just been on a successive quest for drugs, some means of feeling good or for just numbing the pain of life. Collectively they realized that they had nothing to live for except the next drug high or sex. But sex came at the price of sharing drugs and smoke. They only turned to sex when they were really horny or when they scored a lot of dope.

Manny's face lit up. "Oscar owes me two hundred, let's go get it and we can eat and score another ounce."

"You know Oscar is not going to come across with what he owes. He's a rip off," said one of the boys.

"Hey, there are four of us. What's he gonna do? We'll kick his ass and take it," said Henk. "I'll take my piece. That will make him shit in his pants and he'll come up with what we want."

Manny drove his 63 Chevy cruiser. Two of the others got in the back seat, and Henk rode shotgun. Manny took it slower than usual because he realized that he was still screwed up. He worked hard at keeping a straight course and they headed to Oscar's house on South Cypress.

It was an older established neighborhood, built in the years just after World War II ended. The original owners had long since died or moved on. It was still the era of raised floors with concrete steps to a small front porch. It was a working class of mixed nationalities, mostly white and second or third generation of immigrant Mexican families. The yards and houses were well maintained, much better than those on Nocta where Henk grew up.

Oscar saw the car pull into his driveway. He quickly locked the front door and pulled the blinds closed. They were only open enough so he could peek out; he didn't want anyone to see in. He knew there was trouble out there. He owed Manny. The crazy gringos with Manny were real bad dudes. He thought they were Aryan because of their tattoos, although they had not ever said anything. He was afraid of them.

Henk saw the slight movement of the blinds, so he knew someone was at home. He expected that the door would not open and that knocking would bring no response.

Manny got out as he said, "Wait here. I'll be right back." He went to the front door.

Henk got out of the car too, and headed around the house to the back door. He opened the gate and turned left to the concrete steps at the back door. He heard the growl before he saw the grey pit bull coming to check him out.

Henk saw that he was too far from the door to get in, even if it was unlocked, and the gate was latched. He thought the dog wanted to tear him up. Henk yelled at the dog, but it kept coming toward him. He needed to move fast. The back door was most likely not locked since the owners expected that the dog, with his big teeth in his big head, was all the protection they needed.

He pulled his gun out when the dog was beginning to lunge for his leg. Henk fired the .22 caliber pistol, putting a round hole directly above one of the dog's eyes. The pit bull dropped at his feet.

Henk heard footsteps and running inside the house, so he jerked open the door and stepped in. His pistol was still in his hands. He met Oscar face to face in the kitchen. Oscar was alone.

Henk's face broke into a huge grin. Oscar's face paled. It was almost as white as this blond gringo that was staring at him with an evil look on his face.

206

"Get the fuck out of my house," screamed Oscar.

His eyes widened and fear gripped his heart as Henk raised his gun. He began to back up, his bluster was gone, now he hoped to get into the hallway and make a run for his bedroom. He did not have a gun, but hoped if he could get to his room he could get out the window and be over the fence before he got shot.

Henk had the gun pointed at him and both of them knew escape was out of the question.

Henk said, "Why did you not let Manny in? He just wants what you owe him. Now you can give it to me."

"I don't owe him anything. He sold me some bad dope, so screw him."

"This is not the way to talk about somebody who is your friend. Come on, give me the two hundred and we will be on our way."

"I don't owe him two hundred; it was only a hundred and I don't have that much anyway. I have fifty and a little hash. You can have it, just go."

"Empty your wallet on the counter here," ordered Henk.

Oscar took his wallet out with shaking hands. He knew he was in deep shit because Henk would find out he had lied. Trying to keep some of the money from falling out, he shook the contents of his wallet onto the kitchen counter. Over a hundred dollars were spread out for Henk to see.

"Holding out on your buddy are you? That's not nice chump." Henk raised the gun and pointed it directly at Oscar's face. They were only four feet apart. Oscar knew Henk could not miss at this close range.

"Please, just take it and the hash and the baggie in my bedroom. I am sorry. Please take it and go. Then Manny and I are even," pled Oscar.

Bang! The bullet hit him just about dead center in the forehead and Oscar crumbled to the floor.

"Shithead, you shouldn't have lied to me," muttered Henk as he scooped up the money and removed the other currency from the wallet. He found Oscar's room and located the stash of dope in the sock drawer, taking a vial of hash and two bags of marijuana.

Henk went out the way he came in, and met Manny as he came off the porch. They both got in and drove off.

"Slow down, you want the fucking cops to stop you!" yelled Henk.

207

Manny looked at Henk with fear, "I heard a gunshot, did you shoot him?"

"Hell yes, I shot him! He was holding out on you and lied to me, the dumb shit."

They got back to Manny's house and all went inside to decide what to do. How long would it take before somebody called the cops? The cops would be there to talk to Manny, because Oscar's neighbor came home and saw the car. Maybe somebody heard the two gunshots.

"Oh, crap we are in trouble."

"Here is the dope. I am keeping a hundred. Bring me to my house and I will figure out what I am going to do and where I am going. That way you can tell the cops I am gone but you do not know where to," said Henk.

Henk walked into his home, and went directly to his closet. He removed the .22 caliber rifle and two boxes of bullets. He loaded the pistol and the rifle, made a sandwich, and waited until dusk.

Before anyone came home he put on his warm Pendleton flannel shirt, wrapped his rifle in a towel, grabbed the bag of sandwiches he made and left out the back door.

Chapter 41

July 1977

"Cal Jam a Huge Success," read the headlines of the Daily Report and the Pomona Progress Bulletin. The city was very pleased with the outcome of the concert. "There were no arrests and no serious injuries or problems. Traffic was the major concern, but with the aid of surrounding agencies the traffic leaving the event was orderly and all roadways were back to normal in a few hours."

"The concert brought new life to Ontario Motor Speedway and boosted the local economy with millions of dollars."

That was the official quote from the city's mayor. Based on this success, the city might even have another event like it.

Jack expected this evaluation and also expected lots of phone calls and comments from OPOA members. For days he could not walk the halls of 200 N. Cherry without being confronted by OPOA members who demanded to know what the association was going to do.

"How can we stop this?" was the standard question. "We created a free for all so any pothead and doper could come to our city and use drugs freely, with no fear of arrest. We bust people every day for the crap that went on. Why are they planning another fiasco?"

"Money," responded Jack. "It is all about money: money for the Speedway, money for the investors who are all big wigs in Ontario and Upland, money for the economy, and big money for the promoter."

"Sacrificing honor, ethics, and morals is okay for a few days as long as it brings in lots of money!" said Ray. "We need to call a Board meeting. Too many of the association members are upset and they want to make it known that OPOA opposes another rock concert."

The Board did call a meeting. The meeting was moved from the police station conference room to the Elks Lodge to be sure it was not recorded or listened to. Jack gave each Board member floor time to speak their piece, with the assurance that no matter what the stance was, it would be heard and kept confidential.

Each Board member was opposed to having another Cal Jam.

Six voted against another concert. One voted for the concert because he did not want to fight City Hall.

"We will lose anyway, so why fight it," he explained.

The other six looked at him with disgust. "If we do not try, of course nothing will change. We will just have to come up with the right presentations. Maybe people will listen to what really happened at Cal Jam I."

A letter was drafted and approved by each member. The letter would be presented to the chief and a copy would be sent to the city manager. It was brief but direct.

We, the OPOA, are opposed to the city hosting another rock concert such as Cal Jam. We made an oath to uphold the law and are opposed to setting a day or days aside during which there is no enforcement for violations of Health & Safety and Penal Codes. The concert sets a poor example for our youth by exposing them to drugs and open sex. This makes it appear that adults approve of drugs in venues that are making money for the rich.

ack and Chuck presented the letter to Chief Brookings. They handed it to him when they entered his office. He read it before he offered them a place to sit.

"You cannot oppose a concert. It is your duty to do as you are assigned."

"Sorry, sir, we object on moral grounds and will ask to be excused from working there. You know that people died there and that drugs, nudity and sex were rampant, in spite of what the official report says."

"You will work this when ordered. The city wants and needs this event, so we will do as told."

"Yes, sir, we will do as ordered, but we will not volunteer and we will publicly oppose the concert. May we have your permission to appeal to the city manager?"

"Do not waste your time or mine. This concert will happen. I would rather we did not have to have the concert but I will enforce the directions given me. I suggest you do the same. Do you hear me and understand what I am saying?"

Jack and Chuck got up and left. This was what they expected, but it was only right to let the chief know the sentiment of the officers who worked the streets and the Investigations Bureau. They knew the fight was on. They also knew that their jobs were in danger. They understood precisely what the chief said.

A few days later, the briefing sergeant handed Jack a phone message with a number to call, and instructions to ask for Lanny.

"What's this about, who is Lanny?" asked Jack.

"Don't know, nobody told me. The chief's secretary gave it to me to give to you."

Jack went into the bureau to make the call.

"Lanny please," he said when a nice-sounding young lady answered, "Big Apple Productions."

The light went on. Jack realized he was calling the promoter of Cal Jam. This was going to be interesting. Jack wondered what he was going to say.

Lanny came on the line. "Good morning, Mr. Hillberg."

Oh my, Mister, thought Jack. People who called him mister were either very young adolescents or someone who wanted something. This phone call was about wanting something.

"Yes, sir, how are things in New York? To what do I owe the honor of this call?"

"Things are great here. I am going to be in Ontario next week. I would like to meet with your board to explain the benefits of Cal Jam II. Would it be okay to meet for lunch?"

Jack knew the pressure was on. Somebody had already notified the promoter, and he was going to get active before any negative stuff hit the press. Jack knew they would have to attend this meeting just to show good faith and demonstrate that they were willing to listen. He also knew, or at least thought, that some kind of enticement or pressure would come with the lunch.

"Wednesday, at noon, at the Canopy, works for you?" he asked. Jack wanted this meeting on his own turf, not where Lanny could control the event.

The meeting happened as planned. All seven Board members ordered Texas Burgers and iced tea. There would be no alcohol consumed at this meeting. Who knew what evil lurked or who would be told about what was done. Lanny, real name Lander, ordered a plate of fries and a cocktail, seven-seven on soda.

"Guys," he started out, "This concert is a big deal and will benefit the city and you. The chamber of commerce wants it, the Speedway wants it, the city does too, and your chief is for it. What is your objection?"

"Well, sir, we have this hang up about crime and drugs coming to our city for a weekend free for all. It sets a bad example for our youth when we allow drugs to be used freely when enough

211

money is paid," explained Jack.

"Come on guys, you know there is not that much drug use involved. Besides, they are going to be using drugs that day anyway; if not at Cal Jam, then someplace else. We just give them a safe place to enjoy their favorite bands. Sure we make a profit, I hope."

No one responded. Everyone was busy eating and avoiding the question. This was what they expected: rationalization. Crime happens anyway, so why not make money when you can.

Lanny picked up the conversation again. It was obvious that he had not sold his philosophy but yet he was not certain. Now was the time to throw in a carrot, a lure, a temptation, work on the avarice of common man.

"Have you found a place to buy for the Association to have its own clubhouse? What are you looking for, a house, office building or what? Did you like that historical house with the pool and guest quarters? It has a nice meeting room, a room for games, and bedrooms for officers to crash? How much was it?"

Jack looked up, wondering how much this guy knew. Clearly, he had done his homework.

"The asking price is sixty-eight thousand. Have you seen it?"

"No I haven't, but I was told about it and drove by. It looks real nice with the natural stone exterior and old trees. I can get you that clubhouse, if you want it. This concert could be good for everybody. What do you think? Can we agree to work together?"

Jack looked at each person to read their reactions. There was no clear response. Some seemed interested, two seemed pissed, and the rest were stoic.

"How about we get back to you?"

"Sure, you need time to think about it. Think about how nice it will be to have a clubhouse. You have wanted it for years and you are really close and I can help. When will you get back to me? You can make the decision without having a membership vote, right?"

"We can decide. That is what they voted us in for. How about we let you know in three days?"

"Great!" said Lanny as he picked up the check. "If I do not hear from you by Friday, I'll call you." He left the group to finish eating and talking.

All was quiet until the door closed.

"How did he know we are interested in a clubhouse? Has he

212

talked to any of you?" asked Ray.

Everyone said, "Not me."

Someone added, "Never saw him or talked to him. Somebody up in the front office must've told him. You know he has the chief's ear and the city manager's ear."

"He has done his homework. What else does he know about us as a group or about us individually?" mused Jack. "What do you think, gentlemen?"

"Pretty tempting," said one guy.

"I think we should go for it. It is going to happen anyway, so why not get something out of it?" said the one who voted for the concert. That fit with his attitude-the concert was inevitable, so why not get a clubhouse besides?

"Bullshit, we are not for sale!" said another.

"I am sticking with what we said. This is a matter of honor and integrity. Money is not the issue," said the fourth guy.

"I put on this badge to uphold the law, not to sell out for expediency, money or power. I say, Hell no!" said the fifth.

"Screw em! I agree. We are not for sale. What do you say, Jack, you're our leader?"

"I may be president but my job is leading, not influencing you to do what I want. I am opposed to the concert and I am very pissed that they thought they could buy us. We are not for sale. Do you want to vote now or wait a few days?"

The unanimous vote was, "Sorry, but no."

Three weeks later Jack answered the phone at home.

"Hi Gladys, how are you?" It was his realtor calling. Gladys Lipson had sold Jack several houses and was a partner with him on several more as investment properties.

"I'm great, Jack. Wondering if you have time for lunch Saturday. You are off then, right? I have a friend in town who I would like you to meet to discuss doing some business with."

"Sure, I can make it; how about the Spunky Steer?"

"Not this time, let's do Marie Calendar's."

"Got it, see you in a couple."

Saturday Jack walked into Marie Calendar's on Philadelphia in Chino, just a few minutes early. He was not early enough. Gladys met him at the door and guided him to the separate dining area they used for meetings or small family gatherings.

Jack almost stopped in his steps, but recovered soon enough to hide how startled he was. There, getting up from his chair was

213

Lanny.

"Good to see you again," he said. "Gladys thinks a lot of you and thought it would be good if we had an opportunity to discuss some things."

Jack took a seat and ordered a glass of water.

"I ordered you a Frisco Burger," said Gladys. "I know how much you love them. You have one almost every time we are here. I have a house to show in an hour, so thought this would save some time."

"You can almost hear the door slam when Gladys talks- another house sold," said Lanny, giving his takeoff on the Coldwell Banker Reality advertisement.

The food came and Jack picked at the burger. His gut was in a knot. He did not want to talk to Lanny, did not want to be seen with him, and now his own partner had arranged this meeting. He couldn't keep up with his thoughts. *How the hell did Lanny find out about my investments and that Gladys is my realtor and venture partner? The jerk lives in New York! How does he get all this information?*

"Gladys says you are a great guy and have standards, which she and I admire. I am Jewish and she is Mormon and you are Christian, so ethics are important to all of us."

"Thank you, I do try to do the right thing."

"Gladys says she is very involved in politics and in the schools here, trying to be a good influence. She thinks Chino needs leadership that has your morals and ethics. She cannot run for public office, but thinks you would make an excellent councilman."

"Who, me? I don't have the contacts, time or money to run for office."

Lanny continued, "You both have talked about your interest in the council. You would be perfect! You have been active and you have had numerous write-ups in the newspaper about the cases you worked and arrests you made."

Jack put the burger down. He had not taken more than two small bites. He stayed cool and did not get flustered, but Lanny saw the reaction and made an assumption.

"If it is the money you are worried about, don't. If you agree to run we will invest money and training into it. I'll guarantee you will win. In fact, I will make sure you will win. We can make it happen. The money part is covered."

Both Gladys and Lanny looked at Jack to see his reaction to having enough funds to run a successful campaign. When he didn't see the excitement he expected, Lanny picked up the conversation again.

"I see you have reservations. This is not about Cal Jam. I like to help good people, like Gladys here. There are no strings attached, Jack; purely an investment in the community."

"Wow, I am honored. This is something I was not expecting. Wow, that is something! Me, a councilman? I need to share this with Gail. Can I get back to you or Gladys in a few days?"

"Sure, here is my card. Love to see this happen, couldn't happen to a better guy. Good luck with your wife."

The food was left uneaten. Jack's guts were in a real knot. Sure, no strings attached. *It was all about community and altruistic values,* Jack thought to himself. He thanked Lanny for lunch and the kind offer, thanked Gladys for thinking so highly of him, and left.

Jack slammed his fist onto the steering wheel of his 56 Ford pickup. *The chump thinks I am for sale!* He must think that everyone has a price and that this is my price. Does he really think he could do that and get away with it? Yeah, probably, guys like him have lots of connections and means that nice moral and ethical guys like me do not have. How much money is he willing to stake on this? Jack calculated the amount in his head; Sixty some thousand for a clubhouse, another fifteen thousand for the campaign.

"Shit, I don't even make fifteen thousand a year."

When Jack got home he told Gail he was a great person and she should be pleased and honored to be his wife.

Gail looked at him, "What's gotten into you? Been smoking something funny?" Then a smirk went across her face. "Okay, what's up, what happened at lunch?"

Jack told her the whole story and told her he was not going to accept that offer or any other offer where he would be beholden to someone, especially not this New Yorker.

Gail looked worried. It was not because of the idea of running for office. She was concerned about how much was known about their lives, their habits, business and family. "Can we trust these folks to leave us alone? What part does the police administration, the city manager or city council play in this? What else do they know? Who feeds the info? Are you still being followed? If you

215

say no what will they offer to do next? Honey, I am afraid for us."

Chapter 42

September 1977

"Gentlemen!" Ontario had only three female officers at the time and none were in attendance at this meeting. "Gentlemen, this meeting has been called in response to the latest events regarding the promotion of Cal Jam II. I am pretty sure this meeting is not being recorded, however, be aware that what is said here will be known by the chief of police and the City before the day is out."

The City had become the catchall phrase for anything in city government; thus the term included the city manager and his staff and the entire city council and the police administration. The association had friends who sat on the council, but they were politicians, so trust was limited.

Jack held a letter up to show the men what he was referring to as he continued with the presentation. "This letter is a letter from the department's management team and office personnel supporting the chief and the rock concert. It says that the below signatures support the chief of police in leadership and support him and the City in support of hosting Cal Jam II.

"This letter is intended to show the City that support for the concert does exist in the department, as opposed to the position you and your Board has taken, opposing this event. The chief has visited briefings for each shift and the bureau to promote the importance of the event. The financial needs of the Speedway and the economic gain for the City are used to promote the concert. Insinuations or enticements have been made that the revenue would bring better equipment to the police department.

"This meeting is public and any member is welcome to attend and speak up. I just ask you to stick with the issues and not drift to personalities or accusations. Let's stay with the facts. Those of you who are still in your probation period should refrain from speaking. I ask this for your own protection. You may be sure that someone will repeat what is said and done here, so be circumspect in what you say.

"If you should desire to make a motion, the vote will be secret. This is for two reasons. One is to give you complete freedom to vote as you wish with no coercion. The second reason is to protect you from anyone who would hold that vote against

217

you when it comes time for promotion or discipline.

"We are not going to do what the administrative staff did with this letter. This letter has the signature of every field supervisor, every command staff, and every non-sworn staff including secretaries, dispatchers, file clerks and office managers. The only persons omitted were the janitors.

"How does one get all these people to sign a letter about something as controversial as the concert? We all know one or more of these people have voiced opposition, yet they signed the letter. Did they sign it willingly, without coercion, as it says in the letter?

"What would you do if you needed your job or were hoping for a promotion, and the deputy chief came to you with this letter and asked you to sign it? He did not leave the letter for them to scrutinize, he stood there waiting for the signature. The pressure was on and they signed it, which is what most of us would do."

There was a lot of grumbling and talking going on amongst the men. Jack waited for the group to finish digesting what the management staff did. These guys experienced pressure every day when they were on the streets. Everything they did or said came under the microscope. All it took was a complaint from a civil rights advocate or someone who claimed to have friends in the city, or someone who just got pissed off and claimed they were tax payers so they should not be cited for speeding or arrested for drunk driving. Someone is always looking over your shoulder.

Jack got lost in thought about that, recalling working a security detail at the airport. A black limo was parked in the three-minute zone and no one was around. He was lax about enforcing the time limit on parking there because three minutes was often not enough time. He went on with his tour of the terminal, and then walked back along the curb. Thirty minutes had passed and the car was still there. He waited next to the car, hoping the driver would see him and move the car. After another five minutes Jack took out his citation book and wrote the ticket. If it was paid on time the fine was five dollars.

A half hour later the driver of the limo approached him. In his hand he held the citation. "Did you write this?" he asked.

"Yes, sir, I did."

"Do you know who I am?"

"No sir, I do not know and it would not make any difference. It is a three minute zone and your car was there over an hour.

You're lucky I didn't tow the car."

Sputtering in anger, the man cursed. Almost yelling, he said his name and stated, "I am a friend of Richard Nixon and am here to pick up some important people to take to the San Clemente White House."

"Do you know Jack Hillberg?" asked Jack.

"No, who the hell is he?"

"That's me, sir. That is who you should know if you want respect. So move the car and pay the ticket."

The room became quiet and Jack refocused on the meeting.

"Gentlemen, we are not like the administration. We do not impose the will of the Board upon you. We are here to represent you and carry out your directives. But be aware that battle lines are being drawn and pressure will come down."

"Do we have to work the concert?" asked a patrolman.

Jack turned to the PORAC-provided attorney for the answer. "Yes, we do. We will obey orders."

"Can we still make it known that we oppose this concert, and why we oppose it? Can we go public and gather community support?"

The attorney, Benjamin Finkel, stood and explained the situation. "There are legal avenues for the association to inform the public, especially groups like churches and service clubs, regarding what happens at rock concerts, and regarding the authority of the chief to provide the security for the city and those who visit the city."

Finkel continued, "You must work any position or duty assigned to you. However, that authority is limited to this department. Other departments cannot be ordered to work the concert. They can only be ordered to work in their city when an emergency exists. Having a rock concert is not an emergency. It is a planned event."

One of the old-timers stood up. "You know I am near retirement. I just have one year to go before I pull the plug. In all my thirty-two some years I have never seen the city or the previous chiefs approve anything that would set aside laws or promote depravity. We have our youth to think about, even if no one else does, and we have to think about the honor that goes with this shield," he said, tapping on the badge that was pinned to his uniform.

"May I make a motion?" he said, looking at Ben and Jack.

219

Ben nodded.

"I move that the OPOA make a public statement opposing the concert and that we authorize the Board to take appropriate actions as needed."

The motion was seconded. Squares of paper were handed to each person in attendance. Faces were grim. Some showed fear and others were angry that they had been put into the position of having to take a stand for justice and doing right. That was the job of the elected officials.

There was silence as each man wrote a yes or a no on his ballot. Yes votes opposed the concert and no votes abstained from taking a position. The ballots were brought to the front and given to Ben to count, and then he would confirm the result with Jack.

"Gentlemen, we have a clear majority. Eighty-four yes votes and thirteen no, with one abstention. I am pleased that no derogatory comments were made. We now need to stick together and remain objective. If this had been a fifty-one percent vote the Board would recommend not proceeding. This issue is too volatile to address with a small majority, but you have made a clear statement. We expect troubles to come but we will honor your wishes."

Chapter 43

Briefings were somber events the next day. It was apparent that the chief and the administration had been told about the meeting and what had transpired. Was there a rat or even several rats? Did someone manage to record the meeting?

It did not matter. Everyone had pretty much conducted himself professionally and respectfully. Frank had told everyone that shit was going to come down and it did.

"There has been a disregard to policies of late," intoned the sergeant. He did not look up and face the men. He was just following orders. After all, it was not like he agreed with this. "Helmets must be worn at all times when you are outside your unit. Code seven is strictly limited to thirty minutes. No more going out of your beat to eat."

"Aaw come on Sarge, you mean we can't go home to eat?"

"Sorry guys, that's the order. If you want to eat with your family they can bring a lunch to the park or meet you someplace."

"What kind of shit is this? We can't afford to buy meals out! Who goes to parks in the morning when the grass is all wet? What about the guys on swing shift? Do their families have to come out at 9pm to eat? This is crap!"

Sarge did not reply. He also did not read the other policies that were made or would be enforced. He knew this was enough for one day. The rest could wait till tomorrow.

On Monday, the sworn staff was called in for a special meeting. The attitude in the station was somber. Many of the non-sworn staff smiled, and some made comments to members of the OPOA Board to show support of the action they took or to apologize for signing the letter.

"What was I going to do?" said Betty. "He was standing right there, waiting for me to sign."

The narcotic sergeant contacted Jack. "10-87 at Walter's. Okay?"

Walter's was the coffee shop/café on Euclid. Walter's and the Thunderbird Lanes bowling alley were the only places open twenty-four hours for food. Chuck, the cook at Walter's during the night shift, loved to have officers come for lunch or coffee. His jokes and corny comments helped during a boring night. You could count on Walter's to provide a free cup of coffee, no matter

221

what time of day it was.

Two of the waitresses there were better than average looking. In fact, Di was drop dead gorgeous, but most guys did not look her in the eye. Her big attractions were just a little lower than that. She was proud of them too, showing off a little extra when she leaned over to pour coffee or serve food. It was no wonder several guys hit on her. She stayed cool, but did land in bed and had six-month affairs with two different patrolmen, at different times, of course.

Jack walked in when he noticed that the supervisor's unit was already parked out back. It was not the same sergeant who he saw having sex with the dancer at Satan's. This one he trusted.

Like every cop, the sergeant chose the corner booth and sat facing the door. Jack didn't mind sitting with his back to the door. This was a safe place and one of the best was protecting his back. Bill was always alert. He seemed casual, but his eyes saw everyone coming and going.

The coffee jug was already on the table, with two cups and two glasses of water. They would not be disturbed unless they motioned the waitress over.

"How have you been? Miss working with you. We had some good times working dope," said Bill.

Jack wanted to get right to the point. He hated wasting time beating around the bush. When there is an elephant in the room he wanted to deal with it.

"What's up, Sarge?" asked Jack. "Something must be cooking. Did my name come up in the staff meeting this morning?"

Bill smiled. It was a smile that Jack learned to recognize after working narcotics with Bill for nearly three years. It was a smile that said, "You're right, I am busted," with just a little bit of embarrassment thrown in.

"As long as the rock concert and the association are around, your name is involved." He shrugged, "That is okay with me, but not everybody is happy about it."

"But that is not why I am here."

"Oh, really? That is about all anyone wants to talk about lately, so what is this about?"

"There is a promotional exam coming up in three weeks, for sergeant. Have you applied for the test?"

"No sir, I have not," replied Jack. He had no interest in the promotion, but refrained from further comment or explanation.

222

"We, er, I think you should take the test. I've seen your work as a team leader first-hand, and observed how well you coordinated investigations and raids. You work very well with officers from other agencies and are well respected. You should take it. You will get the promotion."

"I am sorry, Sarge. The promotion has no benefit for me. I like what I do. I love the streets and the people on them. I would lose vacation seniority; my shifts would be two midnights, two swings, and one day, with Tuesday and Thursday off. One of those days would be used up adjusting my sleep schedule. You can see I have thought about it, but it is not appealing."

"It is one more step up that needs to be taken if you want to move up, and the pay increase is three hundred dollars a month. Try it. You'll make it and next thing you know you will be promoted again, or at least be able to work the shift of your choice," he urged.

Jack realized that this was not just a friend urging him. It must be something the staff discussed today. He hated to hurt Bill or argue with him. He hesitated to say it, but there was something else brewing. Jack decided to spin this on a little further to see if what he thought was correct.

"The pay increase is nice, but on my days off I pick up more than three hundred doing construction work. I make more than three hundred every Monday and every Tuesday," he said, smiling.

Bill didn't say anything for a moment, "It's not just the money, Jack. You will make a good sergeant. I guarantee you will make it."

Seeing the frown and doubt on Jack's face, Bill halted. "Take the test, please? I don't want to see you lose your job."

"Whoa!" thought Jack. This was getting serious. His suspicions were probably right. It was time to find out. "This is about me being president of the OPOA isn't it? The plan is to promote me because then I will no longer be a member of OPOA, but the Management Association, right?"

Bill slumped ever so slightly, but Jack noticed it. Jack knew he had hit the bull's eye.

"It is not like that Jack. Just take the test. It will be good for everybody and you will make it, I promise."

"Bill, I like you and love working for and with you. You guys have done your homework. There are only two or three of the management staff that I would be open to listen to and respect enough to care about what they would say, and you are one of them. But you know me. I hate being pushed or used. Come on, you know I am not for sale. I have a lot going for me, you know that and I know that. I will not sell out. I was looking for a job when I found this one."

Shaking his head, Bill attempted to explain, "It is not like that Jack. I just wish you would go for the promotion." But he was no longer looking Jack in the eye. Jack now knew the truth.

"Sarge, I am sorry, but I just cannot do it, at least not now. I am sure this offer will not be there a year from now. The troops are all watching what is going on. There is a tremendous amount of uncertainty and distrust of management and the politicians that are pulling the strings. So if something happens to me," he shrugged, "the morale will plummet further and it will endanger lives. If I take the promotion the guys will all say I sold out and I would lose their respect."

"What do you mean, endanger lives," he asked.

"Everyone knows that it takes a man's full attention to be safe on the streets. That is why you sat down where you did. When guys are distracted they forget to be vigilant. Every time an officer is under the gun or is being screwed with, he becomes less vigilant. It takes confidence and clear minds and hearts to be alert and safe on the street."

Chapter 44

There was a somber mood in the Canopy that day. Jack and many of his friends decided to do a little debriefing before they went home. Jack had told them about the offer of a promotion.

Pete, Jack', Ray, Jeff and Ken came too. They had the day off but wanted to catch up on the bull and hear the latest gossip. The anxiety about the up-coming rock concert was growing. The hassle of traffic control was far worse than any other event at the Speedway. Six or more hours of standing on hot asphalt, trying to keep the worn-out dope smokers from getting into crashes at intersections was not considered as fun. The officers could not drink enough water to stay hydrated, and there was no place to pee. They just had to hold it until relief came or hide behind the door of the police unit to relieve themselves.

Maybe the Speedway Board and City Council should take a turn at traffic control. They would most likely put port-a-potties and an ice chest with water at each site.

"Tell us what this promotion is about," said Ken. "I've been hoping to take the Sergeant's exam. Is there really an opening? Or are they holding this exam just for you? Do they expect a near future opening?"

"Probably having this exam just to get Jack out of the association, hoping the rest of us will not have the guts to oppose the concert," piped in Jack'."

"Who knows guys? Let's talk about something else. I am really tired of all this and you guys are too. If we keep worrying about what the chief and city are up to we'll get our heads all screwed up. We need to stay alert and on our game or we will wind up dead like Ricky."

That was the wrong thing to say. Everyone started telling stories about the deaths they witnessed.

Ken began the stories with the first death he encountered. He was working graveyard shift. It was a dull night with just a hint of fog. As he drove down Sultana from Mission Boulevard he noticed a car that was parked too far from the curb.

"I just went on by," he said. "Then I noticed the front end was against a parked car and there was damage to both vehicles. Shit! Now I had to check it out. No call about a collision had come in, but it did look like fresh contact.

225

"I backed up, put on the caution ambers, and lit up the car with my spotlight. I walked up to the driver's side, the driver was slumped to his left like he was sleeping. But I knew he wasn't because he had a gash on his forehead and blood was still oozing out and running down onto the floor. The car reeked of alcohol, and since it was three-twenty, I figured this guy had closed a bar and never made it home.

"The ambulance came and took the driver to San Antonio, and Bill & Wags towed the car. After that I went to San Antonio Hospital."

"So, was he dead?"

"No not then. When I got to the hospital Emergency Room the nurses showed me which curtain he was behind. He was breathing a bit shallow, but looked okay. I got his name from the receptionist nurse and decided to call the guy's wife to let her know.

"I started writing my report while I waited for her, and then got a cup of coffee. When she came in, I brought her to the cubicle and talked to her while she looked at her husband and held his hand.

"He was the manager of Ontario Gardens, the low rent development at 1900 S. Campus. She said, 'He loves to drink and I cannot stop him.'

"I left her with him and returned to my cup of coffee. I was standing there talking to the nurse when a scream came from the cubicle and the wife came running out, 'He's dead. He's dead, you got to do something!'

"The nurse and a doctor rushed in and I was right behind them. Sure enough, he had stopped breathing. They hit him with the paddles, making his corpse jump, but he was gone."

"Traffic deaths can be the shits," intoned Jeff.

"The worst one I had was at Holt and Euclid, just a half hour before shift change. I was looking forward to going home to see my wife and watch the Tonight Show with her. Fact is I was on the way to the station when the call came.

"This kid, turned out he was just about twenty, ran the light going east bound. He got T-boned by a pickup that was going south. Fortunately, the pickup was going slower than the car, and it landed up against the Wells Fargo Bank.

"The car did not do so well. He spun around one hundred eighty degrees and crashed into the power and light pole. The driver must have been knocked unconscious because he was still behind the wheel when I rolled up seconds later. I had the lights on already and I stopped in the middle of the intersection by the south island. The car burst into flames just as I exited my unit. Before I could get to the car I heard a long scream and the windows blew out. There was nothing to do except wait for the fire truck to put out the fire. What a mess! The ambulance guys put the charcoal mess in a bag and took him away. I will never forget the smell of burning flesh."

"Damn, you guys are morbid," griped Jack.

"Have you seen suicides?" asked Ray. "I had two last month. Ten years on the job and no suicides and then two inside of four weeks.

"One was just a kid too, just sixteen years old. His mother came home for lunch and she found him. He was supposed to be in school but came home after she left, stuck a .22 rifle against his head, and pushed the trigger. It was a mess, with brain matter splattered on the wall and bed."

"What makes a kid do that?"

"Chief Finley gave some sound advice when I hired on," said Jack. "Do not try to figure the why and how come for all the crap you will see. There is no end to the stuff people think of doing, so just take care of your end of the deal or you will go nuts just like the people you are trying to figure out."

"Yeah, I understand, but sometimes you just wish there was something you could do to stop the weirdness or the harm people do to themselves. Chief Finley must have given that word of advice to everybody. Did he tell everyone that what those people needed was Jesus, too?"

"He was probably right. Wish we had him back as chief," said Pete. "What was the second suicide?"

"Oh, that was on old man. He was seventy-nine and found out that he had inoperable cancer, so he went into his bedroom and ate his shotgun. That was an even bigger mess-pieces of skull, hair and brains on the ceiling, the walls, and everything it fell down on."

"Too much detail for me. I came here to be cheered up, not to contemplate suicide. I sure would not make that kind of work for my wife or family. Drink up! I am going home."

"Be careful out there; remember there is a God."

Ray and Jack walked out of the Canopy together. As they

227

approached their vehicles Ray said, "What's on your mind, Jack? Those death stories bothering you or is something else eating at you?"

"It is a mixture of stuff. Those death stories reminded me that when one of us dies all of us hurt and we place a black band around our badges. That band makes me feel as if my heart is getting squeezed, squeezed until it hurts to think about the one who is gone. That reminded me of a death that it really hurt me to witness."

"Okay, let's have it. What death was that and why is this the first time I am hearing it?"

"This death was about evil and Satan. Sadness grips my heart, like that black band, every time I think of it. I am still trying to make sense of it and trying to understand how it works." He stopped a moment. "Don't look now, but we are being spied on. There is blue van at two o'clock from you that was here the last time we were here and it followed me."

"Anyway, it was my first call of the day, 7:05. Just when I was checking out the unit the call came of a medical assist, possible death.

"I rolled over to Mira Monte, getting there at the same time as the fire fighters. They grabbed their medical bag and we three rushed to the front door. We did not knock because this nice looking young lady opened it. She was about twenty-four years old and had long brown hair. What was striking about her was the fear or dread in her eyes. She led us to a bedroom. On the way there she told us it was her baby's room and her baby was not breathing."

"The firefighters went in first and one immediately felt for a pulse while the other took out a stethoscope. Finding no heartbeat, they started resuscitation.

"The mother started to cry. Then she began to sob, 'My baby, my baby!'

"I stood back, watching the medics and the mother, surveying the room. I was looking for anything that was out of place or any indication that what seemed to be a crib death might actually be a homicide.

"The medics began to undress the baby. They were also looking for trauma. It was also easier to apply compression to the chest without clothing in the way. After they undressed the baby they saw signs that rigor mortis was started. The body was

228

stiffening and blue was spreading across the bottom of this baby.

"The mother saw that and screamed in terror, 'Oh God! My baby, my baby! Please, please God, save my baby!'

"Her crying out to God seemed so out of place in that room, because right above the crib there was a 3x5 poster of Satan. It was just a caricature of Satan, with horns, pointed tail, and a pitchfork in one hand. He was dressed in an Uncle Sam suit, and like Uncle Sam, was pointing his hand at the viewer, with the caption, 'I want you.'

"I was thinking, *Why are you calling out to God when you invited Satan into your child's bedroom? It is not God who took this baby's life. You and your husband gave Satan the priority in this room.* That black band we wear reminds me of the power of darkness, where Satan rules. That darkness restricts life and ruins what is good.

"It was kind of like that guy who was staking us out. To me, that symbolized the corruption in our city that allowed evil but puts on a face of wanting justice and wholeness for our citizens."

After a few minutes they both got in their vehicles and left.

As Jack left he headed south on San Antonio, turned right on Holt, and looked in his mirror. He and a black Cadillac were the only cars on the street. He turned north on Mountain, checked his mirror again, and saw that the Caddy was still there.

Hmm, do I have a tail? He continued north, keeping an eye on the car. The Caddy dropped back a block and then pulled closer, several times. Jack made a quick left turn from the right lane, into the Thunderbird Lanes. The Caddy went past. Jack gave himself a mental kick in the butt, *Don't be so spooky or suspicious, dofus.*

Jack drove to the back of building and then slowly turned to go back to Mountain Avenue. He spotted the black Caddy. It drove by and parked at the gas station.

"Shit, I was right," he muttered while he turned to the rear of the parking area. He knew there was an open space in the chain-link fence, where he could go into the apartment building's carport area. He considered parking in a visitor spot to give the tail something to check out, but thought better of it. You never knew what a tail would do. He drove around the last building and was long gone before the tail figured it out.

229

Chapter 45

May 1978

The OPOA Board normally met on the first Tuesday of the month in the PD conference room. They decided to hold the meeting at the regular time and place, even though the main topic would be the coming rock concert. Six of the directors were trust worthy. Beyond the shadow of a doubt, they would keep what was said and who said it confidential. Jack had doubts about one guy. Although he had voted like all the others, he was also known to have aspirations. It mattered little if Internal Affairs recorded the meeting or if a snitch informed the chief, either way the info was out.

The usual matters were disposed of. They approved the minutes, and received financial reports and communications. Then the rock concert was brought up.

Jack advised everyone to be circumspect with their words and to stay with the topic and the facts. They all knew he was concerned about their reputations and careers. He did not want anything they said to come back to bite them. Looking up at the ceiling, they nodded their understanding about his caution. Just because secretly recording the meeting was illegal did not mean it would not happen.

They all knew about the impending lawsuit that was filed by a half dozen officers who had been secretly videotaped in the locker room. Supposedly, the video camera was installed to catch a thief, but it was the chief who authorized it and none of the detectives initiated the surveillance.

"Gentlemen, the members do not want this concert and they expect us to do what we can," said Jack. "What is your pleasure?"

"We have to work it. There is no way we can avoid it," said Potaro.

"City Ordinance states that one officer is required for each one thousand persons in attendance. If three hundred thousand come, as expected, we do not have enough officers, even if every reserve, cadet, and explorer worked and if days off were cancelled," said another. "Three hundred officers are needed and we can only muster about one hundred."

"That means the city will recruit from surrounding agencies,"

231

said Potaro. "If they offer us time and a half pay there should not be a problem finding enough officers."

"This is not about money. It is about providing a free-for-all drug fest. I bet if other officers knew how we felt and what our membership wanted they would honor a request to not volunteer," offered Chuck.

"PORAC has the names of every association in our area and the names of their presidents, so we could write them a formal request not to work the concert," suggested Jack.

As the idea was tossed around the room, the secretary began to write. He listened and wrote, without saying a word or responding to anyone. Finally he looked up and said, "How about this?" Then he read the draft he had composed.

Dear brother officers:

The Ontario Police Officer's Association requests your support in opposing the proposed rock concert, Cal Jam II.

We are opposed to this concert for ethical and moral reasons. The reasons are that we are opposed to inviting people to come to Ontario to use drugs and narcotics with the knowledge that they will not be arrested. We are opposed to creating this influence upon our youth who have not used drugs and should not be exposed to rampant usage or open sex or open defecating and urinating.

The last concert had two bummer tents that were filled with overdoses and those who died were sent to local hospitals. Their deaths are recorded as DOA and not attributed to the concert.

Our membership will be ordered to work, but you cannot be ordered to work. Therefore, if you do not volunteer, this concert will not take place.

As brother officers, sworn to uphold the law we request that you decline to volunteer.

All who were present approved the letter. The secretary went to the association typist while the rest waited. When he returned with the letter on Association letterhead, every director signed the document. As Ray said, "We all need to sign this or else we are throwing our president under the bus."

The letter was sent to the associations of each police and sheriff department from Bakersfield to San Diego. The neighboring associations had already promised their support, so

232

Chino, Upland, Pomona and Montclair would ask their membership to boycott working. They decided to send a courtesy copy to Chief of Police Brookings to inform him.

"Might as well, the city and the chief will know about this before the stamps are on the envelope," said Ray. "So, we may as well tell them and show that we have the balls to do this."

"DOUBLE TIME PAY FOR CONCERT," screamed the headlines of the Daily Report.

It had taken only three days for the council to react to the letter. It quoted the city manager as saying, "We are not concerned about the opposition of the association. Our officers will be ordered to work, and those from other departments will gladly volunteer to work. We are only offering double time pay because we need so many officers. These officers need and want the money."

Jack had to be in court that day. After court was closed for the day Jack drove his 56 Ford custom pickup home. He was thinking about the headlines and the letter; he did not notice the car that was following him until he was half way home. As he glanced at his right side view mirror he noticed the green Oldsmobile a half block back. It stayed in the same position for six or eight blocks, always keeping two cars, not more, between them.

"Could be anybody. Let's not be paranoid," Jack said to himself.

He put his blinker on and made a left turn. The Olds went on by. Just as he thought he was not being followed, he noticed that a blue Ford four-door sedan had turned onto D Street too.

Jack turned right onto Boulder and left onto Holt. Sure enough, the Ford followed but turned right on Holt. Then he noticed that the Olds was back there pacing him again.

"Hmm, am I paranoid or have they improved their tail?" he mused. "Wonder how many there are?"

He turned into the parking lot at King Cole Market, parked, and walked into the store. He bought a bag of chips and a strawberry soda. He watched who came into the store that might look suspicious. He didn't see anyone. He waited inside the door to scan the lot for a car with a driver and no passengers, who had his engine running. There were none in the lot, but he noticed three cars like that parked on the street. One was facing each direction on Holt and one was facing south on San Antonio.

233

What next? Do I lose them, take them on a wild goose chase or just go home? These guys know where I live. He was sure that the third car was the gray Chevy that was parked down the street from his house last Saturday. That day he and Gail were together and he drove through McDonald's to see who was there. Gail asked him why he had a sudden need for a coffee. They had just finished a late breakfast with three cups. He made the excuse that he just liked McDonald's, and wanted something to drink during their ride to Rialto. He knew she was wise to the fact that something was going on, but she had learned to not ask questions, especially questions she did not want the answers to.

What was it that they wanted? They already knew where he lived, what church he attended, and about the side work he did in construction. They knew his realtor and likely knew the investment properties he owned. They knew he did not drink to excess, gamble or chase women. If they wanted to kill him it would not take two or three cars tailing him around town. Were they just hoping to find something, thinking that every man had a vice? Or were they there just to put fear into his life? Screw'em! As long as his family was safe and they were not planning to take him out he just didn't care what they did. But the pressure was there.

Phone calls and letters arrived at the OPOA post office box. First a few, and then the amount increased daily until virtually all of the associations had promised support and would be encouraging their members to not volunteer.

The secretary called for a quick conference of the Board to inform them of the results. Jack had asked him to do this so they could gauge the response of each director, thinking Potaro would show disappointment, revealing that he was likely the snitch.

They met at Walter's for this meeting. Jack knew the results, but he and Bill were the only ones who knew. Potaro walked in next to last. Jack and Bill looked glum and disappointed. When he saw this, Potaro's lips turned just a little bit toward smiling.

"What's up, letter didn't work did it?"

"No, not like we expected," replied Bill.

"I knew it. Everybody likes to make a few extra bucks and the double time offer made the difference. We should never have opposed this, you really messed up the whole Association," he said, looking at Jack. "The chief is going to make your life rough."

Jack smiled back, "The letter did not do as expected. It did more than we hoped. Practically every association is behind us. Now we wait and see how much influence they have on their members."

Potaro said nothing more. He knew he had been found out. His love for money and desire for promotion revealed his true character. He wasn't any better than the guys in the bureau who had sold out to the Mafia for women and pleasure.

Two months went by as the city and the chief attempted to influence other cities and police chiefs to encourage their officers to volunteer. The labor movement among associations was growing too strong for the chiefs to have that much influence. The Police Chief's Association passed a resolution in support of Cal Jam II, but it was the officers who needed to volunteer, not the chiefs.

Two other Board members noticed that they were being followed from work and that the parking lot at the Canopy had been staked out. An old Astro van was parked there off and on for a week. It was always parked with the side window facing the entry and they were probably taking photos of guys leaving with women. Or maybe they had someone with a wire recording conversations. Who knew? Luckily, none of them had girlfriends except Potaro, and he did not go to the Canopy.

When only thirty volunteers signed up to work Cal Jam II the battle was over. The concert promoters quietly withdrew the application. The Daily Report stated that the concert was cancelled due to economics and other commitments that the promoters needed to attend to.

Two weeks later Jack was testifying in court and the bailiff handed him a note. The note was from the chief deputy DA's secretary. It said, "Report to the Chief of Police's Office immediately after leaving the court."

Deputy DA Gonzales saw the note but continued taking notes during the defense attorney's cross-examination. When the defense rested the judge said the trial would continue the next day for closing arguments. Before Jack could get up and leave, Gonzales grabbed his arm.

"What's up, you in trouble? I've heard some rumblings about you being blamed for killing the rock concert."

"I heard that too, but it was not me. The entire Board voted and planned the opposition. Chief is under a lot of pressure, so there is no telling what this is about. What have you heard?"

235

replied Jack.

"Not much. Just heard the chief deputy on the phone saying he had not given any advice or comments about the concert and that you worked hard at gathering support from the Sheriff's Protective League. I think he was talking to the city attorney. Let me know if I can help. Most of us in the DA's office are behind you, we just cannot say much."

Jack drove to the station wondering what he was facing. He knew he had not done anything that could result in discipline, either on the job or off the job. He came into the building through the north door and he suddenly had the urge to use the restroom, which was just inside the door. As he came out of the restroom the watch commander, Jake Holmes, was coming in.

Jake's face grew dark and anxious when he saw Jack. "Chief is waiting for you," he said. Then he quickly went in, closing the door behind him.

Does everybody know what is up but me? wondered Jack. *Shit" I might as well hurry over and get this done.* He headed to the chief's office. He noticed that many eyes followed him as he went down the hall past the watch commander's office, the office pool and break room; or was he just paranoid?

He stepped into the chief's secretary's office, smiled, and said, "Hi Marge."

She did not smile back or respond. She simply picked up the phone and notified the chief that he was there. Then she spoke, "You may go in," and pointed to the door.

The door of doom was what Jack saw, but he opened it and went in.

The chief stood up as Jack entered. He was holding a white paper that looked like a letter.

Shit! I am getting fired, thought Jack. Across the office, still seated, was the detective bureau captain. Jack looked back and forth at the two men, trying to get a read on just what was going on. This was high-powered stuff.

Before anyone spoke Jack paused at the door. His hand did not leave the knob. "Do I need to have a lawyer or representative?" he asked.

"No, no, nothing like that," responded the chief. "We have been thinking about the problems we have with an area that the bureau has not been able to address properly. Captain Hasler and I have come up with a plan to meet those needs and to further assist

236

you with broadening your experience and helping your career."

Jack released the door, allowing it to close .Meanwhile he watched the face of both the chief and his captain. Captain Hasler was somber; no smiles and no frowns, but he was not willing to look Jack in the eye.

Snake or wuss, thought Jack. Either way Jack's respect for him was going downhill fast.

The chief extended the letter to Jack. "Here is the plan for your next assignment. I think you will be pleased."

Jack kept his eye on the chief as he took the letter. He saw the animosity and the hint of a smirk playing along his lips and in the way his eyes narrowed. Looking down at what he was given, he saw a job description for his new assignment. "Malicious Mischief Investigator and Garage Sale Permit Enforcement."

Jack almost sputtered in amazement at this ridiculous assignment. He caught himself before he looked up and said anything. It was the same thing they did to Bob and Ken a few years ago, same assignment and everything. He saw the expectation on both faces. *They are hoping I'll say something stupid so I can be charged with insubordination,* he thought. Keeping an impassive face, he looked the chief in the eye.

"Thank you sir, I will do my best." He turned to leave before he did say something stupid.

Captain Hasler stood too. "Ray will be your partner. He is being given his notice by the sergeant. Your days off will be Sunday and Monday so you can work the garage sales on Saturdays and interview the teenagers at home when the parents are there. This will round out your experiences and be good for your career advancement."

"Yes, sir," said Jack. He saluted before he backed out the door. The secretary either went home or was not at her desk. *Smart,* thought Jack, *she probably sees through this bullshit too.*

These changes in assignment had never been mentioned as Career Development before. Jack realized that they wanted to make sure he knew this was payback time. He and Ray had the best percentage of clearing cases in the bureau. They worked the hardest and longest hours, and now they were going to the lowest grade of crimes. Crimes that no one paid attention to unless it was graffiti or huge amounts of damage, and then the gang detail was the one that handled it.

Monday the entire department would know that he was

discarded into oblivion. The troops would get the message. Do not ever cross the chief or City Hall.

Yard sales! The fine was what? Twenty-five dollars? Even if every yard or garage sale in the entire city were cited, the amount collected would not be enough to pay for one detective, much less two. Shouldn't code enforcement be doing this work? Their pay rate is half of a sworn peace officer.

He left by the back door and headed for his pickup. Ray was standing next to it. Ray had a huge grin plastered across his face.

"Really pissed them off, didn't we?' he laughed.

Jack started to laugh too. This was so crazy. They hugged each other realizing that the city would be sorry they did this. It would take only a week or two before the increased case load of the other investigators would force a reversal of this order.

That was exactly what occurred. Two weeks later, they were returned to the bureau to work burglary. But the message was delivered and understood.

Chapter 46

October 1978

It was a dank foggy morning. The sky was clear but the ground fog made the grass and cars parked outside wet with dew. Henk knew that this moist air would soon fade away into another sunny Southern California day. Meanwhile he would look normal wearing his long waistcoat. He needed the coat to hide the .22 caliber rifle he was carrying. With the collar up and a knit cap on his head, he figured he would not be spotted or recognized.

He started walking. Everybody he had called refused to give him a ride. Each one had some excuse for not to being able to help him, but he knew why they were refusing. It was his own fault. He should not have lost his cool. *But what the hell*, he figured, *the chump should not have ripped him off or lied to him.*

He needed some money to get out of town. His family had not answered the phone not that they would have much money to give him, but at least they would give him a ride so he could get more money and a ride to the bus station. He had a friend that lived near Yak, Montana, who would give him a place to hide out. No one knew where Yak was, and there were lots of cabins out in the woods up there, where he could survive for years.

His buddy worked at the Dirty Shame Saloon and would help him get food and beer. He could grow his own weed and do very well. He might pick up some work doing odd jobs and construction, and then get a new ID. Thinking about that almost lifted his angry, dour mood He almost felt hopeful about a bright future but he needed a couple hundred bucks first, and to get to the bus station without being spotted.

He started off walking west on State Street. There were not many cars there, and the railroad tracks on the north made this a fairly safe way to get to Magnolia. Then he went south through the semi-agricultural area to where an acquaintance lived, just around the corner on Philadelphia.

The pot-smoking meth dealer would have a stash of a thousand or more dollars. If he was nice, Henk figured he would take only part of it. If he was a jerk? Well, then he would shoot the punk and take it all.

Meanwhile Ricky came into the police station to work for his buddy. It was Ricky's day off, but Mike had family from Oregon coming to visit so they had agreed to switch their days off. Ricky checked his unit and thought about checking the shotgun, but he figured it was checked by the previous shift, so he ignored that.

Ricky began his shift by going south on Euclid. He stopped at the donut shop by the Southland Market. He figured he would grab a cup to wake up and tune his brain to be alert. Then he would cruise the schools. He had a thing about keeping pedophiles away from schools. Writing a ticket for speeding in the school zone was always good too. Just gotta protect the kids.

He cruised Ontario Christian School, and then headed toward Cypress School. He turned left on Francis, cruised to Ontario High, and then went south to Ontario Christian High. He never got there because the radio jolted him from his reverie. He had not been paying attention to what he was doing; he was just driving and thinking. Thinking about what was going to happen, about crashing the unit.

Was he going to be suspended?
How many days off would that be?
Or would he be terminated?

He hoped termination was not one of the possible considerations. That would really mess up his chances of being hired by LASO.

What is taking so long, he mused. *They are killing me with this waiting. My wife is anxious and crabby too. I don't blame her; it is not her fault that I got into the crash or her fault the process is taking so long.*

He shook his head to get rid of the cobwebs.

The transmission was the patrol sergeant, reporting that he thought he had seen Henk Mueller walking south on Magnolia. Tom was on Francis and had just crossed Magnolia when he spotted a guy he thought was Henk, walking south from Francis. He was going to turn around to check him out. Roll a backup!

Ricky picked up the mike, "One O Two rolling from Palmetto and Philadelphia."

He turned west, had a green light at Mountain, and turned north on Magnolia. He drove slowly, keeping his eyes out for anyone on either sidewalk. Then he spotted the other cruiser, coming south from Francis. Henk spotted the sergeant and began running. He was next to Inland Christian Home, but decided to go to the apartment complex just southwest of there instead.

240

As Henk turned to run into the apartment complex he spotted Ricky's cruiser. He was running fast now and he took his rifle out from under his coat so he could run faster. With his rifle in his hand, he ran between the buildings, hoping to get out of sight and hide.

Ricky slid into a parking space next to the curb, unlocked the shotgun, grabbed it, and got out. He did not wait for the sergeant. He walked into the complex alone.

Tom saw Ricky going into the complex and screamed, "NO!"

Of course, Ricky could not hear him. Tom grabbed his mike and called for units to cover the south and east side of the apartment complex. District three, five, a detective unit doing some preventive patrol, and a Chino police unit were all rolling in response to Ricky's transmission that he had seen a long-haired man wearing a plaid coat run into the apartments with a rifle. Maybe it was Henk Mueller, who was wanted for the investigation of PC187 last night.

Ricky had his hand-held radio in one hand and the shotgun in the other. He was broadcasting his location and the direction the suspect was going.

Henk heard the radio traffic and panicked. He knew the place would be swarming with cops in a few minutes. He had to find a way out! Just then he saw a lady carrying a baby come out her front door. Quickly, he pushed her aside and went into the apartment.

As he was about to shut the door, Henk saw Officer Augustino. He was walking across a large open area, apparently looking for him. Henk knew that if he were spotted he would be trapped and caught. A chill ran down his back as he realized what he needed to do to avoid arrest. Calmness took over, just like last night. He smiled to himself about how cool he was. Calmly, he raised his rifle, carefully aimed and took a shot.

The resident of the apartment screamed as she saw what was going on. Clutching her baby, she scrambled away. Half crawling, half running, she held her baby tight as she watched the officer crumble to the ground.

Quickly she dodged around the corner so she would be out of sight of her front door. Safe for now, she too crumbled to the ground, sobbing. Sobbing for the officer she saw get shot and sobbing with relief that she and her baby got away. Gathering her things, she knocked on the closest door and continued knocking

241

until someone answered.

Still crying, she related what was happening and asked the man to call the police.

Ricky had seen nothing and never heard the scream. The bullet entered his head just in front of the earpiece of his helmet, striking him in the temple. He was dead before he hit the ground.

The switchboard lit up like a Christmas tree with calls about an officer shot.

No, he was not moving.

No, we do not know where the shot came from.

No, we do not know who did it.

Please, please roll an ambulance. This is awful!

The only person on the radio was the Ontario dispatcher. Everyone knew to stay off the air unless they had pertinent information.

Officer down! Officer down!

Every police unit and detective was on the way to south Magnolia. The ambulance company had monitored the call and was on the way before the phone rang. Even tow trucks were on the way. They had no idea what they could do, but felt the need to be there.

Henk closed the front door of the apartment, locked it and ran upstairs. He turned off the lights in the bedroom, pulled back the drapes, and opened the blinds just enough to see out. He saw the officer sprawled out on the grass. His shotgun was lying out of reach and his radio was underneath him.

Henk grinned to himself with satisfaction. "Stupid Jerk," he muttered.

He quickly went to the other rooms to see what was happening outside. He said to himself, "Should have taken that woman inside with me, now she will tell the cops where I am, damn it!"

"Suspect is in unit 1378," blared the radio. "The resident says the suspect is alone in the apartment. She is safe nearby, on the phone now!"

The detective unit arrived on Magnolia. They left their car on the street near the patrol car. Looking at the unit numbers, they approached the complex. They spotted Ricky lying about twenty feet from the building and thirty or more feet from where they were standing.

No words were said. They knew they had to get Ricky.

242

Hopefully he would survive if they could get him to the hospital soon.

Henk returned to the front bedroom and saw the two detectives. "What the hell!" he muttered. "May as well take some more out; they are going to kill me anyway, a few more won't hurt and it is fun shooting pigs."

He opened the blinds and the window. The movement was seen, and just as he pointed his rifle, one detective fired a shot from his .357 Magnum. Henk saw the flash and pulled back. The shot hit the stucco a foot away from the window.

Knowing they had just a few seconds, the detectives raced out to Ricky. They each grabbed an arm and dragged him along to safety, just as they heard two shots from the .22 rifle. One shot struck a car that was parked at the curb and the other plowed into the lawn. The detectives left the shotgun and radio behind to mark the spot where Ricky was laying.

The ambulance arrived and loaded Ricky up. As the ambulance left, police cars kept arriving. The entire complex was surrounded and officers took positions behind apartments and inside neighboring units. Some of the officers inside were on the same level as the suspect. They opened windows and pulled back shades. All they needed was for Henk to show himself and he would be a dead man.

Twenty plus officers were praying. They had two things on their minds and in their prayers. "God, please save Ricky" and "God give one of us the opportunity to bring justice."

They knew that justice was difficult to administer. It was best to let the court system handle this but they also knew that Rose Bird was on the Supreme Court and she was an advocate to end the death penalty. Death was the only justice a police officer saw as appropriate for a cop killer.

The radio broadcast said that Ricky was in very serious condition, but they knew that was just a euphemism used to soften bad news. Ricky was dead and they knew it in their guts. Their guts were in knots. Their faces were grim. One of us was dead.

This was something each officer realized could happen, on any day, to any one of them but the reality was hitting home that today was the day and it was Ricky.

"Please God; let me blow that dirt bag away."

"Do not shoot. Do not shoot! Negotiations have been established." The message came across every radio.

The PD did not have an official negotiator in those days. The job was given to the watch commander. The lieutenant's office became the command center until it was determined whether a command post should be set up near the site. The chief of police was there to listen and instruct. The window between the WC office and dispatch was open to facilitate listening to radio traffic, and the phone conversations that were coming and going in dispatch.

The lady whose apartment Henk commandeered gave her house phone number to the watch commander. He called, but no one answered. When the answering machine picked up the call, the lieutenant left a message.

"Mr. Mueller, please pick up the phone. This is Dan at the police department; I want to talk to you. We do not want to hurt you, please talk to me."

The patrol commander was on the way to the site with a bullhorn and a sniper rifle. The plan was to use the bullhorn to get the suspect to answer the phone and be talked into surrendering. If that failed, the sniper would take him out when he was spotted. That is, if another eager cop had not already made the fatal shot.

Meanwhile, the ambulance arrived at San Antonio Hospital. They did chest compressions on the way, but there was no response. Ricky was wheeled into emergency, where an anxious team was waiting. Many of them knew Officer Augustino from the times he came to follow up on injury traffic collisions. They liked him. He was good. Now his life was in their hands.

When they saw him they knew his life was already gone and there was nothing they could do except weep, which many of them did, openly crying and hugging. They wheeled Ricky into the corner, pulled the curtains closed around him and waited.

The watch commander dialed the number again.

No answer.

Thirty officers were waiting for an opportunity to be a hero. None were calling for surrender. They were waiting for a good shot or for the negotiator to complete his task. They did not know that contact had not been made until they heard the commander on the bullhorn telling the suspect to pick up the phone.

Back in the WC office, they heard the bullhorn over the radio and placed the call again. This time Henk picked up the phone.

He said nothing. Just waited and listened.

There was twenty seconds of silence, and then the lieutenant introduced himself. "Mr. Mueller, you are in a tight spot, you need me to help you out."

"Fuck you! You are just going to set me up to kill me." He hung up the phone.

The phone rang again, and he picked it up.

"What?" he shouted. He was nervous and afraid. He was trapped and there were cops everywhere he looked, all waiting and wanting to shoot him. All of a sudden he did not want to die. He slid to the floor in fear. Fear of being seen through the window and fear of giving up. He was a tough guy. He could not give up.

The voice on the phone began to talk to him. It was an assuring voice, calmly talking, with no threat or accusation. "What can we do to help you understand that we will not hurt you? Please give up and come out."

"I am not coming out with all those guys out there; they will shoot my ass as soon as I come out the door. Make them all go away. I want to see them leave."

"I cannot do that. If the guys all leave you will escape, and we cannot allow that. Throw your gun out the window and come out the front door with your hands on your head, and I promise you will be safe."

"No way in hell. I do not trust any of you."

"Sure you can trust me. We could have sent tear gas into the place and stormed it. Then you would have been shot on sight. We have not done that, right? So give up. You have no chance of getting away. What can I do to assure you? Who do you trust?"

"I trust my mom and my sister. They are the only people in my life that have not hurt me."

"Okay, if your mother comes with us will you come out to her? She will trust us and you will see her, okay?"

The phone went dead.

"Shit," muttered the lieutenant. "He hung up."

What was actually happening was that Henk was sitting on the floor, his head in his hands. He was shaking with dread. There was no way out, even if he shot more cops. *Maybe I should just shoot myself?* He picked up the rifle, looked at, and realized that he was not capable of suicide, not even suicide by cop. If he gave up he would get the death penalty for sure. "What do I do?" he mused. "I have nobody to trust or take care of me." All of a sudden his dysfunctional childhood overwhelmed him.

The phone rang again. He picked it up and his mind was

made up. He knew what he wanted to do.

"Mr. Mueller? I have talked to your mother. She is on her way to where you are. Will you talk to her?"

"Yes, I will talk to her. If she says it is safe for me to come out, she needs to come to the front door and walk out with me."

"That is good. An officer will be with your mother when she comes to the door."

"I do not want an officer, just my mother!" he screamed.

"You know we cannot send just your mother. You could take her inside as a hostage. That would get me in big trouble with the chief. How about if the officer is a command officer, lieutenant or captain? Would that work?"

Silence.

The WC waited. He knew this was the critical moment. Talk and blow it or keep quiet and blow it. He waited.

He heard a sigh.

Hope stirred in the WC's heart.

"Okay, send mom with a captain who is not gun happy."

"Okay, just leave the gun in the bedroom and come down."

Twenty more minutes went by before the mom showed up. She met the captain on the street, and then side-by-side they walked to the door.

Slowly, the door opened. The suspect looked both ways, and then as his mother stepped onto the porch he came out.

The sigh that came from everyone who observed or listened on the radio was almost audible, and it felt like a draft of wind as relief spread around.

The standoff was over!

The forensic team stayed to collect evidence. They took photos and collected bullet casings. Everyone else returned to their duties. However, nothing was normal. The patrol cars 10-87 various places to discuss the event and the detectives did the same. The official word was that Augustino was gravely injured. No one was using the "D" word.

The two officers that pulled Ricky's body to safety were interviewed and kept away from the public. No one but the hospital, the chief, and his admin staff knew Ricky's condition.

Television crews were swarming around the hospital and the police station. Anyone who came out of either building was grabbed to ask for information or an interview.

"What happened?"

"Is the officer dead?"

"How do you feel about this terrible shooting?"

The media continued with rapid-fire questions.

No one dared or wanted to venture out of the police station. Those who needed to leave used the back door that led to the parking area for black and whites, because that area was cordoned off from the news. The chief went back there to get a car to use to make the death notification visit to the widow.

Chapter 47

Chief Brookings and the newly promoted Lieutenant Washburn made the long drive to the Augustino home that afternoon. It was not a long drive because he lived so far away, he lived less than a half mile from the station, but a long drive because it was the most dreaded and painful call a chief had to make.

The lieutenant was confident it would be an easy call to make. They would express sympathy, promise to help with the legal matters, and offer to be there if the widow needed anything. The chief was hesitant. He realized that Washburn was brash and sometimes disconnected from the reality of how people felt. Besides, he had this nagging ache in his gut that told him Carly might be angry and hurting.

He also realized that Washburn was not one of the favorite staff members. Many of the cops remembered the incident of the gun and vehicle verification forms and referred to the lieutenant as a crook. However, he did place high in the promotional exam process, number two or three, and the city manager had pushed for Washburn. Washburn was the first to volunteer for this difficult visit and he expressed such confidence that all would work out well that the chief accepted his offer to come along on the notification.

When they drove onto Ricky's street they saw how well kept the houses and yards were in this almost historic section of Ontario. Many of the homes were built when this was the edge of town, in the late nineteen twenties and into the early forties. They were modest three bedrooms, two bath homes built back in the day when they still had parlors and studies. These houses were on the pricey side when they were first built. Local granite rocks were used for foundation stem walls. The siding was rabbited redwood and stone veneer for the front porch.

Nice people lived on a nice street. They sat and visited with neighbors on their front porches or exchanged greetings with people who walked by. Everyone enjoyed the shade of the old trees that created a canopy over the sidewalks and almost touched the trees on the other side of the street.

The chief and lieutenant parked in front of the house and checked the number to be sure they had the right house. They both

249

touched their shields to feel the band of black velvet. They were somber when they exited the unit.

As they walked up the front sidewalk they saw someone lift the blinds to see who was coming. After a quick peek the blind dropped back in place. Washburn pushed the doorbell. It was a pleasant doorbell, one that played a short tune to announce that a caller was at the front door.

No one responded.

They looked at each other with a question in their eyes. They knew someone was home.

"Probably not dressed properly for us," said Brookings.

They pressed the bell again. Carly had seen the police car and immediately knew what message they had come to deliver.

"Go away," was the response to the chime of the bell.

Washburn stood close to the door and said, "Please may we come in?"

After nearly another full minute the door slowly opened, but only a few inches. They saw Ricky's eight-year-old boy there. His hair was tousled and his eyes were a mixture of sad and scared.

"Mommy doesn't want to see you," he said and closed the door.

The grief and shock of knowing Ricky must be dead numbed the poor boy's mother. She knew there had to be an official notification if it were true, but just couldn't face the chief and Lieutenant Washburn. She decided to call one of Ricky's friends instead of allowing the two men who stood outside her door to come in.

The phone on Jack's desk rang. He picked it up and heard a woman sobbing .He waited for the sobbing to end before expecting her to reply to his greeting. As he waited it dawned on him who it was.

"Carly?" he asked.

"The chief and that crook are at my door. I do not want to see him or talk to him, ever!" she sobbed. "Can you come over? Please?"

"Sure, be there in five or ten."

He grabbed Ray and they headed out. They headed to Augustino's home in one of their personal cars. The anticipation of meeting the chief there was a most unpleasant thought. How could they explain to the boss that the widow did not want to see him and would not let the lieutenant in? With huge relief, they saw that the chief's car was not there.

"Poor bastard," goes Jack. "He is really stuck in a hard spot. He cares about the troops but the pressure from the city manager and a couple of crappy councilmen totally make his job impossible to do well."

"That's true," responded Ray, "but he has always said that when the heat is too hot he will get out of the kitchen."

"That is easy to say, but damn difficult to do when you are top dog and have no place to go but down or out of the department, and he only has a few years till he can retire."

"Right, he is stuck between a rock and a hell of a hard place. However, it still is not right that the grunts have to pay the price. We will just have to get more involved in the next election and support a candidate to run against Rojas."

They knew that they could not finish that discussion here. Their ideas might be good but it would not be easy to bring good leadership. Politics bred its own greed for power.

They walked up to the front door. It opened and they continued right into the living room.

"Thanks, young man," said Ray to Marcus, messing up his hair.

Marcus was the second of the three children. There were two boys and the youngest was a girl. The other two were named Trey and Carmen. Carly told the kids to go outside to play, because she felt better now that friends were there.

Carly welcomed them into the kitchen, where they gathered around the table. She was in shock as she poured them a cup of coffee and then sat down. They waited for her to speak, aware of the fact that it was her call and her schedule. Finally, she spoke.

"The chief was here. I didn't know what to do. I have no respect for him and even less for the other guy. I do not want to talk to them. What do I do? Do I have to let them in? Their visit could only mean one thing. Is Ricky really dead? I have seen the news, but they do not know much. It is so hard to believe."

Ray took her hand and gently squeezed it. "Yes, he is. He died doing his job, doing his duty. We can hardly believe it either. I'm so sorry! The chief was here to give you the official notification and to help you in any way the police department and the city can."

They went on to explain what they knew about how it all happened. They hugged her and let her cry for a while. Tears came

251

to their eyes too, although they kept their emotions under control. Finally, she regained her composure enough to speak.

"I do not want the chief or Washburn to speak at Ricky's funeral or memorial service. Will they have to be there? I can't even believe we are talking about this!"

"You do not have to do anything you don't want to do. If you don't want the chief to speak at the funeral he will respect that."

"I don't want the mayor or any of the council to speak either. What am I going to do?" She asked with obvious despair. Her distaste of the political world overcame her. No one had to tell her what she firmly believed in her heart. The pressure of politics and disregard for its effects on the cops who worked the streets was what made Ricky less than vigilant over the past months. She was sure that his last thoughts had been about his future and the security of his family.

"What do you think, Jack?" asked Ray.

"It is her call to make about who she sees and talks to. We, that is the association, can help with planning and running interference for you, Carly. If you would like," asked Jack as he turned toward her.

"We can call the pastor of the church you select, and then you and he can plan the service as you would like to have it. We will talk to the chief to explain your wishes and have him coordinate the things that the department will want to do."

Looking fearful, she asked, "What will the department want to do?"

"The usual stuff like the Honor Guard, presenting the flag to you, a helicopter fly over, arranging and coordinating the attendance of officers from other departments, and handling traffic. Stuff like that."

"That is okay, but I want, and Ricky would have too, just the pastor and maybe two of Ricky's friends to say something. I want to make it upbeat, not formal or depressing. But I do not want the chief to give me the flag. Can Rick's favorite sergeant do that?"

"I am sure he would be delighted to be the presenter, and the chief will probably be relieved that he does not have to do it."

"What church do you want to use? Is yours large enough to hold a thousand or more people?"

"A thousand?" asked Carly with shock in her voice.

"Sure, easily," said Ray. "Departments across the state will send a delegation of two to four. Every officer in Ontario and most of them in neighboring departments will be there. Then you have friends, family, and hundreds of citizens that will want to pay respects."

Carly bowed her head as the tears dripped down her cheeks. She was in awe of the prospect of all these people coming to pay respects to the man she loved, but was now gone. Gone forever.

All three of them sat back and were lost in their own private thoughts.

Ray was thinking about the line of police vehicles. How long would it be? How would they get on the freeway? Where would they park when they arrived at Forest Lawn?

Jack thought about how to present her wishes to the chief. He felt like he needed to create the working relationship it would take to please all the various people involved, and their needs and wishes.

Carly was thinking about how to handle the public's expressions of sympathy and how she would get through the time of pain and anguish. She was thinking about needing to call her and Ricky's parents. She also thought about how she would tell the kids their father was gone.

She said, "Will you guys help me tell the kids? They know something bad has happened to Ricky, but I don't know if I can tell them myself."

Ray called the kids inside, and they had a very serious talk with them. Of course there were more tears. Each one of them had a turn sitting on mommy's lap, crying, and hugging the parent they had left. Thankfully, there were three adults, and the kids took turns on each of their laps.

As they absorbed the news, the kids wanted to know if dead meant that daddy would not come back. That brought more questions to their minds. Patiently, each was answered as well as they could be. Finally, they seemed to understand as much as children are able to.

When he thought the time was right, Ray took the kids out in the back yard while Jack stayed in the kitchen with Carly. They went through the motions of having a good time playing outside while they tried to process the news they had just received. Ray played catch with the boys and Carmen played on the swing. Ray finally went back into the kitchen. Meanwhile, Jack had called family members for Carly, to inform them of Ricky's death.

An hour later, Carly decided to ask the pastor of the little

253

community church that they had been going to for the past year to give the homily. Ricky liked him because he seemed to understand the pressures of being a cop. He was a real people person who understood life. He understood life by being involved in lives, not just by preaching and oozing theology. They had spent many years not going to church, but they went back because they wanted their kids to be grounded in the Bible and have a relationship with God. In the process, they, too, developed a trusting relationship with God. What was good for the kids turned out to be good for the mom and dad too.

Ricky and Carly experienced difficulties at home, and of course Ricky did at work too. The pastor guided them through these past months of turmoil.

There in Carly's kitchen, Jack called the local Calvary Chapel to see if the facility would be available for the memorial service.

"Of course it is," responded the pastor. "That is what we are here for, to be of help in time of need. There will be no charge or fees. It is our way of saying thanks."

Then they contacted Rose Lawn and made arrangements to come in to finalize the plot location and time of internment.

Jack asked Carly if she needed help with the arrangements at the funeral home.

"No, my mother and sister said they would come here later today, and I know they will help me, but thanks."

When Jack and Ray had done everything they could to help her they said they thought they should leave, if Carly would be all right. Carly said she would as she hugged Jack and Ray. "Thanks for doing so much to help and for being there for Ricky and now for me."

"No problem, that is what we are here for," said Ray. "Oh by the way, we will, that is if it is okay with you, set up a memorial trust account for the kids to help with college. Frank at Inland National Bank will set up the account. We will do some publicity and set up how the collecting of funds will go. OPOA will seed this account with a thousand dollars to get it started."

Crying, she nodded her thanks for that, hugged them both again, and sent them out the door.

Jack and Ray headed over to the Canopy for a burger and fries and to discuss just how they were going to approach the chief with Carly's wishes.

As much as they would have liked a beer, they ordered

Arnold Palmer's. "Want a shot with that?" asked Doreen, the barmaid.

"Yes, but no. Do not do that. Sure does sound good though, might need some false courage when we go do what needs to be done."

"Who is going to explain this?" asked Jack.

"What do you mean, who? You are the president. Many are called but few are chosen. You are it buddy."

"Thanks a lot good friend," grinned Jack, "I should have a dozen friends like you."

"Okay, this is what you do. See, I am not throwing you under the bus. I am giving you the words to speak. I just do not want to do it myself. 'Chief, sir, Carly Augustino called when she saw you come to the door. She guessed why you came but could not face you or handle the news you were bringing. When she realized she needed to hear the official news, she called me and asked us to come to her house.

"We went and told her you had come to give her the official notification about Ricky's death and to offer your help. She understood that, but wanted to talk to someone she knew personally, and that is why we went over when she called.

"It turns out that she has some concerns about the memorial service. She is afraid it will become a political and secular event, which she does not want. What she wants is to have a spiritual service that recognizes God and the future hope she has. She wants to thank everyone for caring and reaching out to her and that is it. She is okay with the flag presentation and the Honor Guard. She thinks Ricky would like to have had his favorite supervisor make the presentation. The speakers will be her pastor and she hopes to limit the speeches to his training officer and his best friend. Would that work, sir?"

"That is a great presentation. I will let you do it," said Jack. "I could never say it that well myself."

"You sneaky chump, you are going to make me do it. Okay, but you have got to be there with me."

They returned to the station and went to the chief's office to ask for five minutes of his time. They were ushered in and were invited to sit. That was rare, but they sat and began the presentation.

"Sir, we received a call from Officer Augustino's wife. She saw you drive up earlier. She guessed why you came but could not face you or handle the news she expected. So, she called Jack and asked us to come to her house. We went to her house and told her you had come to give her the official notification about Ricky's death and to offer your help. She understood that, but wanted to talk to someone she knew personally, and that is why we went over when she called. She has some wishes that she asked us to present to you," stated Jack. "Ray put together what she is thinking and asking you for. I'll let Ray present them."

Ray explained what they had agreed upon and concluded with, "If we can help in any way to coordinate the service or assist in any way, we are there for you."

Chief Brookings realized that they were in a tough spot and he was grateful that they were respectful of his attempted visit to the widow. It was fine with him that he had not needed to go through the unpleasantness of telling the woman her husband was dead. He leaned back in his chair. A satisfied smile tweaked his lips as he replied. "Sounds like good ideas. My staff and I are most pleased to help make this service one that she and her children will look back on with good memories. How about a 21-gun salute and playing "Taps"? Would she like to include that, too?"

"That would be great, sir. Those things did not come up in her conversation with us, but we are sure she would approve and be pleased you thought of them and suggested it," responded Jack.

Everyone was pleased at the result and grateful that good things were going to happen. They shook hands and departed. What a day! The death notification had been made, but the whole department was still reeling under the loss of a good cop.

Chapter 48

After shift change, near 4pm, the official news was released. The shooting was fatal. Officer Augustino was dead.

The TV broadcasted the news of the shooting. They showed views and descriptions of the apartment complex. Photos of Officer Augustino standing next to his patrol car were on every station. Channels 2, 4, 5, 7, 9, 11 and 13 all had reporters at the hospital, the site of the shooting, and to interview the commander who took the suspect into custody.

Every officer's home had the TV on to witness the news report. Those whose husbands were at home were watching together. Most held hands or sat close, relieved that they were safe but in anguish for the slain man's family.

Each officer tried to assure his wife that this would not happen to him. He would be more cautious. He would be on top of his game. No one would get the drop on him. Besides, this was such a rare occasion. Ontario only had a total of three officers killed on duty and the department existed for nearly eighty years. One of those deaths was a car crash, not a shooting.

Most of the wives were proud of their men. They saw them as brave and doing good things for society, in spite of the danger. Yet, they feared for their safety and wished they could get safe jobs. But they wouldn't. The cops relished the adrenaline rush and the power to make a difference.

The wives whose husbands were at work as patrolmen or detectives were worried. They turned off the TV to protect the children. Gathering the kids together, they told them something terrible happened.

"Is Daddy all right?" they asked quicker than their mothers could tell them what happened. Fear was in each kid's face as he or she looked to mom for assurance.

"Yes, Daddy is okay, don't worry. Daddy will be home soon," she said, hugging them to her breast. But they were worried. Something was very wrong. They knew that because mommy was crying and hugging them so tight that it hurt. But they wanted to keep hugging because they were scared.

Slowly, the hug loosened and then ended. Wiping away her tears, mother explained that one of Daddy's friends at work died. "A bad man was shooting and hit one of the policemen."

"Is he dead?" they asked innocently.

The tears welled up in Mommy's eyes as she said, "Yes, he is, but Daddy is okay."

The children soon returned to play or homework. Their faith in daddy was strong. He was okay and would come home soon. Daddy always came home. They did not think of Ricky's kids, whose daddy was not coming home.

Some of the wives called each other and got together. They all needed the comfort of someone who understood. Someone who had the same fear they did, but also someone who was impressed with the men for doing their jobs. They did not just do the job, but loved it. When they went to work every day they knew they were keeping Ontario safer.

Gail had that conversation with her son and daughter. She looked at the clock. It was 5:30. Jack should be home soon. Jack

257

did not come home and had not called. Usually that happened when he was on a case and did not have access to a pay phone. As Jack had told her, "When the phone call is from the PD or a police car pulls up in front of the house that is the time to worry or be afraid. Until then just trust me and God that all is right, and I will be home when I can."

Tonight she really needed him home. She wanted the comfort and assurance of seeing that he was fine and in her arms. In her heart she knew he was not working, but he was not coming home either.

"He is fine, he is fine," she mumbled to herself, "but I wish he was here."

Lystra was also looking at the clock, expecting Ray to be home soon. She prepared the table for dinner for the five of them. Then she went about cooking the rice and beef dish the kids liked so well. They all liked it except Antoinette. She hated the peas, but would pick them all out carefully so she would not pollute herself.

"Where was Ray?"

He called when he could, but they had an agreement that no call just meant that he was tied up with work and no phones were available. She knew he was faithful. Their trust for each other was great. She also knew this absence had to do with Ricky's death; he needed to be with the guys, or maybe the guys needed him to be with them.

She remembered the night he did not come home and did not call. It was four in the morning when he returned. He had gone to work that morning at 8am and called her at lunch, but that was the last she heard. He and Jack had received a call from an informant who told them about an impending theft that a burglary team was going to pull that night. They had followed this guy and his partner down to Del Mar, through the coastal harbors, all the way back to Newport. They planned to steal outboard motors. The cops had no way to call home and were outside radio coverage areas for a long time. Fortunately, the crooks needed a restroom, which Jack and Ray needed too. They urinated behind the car, parked half a block away from where the suspects stopped. They wished they could order some food and drink, but were at least grateful for the relief.

Jack had told her, "We cannot just stop at a pay phone whenever we want to. Just remember, God is near, and I will not do anything stupid, Okay?"

258

She remembered all of the times the guys called him for advice. It seemed that he and Jack were the go-to guys that so many officers looked up to. Both had strong convictions and relationships with Jesus, which gave them confidence. That confidence rubbed off or helped the teams when the pressure was on.

As Ray was known to say, "If Jack is not comfortable, I am not going. If he is okay, I am okay."

Finally, at 6:30 she put the food on the table. The kids were starved and quickly ate what she put on their plates. She just nibbled at her food. Her stomach was in knots. She knew this was irrational. Jack was fine, but knowing that Ricky got shot rocked her. She, like every officer's wife, was thinking, *It could have been my husband that is never coming through that door again.*

Gail took her ironing board out. She needed to keep her hands busy and her mind occupied. She took out the ironing, set up her ironing board, and began to work. Soon, her anxiety had her working furiously. The shirts and blouses were rapidly being hung up on the rack. She groaned with anxiety and worked even faster. Both kids were watching her. They realized that something was really amiss. Mom was never like this. She was always cool, collected and happy.

"What's wrong Mommy?" asked her little girl. "Is Daddy okay?"

Her brother grabbed her and took her into the hallway. "Mommy is upset, but she will be okay, and we need to leave her alone for a while."

Bless his heart, he was only seven and was acting like a man already.

Gail overheard her son and burst into tears. She rested her head on the ironing board, feeling strangely good from the warmth that came off it. Quietly, she sobbed. Her shoulders shook as she called out to God. "Where ever Jack is, keep him safe and remind him that you, Lord, love him and I love him too."

She needed that reassurance of belonging to God and trusting Him. She smiled as she recalled how often he had told her, "There is no one or no place that I would rather be than with you."

She knew he would come home.

At midnight she went to bed, alone, wondering how Jack was doing and when he would be home. Restless, she dropped off into troubled sleep, listening for the sound of the door opening and his

259

soft footsteps as he went to the bathroom to prepare for bed. But she did not hear that door or the footsteps.

Lystra waited and waited too. Just like many other wives were tonight. Troubled and restless, she fell asleep after one o'clock.

Chapter 49

When the official announcement came it was not shocking. Everyone knew in their hearts that Ricky was dead, but now the reality struck home. The real pain began; the sorrow was overwhelming.

The afternoon was tough; not much work was done. Everyone just hung around waiting for confirmation of what they knew was coming. Now they gathered at desks, in hallways, the break room, or outside. They were crushed. Their minds and hearts were in turmoil. They knew they should go home but the need to be together overwhelmed them. They had nothing to give so they hung onto each other for strength until they could go home.

Eighty percent of them did not go home. They headed to various places to discuss the day's events, going over the details of what they saw, heard or were told. Some, a few, went to the Canopy. Most went with their closest friends or trusted *compadres* to someone's home. All of the homes they went to provided liquor. They needed to talk and they needed the drink; the drink would dull the pain.

Ray, Ken, Jack', Jack, and Bob all went to Blake Schneider's house. Fifteen guys crowded into the family room. Blake knew he did not have enough liquor or beer to satisfy these guys. But no fear, Ray figured that out and he and Bob came in together carrying a case of Heineken, two quarts of Johnny Walker Red, one quart of Smirnoff, two quarts of Seagram's Seven, and two fifths of brandy, along with a bag of ice.

This could be some serious drinking. Normally this much drinking would lead to loud laughter and jesting. Not tonight. The mood was somber. They were not drinking for fun; they were drinking to drown sadness, dull the pain and anxiety. Each one there recognized why they were drinking and that they probably were going to drink more than usual. They also knew that they did not have to say anything about what and why they drank. They all understood each other's feelings. That was why they were there instead of at home.

At home they had to be strong and comforting. At Blake's place they could rehash the events, lash out, cuss, or just sit and say nothing at all. They were there because they were not able to

261

perform. They needed this time to sorrow with people they trusted and who would not expect anything from them.

There were no mixers. The drinks were straight from the bottle into a water glass, with ice if a guy wanted it. The first drink was an inch or two in the bottom of the glass for those who drank liquor. The beer drinkers took it right from the bottle.

"Can you believe this shit? Ricky was dead when he hit the ground, but we got lied to," began Bob.

"Yeah, probably to keep us from storming the place and strangling the bastard."

"Or put a zillion holes in him."

"Or got ourselves shot!"

"If I had known I would probably have done something to entice Mueller to come to the window with his gun, so I could pick him off," spouted another.

"You know the Chief's words, 'We are here to save lives not take lives.' That is his motto."

"That does not make sense this time. The guy is a killer. He murdered someone last night and then Ricky today. He will get the death penalty for sure. We could have saved the taxpayers a ton of money. He is going to die anyway."

"Not could have, should have," muttered another.

Everyone agreed. Fresh drinks were poured, but this time the glasses were poured half full. This was serious.

"You know Ricky was working a traded day off. He should have been home or anywhere but at work today. Wonder how Mike feels, knowing that Ricky was filling in for him today?"

"Sure hope he is not beating himself up and feeling guilty that it was not him out there today."

"Right, Ricky should not have been there today. Not because of the trade but because his head has not been clear for weeks now. In fact, ever since his crash he has been living in a different world."

"I know the crash affected him, with the fatality and all, but what really tweaked his head was the investigation. He thought they were going to pin fault onto him and he would be canned or given a huge suspension. Hell, he even thought they might file criminal charges. Every day he expected the axe to fall. He waited three months to hear if he was going to be disciplined."

"Come on! Everybody knows it was not Ricky's fault. The dude ran the stop sign right into Ricky's path. No matter how fast he was going, if the dude had stopped at the sign nothing would have happened. Traffic has long ago calculated his speed, why keep him hanging?"

"Sure, that is what we all know, but we know the city has been on the rampage about vehicle damage. Look at what they tried to do to Pete. They tried to railroad him with a phony polygraph."

"It's the shits when you cannot trust your own. That is why Ricky wanted to leave and go to LASO. The trust level with this city and administration is dropping fast. It is tough enough to deal with the street crud, but having to protect yourself from politicians is scary."

"His mind was not on the business at hand. He would never have walked into that clearing like he did!"

The room became very silent.

Each man there remembered times when his head was somewhere else besides the task at hand. How many times had he avoided crashing his unit, or even his personal car, when his mind was distracted?

Distractions were easy to have: trouble at home, hassles at work, a case that was in court and being grilled by the defense attorney about your integrity, all really set them off. That was why the training officers told them to drive ten miles an hour slower on the freeways and five miles an hour slower on city streets when they were going through crisis. "Your defense mechanisms are just not up to par. Be careful out there."

Every face was glum. All of them were thinking, *It could have been me*. It happened so fast. Now Ricky was dead and there was nothing that could be done about it. Anger and pain flashed across their faces as these thoughts raced through their minds.

It was soon eleven and still no one was ready to go home. The shock and sorrow had not worn off or been dulled with the drinks. Glasses were filled or topped off. The bottles were nearing empty, so this wake would last only another hour or two.

"Do you realize that most cops get killed during the day time? You would think the night would be more dangerous."

"Ian Campbell of LAPD was killed at night. The Onion Field said they were taken hostage during swing shift and then driven to Bakersfield for the shooting. Wambaugh sure wrote a hell of a good book there. Wonder if anyone will write about Ricky?"

"Ontario PD had shootings and both fatalities were in the day time. Then you have the lucky ones like George Stone. You remember Stoneface getting shot?"

"Yeah, that was in the morning too, some mental nut flipped out that time."

"What happened? Is that when he got shot in the belt buckle and it glanced off or something like that?"

"The Green Lantern bar, over on East Holt, called in they had a guy who was causing problems. You know the place is a dive when they have drunk clients at nine in the morning and the place is commonly known as the Green Latrine."

"Anyway, Stoneface rolled to back up the two officers. He was working traffic on his Harley, but he figured this place was bad news so an extra hand might be good. As it turned out, he was one hundred percent right.

"When the officers told the dude to leave he got hostile and ran into the back of the bar. They grabbed him and before they could throw him to the floor he grabbed a frying pan off the hot plate and bonked Big Al on the head, knocking him out. He jerked free, swinging the pan, and reached down for Big Al's gun. He had a tough time getting it out of the holster, so he got down on the floor, pulled the gun out and started firing.

"He was not aiming, just firing away at the other officer and at Stoneface, who had just come through the door. Shooting looks easy on TV, but this guy found out he was no Wyatt Earp. Two bullets hit the door, one went into the wall, another went in the ceiling, and then one hit the belt buckle.

"Just then Big Al groaned and the dude looked down. They pounced on him before he got the last shot off. They couldn't shoot him because he was practically lying on Al.

"Stoneface was in shock when he realized why his stomach hurt so bad. He thought maybe he was shot, but there was no blood. He did have a huge bruise and it took pliers to undo the buckle."

Jack piped up with a story about Ricky. "I was Ricky's training officer for a few days when he first came on the PD.

"We were on Sultana when we get called to come to the station, 10-19. It was Sunday night about nine. Not a good time to drive up Sultana from Mission. But we took the short route through the barrio.

"We were half way between California and Sunkist when the first rock hit the right front fender. Before we knew it the air was full of baseball-size rocks, all of them coming toward us. Our windows were open, so rocks came in without breaking the glass. One rock hit the front edge of Ricky's helmet, spinning it around his head. A rock hit me on the wrist, knocking my hand off the steering wheel; at the same time another rock hit Ricky on the shoulder. Those fucking rocks were coming from both sides of the street.

"I goosed the gas to the floor and got us out of range, and Ricky grabbed the mike to call in what was happening. By the time backups came there was no one to be found. We did pick up thirty-four rocks off the street. The unit had sixteen dents. We were fortunate that neither of us got hurt.

"Frankly, I thought that would put a scare into him and have him give up the idea of being a cop. Those rocks did not make police work look glamorous."

They told more stories about long ago escapades, and dangers they faced and conquered. Fears that were debilitating were not mentioned but they were present in the room.

"You know this is going to be analyzed to death and then a training memo will come out. A memo, that we all know, is going to blame Ricky for being careless. Maybe it will give some direction to the supervisor to take charge and keep everybody safe."

What they expected never happened. There was no analysis and no training memo. It was like a bad dream that everyone wanted to ignore and hope it was never mentioned again.

"Wonder if any thought was given to have the city's psychiatrist analyzes the shooting to see what effect administrative pressures play on officers becoming careless. I know we are basically responsible for ourselves but there is validity to the saying, 'we are our brother's keepers.'"

"Just like the city is required to provide safety gear. Shouldn't the city also provide the least stress, so a guy can function safely?"

"You are crazy if you think that anyone is going to think about that or care about that. Shit, you know what they want is complete autonomy to decide your fate. Most command decisions are made on expediency and what moves their own careers up the line. When have you ever seen the council or the chief take a stand for what is right without letting politics cause them to sell out their own moral code, to not be swayed or overly concerned about the fall out? Then you have the Monday quarterbacks that sit in their comfy office and dissect what the cop takes split seconds to decide."

"Hell! You know that never happens. They will throw you to the wolves or under the bus if it protects their job, rank, retirement or electability! Look what the rock concert did to this town. The chief and the council know the moral wrongs and ethical violations, but money, big money wins out."

"That was another thing bugging Ricky. He was one of the front guys opposing it and he thought that was one reason it was taking so long to deal with his crash. The chief will get even with those who made him look bad by killing the next concert. He is expected to control the troops but that did not happen. We effectively stopped the concert and revenge is coming."

"Want to bet Jack, here, is going to get his tit in the ringer? You know they are looking at everything he does."

The sour note turned each officer into an angry man. They were together because they very much believed that they were their brother's keepers. They cared about each other and would protect and help anyone in uniform or who carried a badge.

"It should be us against the bad guys, not us against the bad guys and the politicians!"

Jack got up, "Time to go home guys, it has been a hell of a day and tomorrow we have a job to do."

"Yup, it is after one. The booze is gone and I am glad we got to hang out tonight. Thanks, Schneider."

Jack drained his glass of the last brandy and walked out with the rest. No one hugged anyone. They were too macho for that. But their handshakes were firm and took longer than usual.
Ray followed Jack out, watching to see if he was too drunk to drive. If he was being watched tonight he could be in trouble. So Ray followed Jack for about eight blocks to see if his driving was good and to check for any surveillance cars. There were none, so he turned and went home.

Chapter 50

Jack slid into bed with utmost care not to disturb Gail. He did not realize she had not been sleeping. As he settled in he felt Gail moving close behind him, snuggling real close.

His heart was churning as he thought about not being there that night. But he needed to be with the guys, with people who understood his pain and grief. He reached back and placed his hand on her thigh. She snuggled closer. He felt the wetness of her cheek as she pressed against his shoulder. He realized she was crying. Guilt hit him like a rock, realizing how much she needed him but he had left her alone in order to take care of his own needs.

He turned over and took her into his arms, hugging her to himself.

"I'm sorry," he whispered in her ear, "I just couldn't get away, the guys just needed each other."

She whispered back, "I know. I am glad you are home now."

They both said, "I love you so much" at the same time. This made them both smile. Although it was dark and they could not see, they both sensed that the other was smiling too. They snuggled closer. They continued to hold each other, letting their closeness bring comfort and reassurance. When Gail sighed and relaxed, Jack put his hand on Gail's soft rear and pulled her closer. They snuggled closer and closer. He, because he needed the assurance of her love and his own security, and she, because she sensed his need and wanted to be there for him. She reached for him to encourage him, letting him know she was there for him. With a deep sigh of contentment, they made love. She felt secure that her man was safe and loved her. He felt understood and that she accepted the fact that his pain and anger needed to be dealt with before he could come home and be the husband she needed.

Across town, Ray also slipped into bed. He was exhausted and fell asleep instantly. The sorrow and the booze had taken their effect. The last thing he realized was that Lystra placed her hand on his hip, assuring herself that he was there and he was safe.

He woke up with a start. When he looked over at the clock he realized he was late. Bureau briefing was starting in 20 minutes. His alarm did not go off. Lystra was out of bed and must be seeing the kids out the door for school.

The whole world was a mess and the department was probably screwed up as well.

"Just not going to be worried about it," he mumbled, then stumbled out of bed and headed for the bathroom. As he was brushing his teeth he looked up to see Lystra coming in.

"I thought I heard water running so came to see if you were up." She came up behind him and wrapped her arms around him, placing her head against his back. Ray saw the look in her eyes as she came in. It was a look of anxiety and fear. He quickly finished brushing, rinsed the brush, and put it down.

He was wearing only his pajama bottoms, and felt her face on his back.

Is she crying? He wondered, because he thought her face was damp.

Slowly he turned around and put his arms around her, too. There, leaning against the counter, they hugged. She was hugging him tightly, clinging to him.

He sensed her angst as she spoke. She started off slow but her words came faster and faster as they spilled out of her mouth.

"I really missed you last night. I was so afraid. I just couldn't get it out of my head that it was not you that died, but you were gone and I didn't know where you were or if you were all right. I was alone with the kids and I hated that I was afraid for me when it was your buddy that was killed. I knew you were hurting and I wanted to be there for you, but mostly I just wanted to be with you to know for certain that everything was going to be okay!"

"Whoa, slow down honey that was a real mouthful. I am so sorry I wasn't here. The guys really needed each other. You know how guys are. They don't want to spill their feelings, but you know we needed to be together; guys who were going through the same pain and agony of loss. I just couldn't go home till we grasped some way to handle it."

He kissed her eyes softly to take away the tears that were pooled in the corners.

"I love you and want to be there for you," he whispered.

She pulled back and smiled up at him. She loved his size, all six-foot, three and 230 pounds. He was so gentle with her, quite unlike what she expected he was like when he dealt with the creeps and lowlife. She snuggled her five foot six self a little closer.

"I called in that you were not feeling well today, and told

268

them that you would be late if you went in at all." She smiled impishly. "You needed your sleep too, but now that you are awake?"

"I think I should go back to bed for that needed rest. Do you need some rest too?" he asked. "Or will we put the rest part off until later?"

It was later, as he lay on his side cuddled real close, he tenderly stroked her hair and cheek, reveling in the sweetness of their love. Finally, he rolled onto his back and his mind strayed to the events of the morning and of yesterday. Next to him, Lystra was thinking about the same things. It was good that they loved each other and realized that in their love they met the needs of each other. They had far different needs, but needs that helped them survive in life, especially in the life of a policeman and his wife.

It was good to have a home to come to. To have a place to be loved, to be with someone who did not criticize or nag, someone who never brought up past disappointments or problems. He knew he was blessed to have a wife who somehow understood or grasped the enormity and overriding tension and pain that could only be shared with other cops and not brought home to increase her anxiety and fears. Someone you just want to please and to be with because she completes you as you complete her. Neither one wanted to change the other. Content and restful; that was how he felt. That was why a peaceful home was so nice to come home to. An oasis from the wilderness of police work and life.

He knew he was blessed to have this relationship with his wife. Few cops had wives that innately understood what it took to balance home life with the reality of working the streets. Somehow a good wife realized the anxiety her husband lived in day in and day out. She knew he could not bring that anxiety home. He also realized that she needed to know that he was true blue for her. Being committed to finding that balance was the key to lowering the divorce rate in law enforcement.

At work, disappointments would overtake him. In fact they had the capability of destroying lives and attitudes, making work a place to dread and even hate. He felt sorry for the guys who were counting the years to retirement. Poor slobs who thought they were stuck. They had too much time invested in retirement benefits to leave and yet hated coming to work. They killed time and killed themselves with pity and anger, and they were living

269

with little or no purpose, except to stay alive until retirement.

He smiled because he was grateful that for him work had purpose and was fulfilling. He was grateful that he had good people around him to bring balance to life. It was far too easy to become cynical when he saw only the underbelly of society and the political maneuverings.

Sometimes he wondered how he was surviving. Working narcotics and vice for years, he had seen the dregs of life. Hepatitis, STD, overdose deaths, murders for drugs, informants that ratted out friends and would rat cops out too. He had hung out in bars, drank beer in dives like the Bottom Dollar at Riverside Drive and Archibald, the Green Lantern, Nite Lite, and others. Those places reeked of beer and urine; some were places where biker gangs hung out and earned the wings and other steps in biker's creepdom.

He worked with the prostitutes and their pimps. He worked with those who were strung out on meth or drugged on downers or heroin. They were all screwed up in life, just waiting and hoping for the next thrill or high. The pimps were the real low lifes. They used women to earn them a fancy car, expensive clothes and drugs. They lured them with promises and then kept them enslaved with drugs, threats and violence.

Ray was lost in his reverie. He remembered the big black pimp who thrilled his women with good sex and spent lots of money on them. Then, once they were committed, he would add another woman to his stable to expand his income and power. He always needed more women to work. They gave him ninety percent of what they earned. The pimp needed that money and more to support his three hundred dollar a day coke habit. All went well until one day when he was high and feeling powerful and he started demanding more money.

"Work harder," he said. "Rip the creepy johns off. Empty their wallets while you give them a blowjob," he instructed.

But Jamie had enough. She did not want to work the streets. She wanted to stay at the massage parlor where she felt safe and the girls protected each other. She called the vice squad to ask for protection. She told them her pimp was on his way to her house to hurt her, so was begging for help. He would beat her and threaten her with his pistol if she was not out hustling the street when she was not working her regular hours at the massage parlor.

Ray and his sergeant were the only ones available, so they

270

went to the house where she lived with two other masseuses. One was working, so only Blondie and Jamie were there. Shortly after they arrived the pimp pulled up in his black Eldorado Cadillac.

Ray was on the sofa with Blondie, watching TV, when the door opened. The sergeant went into Jamie's bedroom and hid in the closet. Ray had a moment of fear as he heard the pimp, who was standing behind him, open his revolver and spin the cylinder as he loaded his gun.

"You dumb bitch, why are you not out hustling? I told you what would happen if I came and you were still here," he yelled.

Jamie just looked down and cowered but said nothing. She was afraid she may have done the wrong thing. She would get beat up or shot, and so would the cop that was sitting there.

"Get your ass in your room," he growled. He pushed her down the hallway into her bedroom, where Sgt. Bill was hiding. Ray leapt up, grabbed his .45 Auto, and went down the hallway. This pimp was big, six feet eight, two hundred sixty pounds, and wild eyed. Ray knew they had to act fast and sure, because this guy was loaded on coke and his gun was loaded too.

"I told you to get to work! What are you doing at home on your lazy ass," he yelled. "I am going to mess you up. After today you will do as I say!"

Ray heard her scream, and at the same time he heard the closet door slide open.

"Drop the gun asshole," he heard Bill yell. As Ray opened the door he saw the pimp grab the wall. His hands were at the ceiling, and his gun was on the floor. Jamie was lying on the bed, scared out of her wits. Her eyes showed lots of white and her mouth was hanging open while she screamed.

The pimp began to blubber. Tears were running down his face.

"Please don't shoot. Please don't shoot." The wet spot in the crotch of his two hundred dollar slacks got bigger.

"Real brave when you push girls around aren't you," muttered Bill. "Tough guy aren't you!"

Bill kept his gun aimed at the pimp while Ray cuffed him.

271

Chapter 51

October 1976

It started out as a typical gloomy June day, perfect for a funeral service. June gloom was what the early morning days were called in Southern California, when the inversion layer caused the moisture in the air to be like a light fog that, when mixed with the pollution, caused an overcast day. Low clouds and cool air were there until the sun burned it off in late morning or early afternoon.

The day that began in gloom would end with a message of hope and assurance, as the pastor gave his homily and encouraged the attendees as they faced the future without Ricky. It was time for the memorial service, time for family, friends, the police family and the public to come to pay their respects.

The cars slowly filled the huge parking lot. Both sides of the street were already filled for several blocks in all directions with parked cars. The police cars and motorcycles all parked in the lot. They came streaming in, a solid line down the street and around the corner, leading to the main drag and the freeway exit. Units from San Diego, Fullerton, Los Angeles Police and Sheriff, Palo Alto and San Francisco were there. It looked like every city in Southern California sent a delegation. There were also cars from out of state: Las Vegas, Phoenix, Carson City and one from Dallas, Texas.

There were hundreds of units and motorcycles. They would stretch out over a mile as they later made their way to the cemetery, followed by another mile of personal cars. It was the largest police memorial service anywhere, to date, except Los Angeles. But that was partially due to the fact that there had not been any officers killed in shootings for a long time. At least not a cold blooded shooting like this one where no gun fire was exchanged and the officer was ambushed by the suspect. This officer was ambushed and taken out without notice or warning of danger.

The family was in the front row, with close friends behind them. The uniformed officers from Ontario PD filled the next fifteen rows. All of the seats were filled but the people kept coming in. The walls were lined with standing uniformed officers. They gave up their seats for the citizens of Ontario and the

273

neighboring cities. The blue and tan uniforms against the walls looked like a solid line of protection for those who were mourning.

Everyone looked toward the front, where the coffin rested on its bier. There was no corpse in the coffin because Ricky was cremated, but the coffin represented the reality of death. A photo of Officer Augustino was on the coffin. He was in uniform, standing next to his patrol car. Most likely nobody realized it, but this was the unit he crashed. He did not know then, nor did anyone think about that fact that this unit would be involved in the investigation of his driving and whether he followed policy and DMV laws.

The flag of the United States of America, the stars and stripes that each officer swore allegiance to, covered the coffin. Their solemn oath, even more solemn today, was to protect and serve the population of this great country. There was the photo and two white lilies on top of the flag. It was not Easter, but they were Easter lilies, representing the promise of life after death.

The Honor Guard stood on each side of the coffin. They were smartly dressed in Class A uniforms and wore white gloves and white hats. Every five minutes there was a change of the guard. That was done to give others the honor of serving the fallen officer.

After ten o'clock the people kept coming in. The row of uniforms around the perimeter was two deep, and before the last officer entered the church the outside aisles were filled from wall to pew with uniformed personnel. As the last ones entered the foyer the doors were closed, but they soon had to be opened again for ventilation.

The pastor stepped up to the lectern. Silence settled over the place. The pastor had not said a word but the entire gathering ceased talking or whispering. This was a solemn moment. The pastor abandoned his planned opening comments, seizing this moment of utter silence to acknowledge God's presence.

"Almighty God and Father, we come to you this morning to thank you for your presence here. We ask for your grace to reach us as we mourn and remember our friend and your servant. Lord, grant us your peace."

A sense of calm filled the place.

Every eye and every ear turned to Pastor Rob. He smiled and welcomed everyone, thanking them for coming to share this time of commemoration with family, friends, compatriots and fellow peace officers.

"Peace officers encounter violence; violence that interrupts the lives of a city, work place and family. It is every peace officer's wish and desire to provide safety and security to the city, county or other jurisdiction where he works. To bring or enable peace, they place themselves at risk, just as Ricky did last week.

"So we are here to honor Ricky and to share the sorrow of his death with the family and the entire City of Ontario. Ricky's training officer, and then his best friend, will share their memories of Ricky."

Tim Yoder, his training officer, began. "From the first day I met Ricky I knew he would be a great cop. He had a sense to know everything that was occurring around him. He was not nervous and not cocky. He was in control and nothing spooked him or worried him. As you who knew him realize, he was laid back and enjoyed life as much as anyone else. However, when he was on duty he may have seemed laid back but he missed nothing that was going on around him."

He paused, and with a slight scratch or broken voice continued, "That is why it is so difficult to grasp what happened. How could this have happened? Sorry, I did not intend to say anything about that."

He went on to recall how well Ricky learned the ropes, remembered all the streets, and never got lost on the way to a call. He always knew which street was a cul-de-sac or the ones that stopped and started and were not through streets. He recalled how thorough and detailed his traffic collision reports were. He never bitched about having to work a TC that was not in his district. He was always there to help.

"In fact, it was a comfort to know that, even if no back up was dispatched, you could count on Rick rolling up to make sure you were okay. I was never so happy to see Ricky as the day I pulled over a car for a minor traffic violation. No back up was sent, but one of the occupants took off running. I chased that scumbag down the street, into the rear yard of a house, over the fence to the next-door yard, and then out the side yard gate. At the gate I caught up with him and shoved him so he fell on his face. I tried to cuff him but he fought. We rolled around in the mud till we were both wore out. I could not get the cuffs on him, but I got one of his arms in a half nelson and my other hand had a grip on his hair. We were quite a sight as I walked him down the street to

275

the unit. When we hit the sidewalk, up pulled Ricky. Was I glad to see him?

"It took both of us to take him down and cuff him. As you know, Ricky was always spick and span. I never saw a guy who could keep a uniform so neat, clean and pressed. He was not excited about getting down on the pavement with this muddy pair, but he did it. Guess what? He did not get one speck of mud on those blues. How he managed that I don't know. What I do know is that he was a great cop, and I always loved it when he rolled up to cover my back. He always did a great job and always took care of his obligations. He was there for anyone who needed help.

"Ricky was an exemplary police officer. On time, good work habits, friendly to all. How does a guy write ten or more citations a day and not get complaints? I asked Ricky that and he just smiled that smile of his, but never gave an answer. That smile and demeanor is what made those who got those tickets realize that this was a nice guy who was doing his job. He let them know they were guilty without berating them or giving an ass chewing. Ricky used to say, 'If you write a ticket, do it, but never chew their ass and give a ticket.'" After many more kind words and remembrances he expressed his condolences to Carly and the friends and family. He closed with, "I miss you already, buddy."

Next up was Ricky's friend, Mike. They had been friends from back in junior high. Ricky and Michael Machado went to parochial school together in Azusa. Mike slowly, almost hesitantly, approached the lectern. It was apparent that he was having difficulty controlling his emotions. He was obviously a dear friend.

Pastor Rob rose from his chair on the podium, walked to Mike, and placed an arm around Mike. They walked together to the lectern. Pastor Rob started by introducing Mike, giving Mike some time to get comfortable and to gather his thoughts.

"Mike met Ricky in the eighth grade when his family arrived in California from Azores, Portugal. Mike spoke virtually no English and Ricky took Mike as his friend, helping him learn English, showing how to do the homework, and being his pal during lunch and recesses."

Mike was ready to speak then. He looked out at the crowd and got the shakes again. He had never been in front of this many people. Everyone was looking at him, waiting to hear something that would encourage their hearts or bring them some cheer.

276

A grin broke out across his face as he thought of something humorous to say. He hesitated. There were a lot of guns out there. He did not want to tic them off. *No, they will be okay,* he thought. He started without looking at his notes or beginning with his planned talk.

"I have never seen this many cops outside of a donut shop," he said. The whole place broke out into a laugh. Quickly, he went on, "unless it was getting coffee at the fire station. I know how much you guys drink coffee. Every day the beat cop comes by the station for a cup and tries to harass us about playing Ping-Pong or polishing brass.

"You already heard how Ricky and I met. You can understand that someone like him would become your best friend. I owe so much to him for those early days and months of being in a new country. We played baseball together, only because neither one of us was tall enough to play basketball or big enough to play football. We loved baseball and continued to play softball and go to Angel games as often as we could. I yell a little louder than he did and drank more beer than he did. He kept me in control and I stretched his fun zone. We made a good team.

"When we married he was my best man and I was his best man. We babysat each other's kids and played ball with the boys and, don't laugh, played house with the girls." Mike wiped away the tears as he recalled the fun times.

"Then we both decided that we wanted to change jobs. I wanted to be a fireman but Ricky wanted to be a peace officer. We discussed this many times. Why be a cop? What makes you want to be a fireman?

"Ricky would say, 'There is no way in hell that I'll go up the ladder truck. Hanging out there in the sky is not for me.' My answer was, 'Sure but I won't have to chase crooks, write tickets or piss people off, and besides that I won't get shot at or shoot anyone. Besides that, firemen are everybody's heroes.' I thought I had him there. Everybody wants to be liked and to be a hero, right?

"Not Ricky. He just wanted to do what needed to be done, do it right and be respected. Being liked was not necessary. 'Besides', he would say, 'you know that God made police officers so that firemen would have heroes too.'

"Ricky you are right, you are my hero, love you, man!"

277

Chapter 52

There was not a dry eye in the church. Carly was sobbing on the shoulder of Mike's wife, Sonia. The kids were crying because mommy was crying. All of the Ontario cops had their heads down, looking at the floor like it was the most interesting thing to study. Almost in unison everyone perked up and wiped their eyes. They smiled because they knew Ricky was a hero.

Pastor Rob opened his Bible and turned the pages to what he was looking for. He looked over the audience. All eyes were toward him. Every pastor wanted that moment when full attention was focused on the pulpit. He chose selections from Psalm 46: 1 – 10, just for this purpose. He began to read.

God is our refuge and strength, a very present help in trouble. Therefore we will not fear, though the earth should change and though the mountains slip into the sea. . . . There is a river whose streams make glad the city of God, the holy dwelling place of the Most High. God is in the midst of this city, she will not be moved; God will help her when morning dawns. . . . The Lord is with us; the God of Israel is our stronghold. Come behold the works of the Lord . . . cease striving and know that I am God.

Pastor Rob began his message. It was a message of comfort and assurance that those who trust God realize that nothing can ever take away the blessing and peace of knowing that God was there when trouble came. He explained that the city referred to in the Psalm was a picture of the hearts of people, the people who had invited God to take a place in their life and hearts.

He explained that the world may be a mess and troubles might be everywhere. There might be hurricanes, tornados, earthquakes, wars and disease, but these things were in this life on this earth. God created man to be eternal. This earthly life was not all there was. The important thing in this life was what was done to prepare for eternity in the future.

"Somehow," he said, "we all know or have some sense that this world was created by a God who knew how to make things work. He made bodies that have hearts, lungs, livers, brains, and immune systems, that all work together. He also made nature work. The exchange of oxygen, carbon dioxide, and water brought life. Some animals live on land and others only live in water. It is a

279

complex world and I cannot explain it all.

"Into this perfect world God made man. That caused a problem, because God made man with a soul. The soul lives forever and becomes part of us at birth, when that first independent breath is taken."

He continued with his sermon, explaining that Satan hated God and therefore tried to destroy what God made. He talked Adam into disobeying God, which was the first sin. God told Adam and Eve that sin would result in death, because only holiness would be allowed in the presence of a holy God. Satan thought he had won.

"God loved his creation and loved mankind. He was not willing to allow Satan to destroy what he created. God developed a plan to undo the results of sin. Sin was a reality but the punishment could be dealt with. God had a hero in mind, a hero who could and would undo sin."

He looked at the crowd and saw that most eyes were focused on his. Very few were looking away or seemed to want to disconnect. This is what Carly wanted him to talk about. This was a vital part of Ricky's life. Since about ninety percent of the congregation seemed interested in what made Ricky the man he was, Rob was happy to tell his exciting story.

"God and Jesus came up with the plan to atone for sin. If a man could live life perfectly, without even one sin, he would qualify to make payment for the sin others had committed. Only a sinless person could accomplish this. A person who sinned could only pay for his or her own sin. This was exciting! When detectives worked a case and there was no known motive, they worked and worked to find the motive. Once they found the motive the crime became easier to solve.

"That was true also with solving how to get us free from the penalty for sin. Jesus came with the solution. Jesus would come to earth as a man to take the penalty, which was due the human race, onto Him. That meant he would die as payment for my sin and for all of the sins of all who accepted his invitation. The motive? God loved his creation enough to die in their place, to pay the penalty for sin himself. Cool isn't it?

"This is what makes Christianity totally different from all other religions: the fact that Jesus paid for your sin. Jesus the Messiah has paid for every wrong thing you thought, did or said. Every other religion requires a person to work to earn righteousness, or to perform certain rituals or oblations. For some belief systems payment is made by doing good deeds or making sacrifices, in an attempt to have the scales at least balance or tilt toward good. The problem with balancing goodness versus wrong is that there is still wrong. When Jesus paid for sin all was forgiven. That is God! He is merciful and gracious.

"Just dying for sin is only half the task. Since death is the penalty for sin then death must also be conquered. Jesus took care of that too. He beat the hell out of death. He rose from the dead so those who trust in Him will have eternal life. No other religion has the power of eternal life.

"The day Ricky died he may have been troubled about things of this life, but he was not troubled about his future life. One of his favorite Psalms was Psalm 27:1-4. 'The Lord is my light and salvation; whom shall I fear? The Lord is the defense of my life. Whom shall I dread?' It ends like this, 'One thing I have asked from the Lord, that I shall seek; that I may dwell in the house of the Lord all the days of my life to behold the beauty of the Lord God and to meditate in His temple.'

"That, my friends, is what Ricky lived by. He laid down his life protecting the people of Ontario and now he is living his future in God's home, the place of eternal and perfect peace."

Looking up as if he saw Ricky in heaven, he said, "Ricky, thank you for being a hero to us all. I will see you later. Love you."

The Honor Guard came down the center aisle. All eyes turned to watch the men come in perfect step until they stopped at the coffin. They snapped to attention, gave a smart salute, and two of them turned to the ends of the coffin. As they picked up the flag to begin folding it in preparation to give it to the widow, the organ softly started to play.

The tune "Abide with Me" drifted over the auditorium. Many recalled this old hymn from days in Sunday school, church, or other memorial services. Rob began to sing the song quietly, but his baritone voice picked up the volume so all could hear him. It was not an orchestrated part of the plan. Rob just wanted to sing the words that William Monk wrote just over a hundred years ago, in 1861, words that still had special meaning today.

Swift to its close ebbs out life's little day
Earth's joys grow dim, its glories pass away;

281

Change and decay in all around I see;
O Thou who changes not abide with me.

Tears swelled in many eyes as he began the third verse:
I fear no foe, with you at hand to bless
Ills have no weight and tears no bitterness.
Where is death's sting? Where grave your victory?
I triumph still, if Thou abide with me.

Hold your cross before my closing eyes
Shine through the gloom and point me to the skies
Heaven's morning breaks and earth's vain shadows flee
In life, in death, O Lord, abide with me.

The heart of every cop tightened. It was as if that strip of black velvet was a boa constrictor around his heart instead of just a black band around the badge. All wanted God to abide with them, with safety and peace.

The Honor Guard waited, standing at attention, during this song. They sensed the grip of sorrow and saw that it was mixed with hope and peace. They paused. When the eyes had been dried and tissues put away, the flag was presented to Carly.

"It is my honor to give you this flag as commemoration of Ricky's steadfast devotion to the City of Ontario, the United States of America, and to you and your children. Thank you for sharing him with us as he served and gave his life in his desire to bring peace."

All eyes were directed toward the front, witnessing this moment. It was a moment of deep sorrow, but also the moment that every peace officer's spouse should receive. She was the mainstay of his life, providing a home that he always wanted to come back to, where he was loved, accepted and encouraged to be the man she was proud of. Sadly, these moments of thanks and respect were reserved for the End of Watch ceremonies, either retirement or, as in this case, the memorial service.

The Honor Guard went into formation, saluted the widow, turned and saluted the coffin and photo. They made a precise pivot and marched down the center aisles to exit the church. The bagpipe began to play a haunting tune as they approached the door.

Slowly, everyone rose and waited for those who had been

standing in the aisles to vacate. Those officers were happy to move and hastened to get outside. The rest of the attendees were slower and less eager. The crowd formed into groups outside, waiting for everyone to get out and for the pallbearers to exit with the coffin. Here groups of cops, sheriffs, highway patrol, and friends came together to share thoughts and pleasant comments.

Funerals were a time for old acquaintances to reconnect and catch up on events in each other's lives. There were smiles on faces of old friends as they greeted each other. Others were standing alone, waiting. Waiting for this event to be over. The grief was hard to handle alone, so they drifted over to join a group of people they knew.

The doors closed on the hearse. Everyone got into their cars and the procession slowly made its way to the cemetery. Motorcycle officers took control of traffic, enabling the long line to move as one unit, snaking its way through the city streets to the freeway.

Many citizens along the route exited their cars and stood patiently waiting. Some saluted. Others were more casual in paying respects. All gave respect to the deceased, but also to those who would carry on. Bringing justice and peace for all!

Epilogue

The department went through many changes in the next year. Many officers transferred to other Agencies: LAPD, LASO, Santa Ana PD, Fremont PD, Stanislaus County Sheriff and more.

After placing first in the next sergeant's exam, Ray was passed over when number thirteen was selected. He knew he was paying for his past involvement in protesting Cal Jam II. He went on to finish law school and went into Criminal Defense law.

Jack' was promoted to sergeant and became the commander of the SED (Special Enforcement Detail).

Jack was fired for his role in leading the campaign against rock concerts. The courts reversed his termination and he was reinstated. The pressure and continued harassment, also known as career development caused him resign. Jack became a contractor and planned to devote much of his time to charities and building facilities for missions in Latin America and Africa.

Councilman Rojas lost his seat in the next election.

The city manager took an early retirement.

The chief retired that year, as soon as his age and years in service allowed.

Jack and Ray maintained their friendship and partnership until Ray died forty years later. They were there for each other whenever the call came, loyal and trustworthy friends for life.

CPSIA information can be obtained
at www.ICGtesting.com
Printed in the USA
JSHW020744120322
23655JS00001B/9